Echo of Peace

A Bioweapon with a Brain

[A sequel to *Casualties of Peace*]

A Novel

Harold H. Lee

ISBN-13: 978-1720939375
ISBN-10: 1720939373

First Edition

Also by Harold H. Lee

Casualties of Peace
Hong Kong Boy

(Available from Amazon.com)

CASUALTIES OF PEACE

GENE EDITING TOWARD A NEW WORLD ORDER

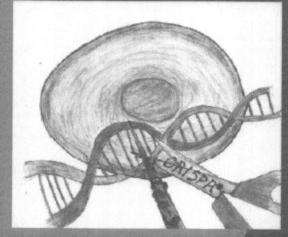

HAROLD H. LEE

Echo of Peace

is a sequel to

Casualties of Peace
A Novel
By Harold H. Lee
Pub.2017

Using the gene-editing technique, CRISPR-Cas 9, a group of molecular biologists create a bioweapon of immense power and use it to force the leaders of fighting nations to lay down their arms.

Global battles stop but there are geopolitical repercussions. The United Nations leads the hunt for the scientists while advanced nations race to develop similar bioweapons.

A race of gene warfare seems inevitable, and the rogue scientists must find a way to stop the impending destruction of humanity seeded by their noble intention for peace.

In this fast-paced novel by Harold H. Lee, we are introduced to the Tennessee Volunteers, a group of friends and scientists striving to make the world a better place. Harold H. Lee brings his years of lab experience and biological expertise to show how today's real advances in gene editing could be leveraged for the common good, and the consequences of such scientific capabilities falling into the wrong hands. This may be a novel, but it could well be a prescient warning...

Acknowledgement

The author is indebted to Paz Layug Reyes for her constant and continuous support in all aspects of the writing. Both Dr. Jack Rary, a medical geneticist, and Dr. Jerry Williams, a physiologist, my graduate study cohorts, have provided valuable suggestions on this and other works. The author is most grateful for their help and their friendship though out these years. The author wishes to thank Mac McPherson for his encouragement for the author to write. Thanks also to Marlene Bergman who has been providing literature in biotech for the author to keep up with the current advances. The author is grateful for the assistance of Peggy Edwards and Miranda McPhee of the Publishing Club, Laguna Woods, CA. Mrs. McPhee has given her time to edit and format this and other works of the author. Without her gracious assistance this and other books would not be in print. For that I am most grateful.

To

Paz

And the duck that brought me luck.

MAJOR CHARACTERS

The Tennessee Volunteers, scientists and friends; all retired.

Bonnie   Ph.D. Radiation biologist.
Harold   Ph. D. Molecular biologist. Molecular therapy.
Jack   Ph.D. An ex-marine. Medical geneticist.
Jerry   Ph.D. Airforce colonel. Molecular physiologist.
John   Ph.D. Molecular biologist. VP, pharmaceutical.
                Ex-board member of the defunct Global Foundation.
June   Ph.D. Molecular biologist.

Harrison   Computer wizard.
Paz   Travel agent. Ex-VP of operations of the defunct
                Global Foundation.

The Phoenix Group

Hector L.   Non-voting member. Psychologist. University of
                Hong Kong.
Jeng, MD-Ph.D. Molecular biologist/immunologist. Stanford
                University.
Li   Hong Kong banker.
Lloyd   Businessman from Kuala Lumpur.
Nelson   CEO of second largest pharma in the USA.
Simpson   CEO of Vouit Pharma, Sweden.
Mrs. Biotti   Italian businesswoman.
Fu   Financier/politician from Thailand.

SAGRC (Sino-America Genetic Research Consortium)

Alex	Ph.D. Molecular geneticist. Environmental Protection Agency, USA.
Calvin	Ph.D. University of Hawaii, ex-FBI, USA.
Lee, K.M.	Ph.D. Molecular biologist, Beijing.
Ms. Mei Mei	M.S. Cell biology and cybersecurity, Shanghai.
Caleb Morrison	President, US National Academy of Sciences.
Robert	Ph.D. Biotechnologist, University of Tennessee.
Somers	Ph.D. Immunologist, Sloan Kettering Institute.
Wang	Ph.D. Bioengineer and technocrat, United Nations and Beijing.

*"We shape our dwellings and afterwards
Our dwellings shape us."*

Winston Churchill, October 28, 1943.

A HILLTOP HIDEAWAY

On a hilltop outside San José, Costa Rica, away from the main traffic thoroughfares, was a cluster of six detached units overlooking the city of San José and a couple of beautiful valleys in between. This hilltop location was always some five to ten degrees cooler than downtown San José and both the coasts of the Pacific Ocean and the Gulf of Mexico. It was less than one hour's drive from downtown. It was a different world—quiet, no traffic noise, no smog, and always enjoyed a gentle breeze even at high noon.

On a clear night one could see the active volcano far away occasionally spurting fire. There were many clear days and nights in Costa Rica due to the fact that there were just a few heavy industries.

One of the units with two bedrooms and a spacious lobby/living room housed the owners, Harold and June, retired molecular biologists from the United States.

The other five one-bedroom units were rented to tourists who had heard about the place by word of mouth. There was no ad and no name. A small number of tourist agents knew this Shangri-La in a very touristy Costa Rica. It was just known as Harold and June's place, or Harold's or June's place. The guests of this laidback guest house were almost all referrals. Those unknown to Harold or June were frequently told that they were fully booked even if there were empty units. No tourists would just drive up.

This no-name place was not a business venture. It was a retirement home with leisure activities. Both June and Harold were well-known pioneers in molecular therapy. When they were not busy with the few guests they had, they wrote their memoirs and futuristic science fiction novels. There were two computers for the guests and general usage in the living room/lobby of this comfortable little hideaway. There was a third computer dedicated to their business side on a long table with a rare one-piece mahogany top that served as a registration counter among other things related to the hospitality business.

At the center of this cluster of six small buildings was a simple pavilion that served as a guest dining room or gathering place, tastefully decorated with native greenery and flowers. When it rained, there were heavy, clear plastic curtains that could be dropped down and anchored firmly to keep the elements out. Guests could see the rain running down the curtains, a sort of moving art. On one side of the pavilion was a large stainless-steel refrigerator and a stove with four burners. That was where all the meals were prepared for the guests. The guests were free to prepare their own meals if they so wished. Ordinarily, Harold would prepare a simple breakfast of eggs and pancakes etc., American standards, which was included in the modest rental cost.

Immediately after moving in, the owners added a patio along the rocky hillside at the back of the bigger unit. The floor of the patio jutted out some ten feet with supports on a solid rock foundation. Underneath this patio was an enclosed space the same size as the patio. Both the patio and the room underneath afforded a panoramic view looking down to the city of San José and the valleys in-between. The patio and the room below were the real hideaway and not open to the public. With very few guests most of the time, this patio and room underneath were well used. The furniture was simple but comfortable, mostly made by Harold, one of his hobbies. There were electronic gadgets for Harold and June to keep up with their sciences and their writing.

June's cell phone jingled. She looked at the caller ID. It said "John."

June put the phone on speaker.

"Hi, John. Long time no talk."

"Yes, long time no business. Do you have a vacancy in two days?"

"Our little place is all booked up."

"New business. Rita and I will be down."

"John, we are retired," June said. "How long will you be staying?"

"Two days at least. Make my reservation for one week. There may be others joining us on and off during that time. I know Harold likes T-bone. We will bring some; and June, your favorite California red, too."

"Oh, yes. I forgot," John continued on the other end. "Can you give your help a vacation for a week?"

"Yes, of course. You will have to do your own laundry and we will take turns to cook," Harold said.

"No problem. See you in two days."

Two days later.

"We have just arrived at San José International Airport. We will drive up in a rental," John called as he left the passport control booth.

"We have been expecting you. Drive carefully. San José is not Washington, D.C., or San Diego. Watch for the potholes. Just follow the GPS and my directions."

"Will do. Till later."

Although June and Harold's place had no name, they gave their guests the name and address of a hotel, the Bougainvillea, at the bottom of the hill. It was a beautifully decorated and landscaped spread of about five acres. Right next to this hotel was a roughly paved road with bumps and potholes leading to Harold's place. There were only a few well-maintained bungalows on this narrow road. These bungalows belonged to rich people in the city who used them as weekend getaway homes. At the end of the road up the hill would be Harold and June's hideaway.

A couple of hours later, John and Rita drove up. Harold and June were waiting for them at the entrance, just a roughly paved parking area large enough for a few cars.

John unloaded a cardboard box. "Here, Harold, your T-bones."

"I'm glad you have recovered one hundred percent from your stroke," June said. "John and Rita, welcome to our Shangri-La."

"It is beautiful. Wow, what a view," Rita exclaimed in admiration.

Harold waved his arms showing the spread. "This is our 5-star hotel! We thought about naming it and giving a name to each cabin. Then we changed our minds. Just a number will do. John, you and Rita are in #1. The rest are booked through the week! We have told some prospective guests that we are fully booked for a month. The tourist season is year-round in Costa Rica. I know John has been here before. Rita, I am sure we will find time to show you around before or after discussing our 'new business,' per John."

John unloaded a case of California red.

"Guys, you must be hungry. Put your stuff in the room and freshen up a bit. See you after however long you need, in the lobby." Harold pointed to their cabin with no number above the door. "We will take you to a restaurant where the proprietor is from Chile, a Japanese/Chilean. She has only four tables in her living room. She cooks really well with a mix of Mediterranean, Chilean, and French. San José has many of these kinds of home-restaurants that only the locals know. And they are very good and reasonable. We can sit there all night and chat."

"Great idea. We always look forward to something unusual. Harold never points us in a wrong gastronomic direction!" Rita said.

NEW THREATS OF BIOTERRORISM

Every nation, big or small, had various quantities of nuclear arsenals. Every nation had the means with the protocol to manufacture a bioweapon that could euthanize a particular person without suffering the pain of death, as long as his or her DNA was known. That protocol had been created by a group of six graduate-school buddies, all molecular biologists from the University of Tennessee. Their noble task was successful in "blackmailing" warring leaders into stopping fighting. The biologists still remained unknown to the world. So did their backer, the defunct Global Foundation.

For more than six years after the release of the bioweapon protocol, the world experienced an unusual calm and relative peace among neighbors that had been hostile to each other. There were no territorial claims or other excuses to point guns at their neighbors and put their fingers on the triggers. On the surface the world seemed to be a Utopia in which most people had dreamed of living. No country would threaten to use its nuclear arsenal or the particular bioweapon for domination or for any other purpose, military or economic. It was because retaliation was as easy as making a gourmet meal!

Had true peace, a new world order, arrived?

Or was it just the calm before a storm?

At the White House at 1600 Pennsylvania Avenue, the president held his usual weekly cabinet meeting. When all the members were seated and coffee was served, the president entered and all the cabinet members stood up.

"Morning, Mr. President—."

"Morning, sir—."

"Please be seated. Defense, please," the president said before he even sat down, wasting no time.

"Sir, we have some recent intelligence," the secretary of defense said. "There may be an obscure group hidden in a small country or some out-of-the-way place trying to modify or improve upon an existing bioweapon protocol to manufacture a more powerful bioweapon to harm a population rather than just an individual. So far, we have no solid evidence. We don't know the motive."

The president paused for a few seconds. "I remember many years ago a small native tribe in the Amazon and a population of hyenas were killed as a warning to us. Is this the bioweapon we are talking about?"

"Yes, sir, your recollection is right," the secretary of state said. "I believe that protocol and a possible modification is the basis for our suspicion."

"Caleb, when the protocol was given to the world, it did not include the technique for affecting a large population, am I correct?"

Caleb Morrison was the head of the Center for Disease Control in Atlanta when that unusual and ingenious protocol of gene editing to produce the bioweapon was developed. Although Caleb was not a bench scientist, he was the most effective science administrator. His talent was realized by many distinguished scientists of various disciplines. For that reason Caleb was elected president of the US National Academy of Sciences. The president wanted him to be in his cabinet.

Prior to being drafted to be a candidate for the presidency, the newly elected president of the United States had been active in basic research in biophysics. In addition, he was active in promoting the publication of scientific literature and jargon to laypersons using non-scientific terms. He continued to promote the freedom of thought based on the well-known Carnegie model—there was no restriction on whatever the Carnegie scientists wanted to undertake. No questions were asked by the administrators about their goals.

Because of his ability to articulate science to the public, he was the first scientist in the White House. He was the third US president without a law degree or a political background. His predecessor had been a professor of history at Yale.

The management of science for progress and public welfare had become a fine art in the United States. That was the result of a president having a background in science. It was not science politics or using science as a political ladder; it was the merging of two widely different disciplines into an effective whole. None of the previous presidents had that vision.

"No, sir. We studied the protocol thoroughly. The facts of the Amazon and safari incidents were in our minds. Somehow, all of us have left that question unanswered," Morrison answered. "We did discuss it somewhat as they were an inbred population that would share genes or gene groups whereas most other populations would not. Since each species shared a particular set of genes, the technique did include such a protocol for a mixed large population. We neglected the population angle. It was like not seeing the forest for the trees. I must apologize, and for my staff as well."

"I understand why and how you might not have thought of that. Although I do not know the specific scientific terminology and the processes, I do understand the salient points of the protocol. I did not do so badly in college biology! When I was at Harvard, there were about twenty of us who met monthly to talk about things, anything that came to mind. Genetic engineering was one of them. Carla, would you try to see if Dr. Young—you know who he is, I believe—is still around?"

"Yes, sir." Carla was personal secretary to the president.

The president had done his homework although it was not on his watch when the deadly but ingenious bioweapon was developed by a group of scientists who were not only well known in molecular therapy; they were all graduates of the University of Tennessee at the foot of the Great Smoky Mountains.

"There are two things I have in mind regardless if the intelligence from Defense is true or not. We need to begin to develop a protocol to counter or neutralize what is probably a bioweapon as a preventive measure. I was thinking that if we know how, we can neutralize or counteract the effectiveness of the prospective bioweapon. Just in case. . . Does that sound logical? At least as a hypothesis, a working hypothesis."

"I think so, sir," the secretary of state answered. "If not for our own national security, we can use it in the same way as whoever gave us the initial protocol from the past episode to effectively maintain the balance of power."

"Gentlemen, we have gone through the nuclear age, now we have gene editing for weaponry. The age of gene warfare? What will be in the future for us?" The president rarely was in a sentimental mood.

Carla entered. "Mr. President, I have found Dr. Young and also Dr. Jones. They are both retired now and have left science. However, Dr. John Jones, a recipient of a Medal of Freedom, occasionally does consultation for pharmaceutical companies, including start-ups."

Morrison said, "Mr. President, I believe we have a new crop of young scientists who can undertake the task before us. In fact, I believe there is a genius, now about twenty to thirtyish, named Alex something in the Interior. Right, Kelvin?"

Kelvin was the secretary of the interior.

"Yes, she takes the approach of using genetic engineering and gene-editing technology to keep our environment pristine, an unusual approach."

"Defense, please gather more intelligence on this rogue nation or group. One point, do it secretly. Use the most trusted investigators. No leaks. I mean absolutely no leaks. And I absolutely mean absolutely no leaks! Caleb and Kelvin, please gather a group of our best young blood to tackle the scientific angle. No announcement at this moment. I will have one later on, that is, if necessary. Carla, what is next?"

"Mr. President, you have fifteen minutes before you see the ambassador from China. I think she mentioned something about what you have been talking about. Just a subtle hint."

"Well, that is not only interesting but a very significant coincidence. Carla, please call the Chinese embassy to delay the meeting for fifteen minutes. I want to get advice now from my cabinet before I see the Chinese ambassador."

"Yes, sir."

"First, I would like for all of us here to be available in case I think you should be included in the discussion with the Chinese ambassador. Of course, I will have to ask her for permission as a diplomatic courtesy. She may want all, some, or none of you to be present. So, stand by in the Blue Room. Carla will call you. Now, Caleb, your thoughts?"

"We should interact with the Chinese National Science Bureau in Beijing. I know the director as well as several young top scientists; some of them were trained here. The best was Dr. Lee. I think we should form a consortium of just the two of us, that is, the US and China." Caleb gave his opinion.

The secretary of defense added his opinion. "I think we should include a security person. I mean a working scientist with a security background who has insight into security and a nose for leaks, for example."

"Good idea."

"Alex is certainly my first choice. With Caleb's help we may choose an appropriate number from the academia," Kelvin said.

"State, please."

"Let us wait to see what the Chinese have in mind. Then we will proceed from there. Such as who will be in the consortium and how to carry out the agendas and mandate. I am glad that China and the US are on good terms. Oh yes, the announcement of the consortium when the members are firmed up; a joint announcement with China."

"Good idea. I have to go now. Stand by. Carla will see that you are comfortable. Oh yes, Treasury, please establish a special account for this. Again, this is confidential. Top secret, confidential. And I mean it! No leaks, absolutely none!"

With that said, the president left the Oval Office followed by his cabinet members who would proceed to the Blue Room.

LINKING TWO SUPERPOWERS

"Madam Ambassador, welcome. Thank you for changing your busy schedule," the president said as he extended his hand to the Chinese ambassador.

"Mr. President, no problem at all. Thank you for agreeing to have this meeting."

"Please be seated. Tea, coffee?"

They were sitting on the comfortable couches in front of the big mahogany desk that had been used by many presidents in the Oval Office. Carla, personal secretary to the president, was standing nearby waiting for orders and the appropriate time to exit.

"It is a warm day. Would it be too much trouble to have a glass of lemonade?"

"None at all. Coming up."

"Carla, me too," the president said.

A few minutes later, Carla brought over a tray with two glasses of lemonade and a few cookies.

"Sir, I will be in the outer office."

"Mr. President, as I mentioned to your secretary, we are concerned by the rumor that some rogue nation or group is planning to extend the bioweapon based on the gene-editing technique given anonymously to the world to be able to euthanize an individual selectively at will for the sake of peace which we have had for a number of years now. We still don't know who this group was. However, our intelligence suspects but still has no real evidence that a new rogue nation or group is developing a more versatile and more deadly gene-based bioweapon. We don't know their motive. We are cautious."

"We also have that same intelligence, not yet verified, and the same concerns. Not only for us, for world peace and humanity. I believe we don't want to start a gene warfare just as we don't want a nuclear winter."

"I believe we should pool our scientific and intelligence resources just in case the rumor is factual."

"Agreed."

"Beijing has instructed me to make two preliminary proposals. One, we will structure a special team to investigate the location of the rumored operation of a group, or a rogue nation or nations. Two, we will form a scientific consortium of scientists to spearhead the gene-editing technique for countermeasures when needed. Both should be kept, as the Americans say, between these walls and the ceiling. At least for the time being."

"I totally agree. Excellent idea. In fact, my cabinet has just proposed the same thing."

"How soon can you get your team together, Mr. President? I took the liberty of including our science advisors Dr. Wang, Dr. Wen, and Dr. Lee with me, I mean they are outside, just in case. You may have met Dr. Wang at the United Nations previously. We think the matter is urgent enough. Even though just a rumor at this stage, it is not too early to begin planning."

"Madam Ambassador, I agree again. In fact, I have done the same; State, Defense, Treasury, and the president of our National Academy of Sciences are all standing by."

"Linking science and politics, *realpolitik* or the politics of science at work?"

"For world peace, a new world order that should have been done long time ago."

The president stood up and went to his desk; he pressed a button. Seconds later, Carla appeared.

"Yes, sir. Madam Ambassador."

"Carla, would you cancel the next meeting on my schedule. I need thirty to forty-five minutes with my cabinet in the Blue Room here. Madam Ambassador, your group should be here too. I believe we have enough chairs. Lemonade for all."

"Yes, Mr. President. Right away."

Minutes later, all the chairs were occupied.

"Madam Ambassador, we had a regular scheduled cabinet meeting a while ago. Knowing what our agenda would be, I took the liberty of asking them to stay in the event we should start a discussion. Or at least we can get to know each other. And I thank you for your agreeing to have my cabinet here."

"Mr. President. Not at all. I, too, thank you for including Dr. Wang, Dr. Lee, and Dr. Wen in the Oval Office."

Introductions and handshakes followed.

"We have our differences, we also share much in common, in the past, now, and probably in the future as well. However, our common goal for a new world order has been discussed on and off at different levels on different occasions. I know the academia in your country, and ours too, has been discussing this topic of gene warfare, I'm not sure it is the right term. I believe, and my cabinet shares my view, that our two countries should put our best scientists together to structure a 'defense,' a preventative measure, proactively, in case some rogue group is successful in developing a new bioweapon affecting the peace and welfare of the world." The president opened the discussion with this lengthy narrative.

"Yes, Mr. President. It is for the common good. Our president in Beijing has also been discussing the same. Yes, we have and probably will continue to have our differences. However, our common goal for a new world order, i.e. a lasting peace, should take precedence. We must put our differences aside. As I mentioned to your secretary, Miss Carla, what we had in mind for this meeting is this. Our intelligence has uncovered a possible rogue group or a small nation that may be able to develop a bioweapon superior and deadlier than that given to us six years ago. I assume, Mr. President, you also know that several top molecular geneticists of international repute decided to retire before their retirement age. And they have disappeared. These unprecedented early retirements and their disappearance from the scientific world are suspicious." The Chinese ambassador gave a slightly lengthier opening statement.

It was a political game.

"Yes, Madam Ambassador. We share your concerns about the suspicious nature of the missing scientists. Their whereabouts are under investigation. I am sure your country is doing the same," the US president said.

"I believe we should work together to annihilate the possibility of a rogue nation or group to disrupt world peace. Mr. President, we propose that a consortium be formed including scientists from both our countries. Dr. Wang and Dr. Lee will be our core representatives. I hope you don't disagree," Madam Ambassador said diplomatically.

"Not at all, Madam Ambassador. We are well aware of the reputation of Dr. Wang and Dr. Lee. On our side, I have proposed Mr. Morrison to lead a team in the consortium. There is ongoing research in genetics in our Department of Defense. I shall include one or two scientists from there. I shall let Mr. Morrison do the selection. OK with you, Caleb?"

"My honor, Mr. President," Caleb Morrison replied.

"Mr. President, I am pleased and I am sure Beijing will be pleased that our countries have found common ground, a common cause to prevent a possibly disastrous malicious action by a rogue nation or group."

"Mr. President and Madam Ambassador. May I make a suggestion?"

"Please, Caleb. Madam?"

"Yes, certainly, Mr. Morrison. We need all the help."

Caleb stood up. "I suggest that this consortium be a cover for what we have just discussed. I suggest that this consortium actually takes on the task of curing diseases, cancer, genetically abnormalities, and other deadly medical issues. Of course, the consortium will analyze whatever we and China uncover as to the scientific intention of this rogue group."

"Excellent idea, Mr. Morrison. You will hit two birds with one stone!"

"Caleb, a stroke of genius!" The president added his comment.

"Mr. President, I am grateful to you and your cabinet. I shall convey what we discussed to our president and premier accordingly."

"Thank you, Madam Ambassador. We shall then get the ball rolling, as we Americans put it."

With that said, handshakes followed. Madam Ambassador of China left the White House with her entourage.

The arrangement to firm up the consortium would follow by appropriate officials in the US and China. A Sino-American Genetic Research Consortium, SAGRC, was born.

For the first time in history, instead of competing with the intent to outdo each other, two superpowers decided to cooperate for the purpose of sustaining world peace, humanity, and health for all walks of life.

Shortly after the meeting at the White House, a joint announcement by China and the US was issued:

The people of our two countries will join forces to find the solutions to cure cancer and other deadly diseases. Our scientists will work together, exchange data, and undertake other scientific endeavors for that task. Scientists in this Sino-American Genetic Research Consortium, SAGRC, will devote their time and talent to this single venture for the good of the world.

Whatever is developed by SAGRC and corroborating scientists will be in public domain. Public and private institutions all over the world can freely utilize the protocols and data to manufacturer drugs or any medical means to achieve the goal of curing deadly diseases.

We believe our combined efforts will save not only many development costs but also, most importantly, will help to shorten the development time for the treatments to save more lives.

There was one hidden agreement between these two giants that was only known to the heads of these two countries. There was a mandate that SAGRC did absolutely no espionage and had no agenda to find this rogue group or groups, or the missing scientists. However, members of SAGRC would evaluate, in secret, whatever was discovered by other covert organizations in both China and the US about the activities of the missing scientists.

The whole purpose was to keep the perpetrators from knowing that SAGRC was involved in bioweapon defense. This was one of the thirty-six war strategies in Sun Tze's classic *Art of War*—keeping your enemy in the dark.

THE PHOENIX GROUP

From the top of the tallest building in Hong Kong the panoramic view was breathtaking. On a clear day, less than half of the time in a year, one could see the Kowloon peninsula and half of Hong Kong Island. At night it was the most spectacular sight. Hong Kong has been called the Pearl of the Orient for many years. With the modernization of China and its economy growing in leaps and bounds, with lights on the skyscrapers the whole region was like a pearl with diamond embroidery.

This building belonged to the Phoenix Group conglomerate, which had diverse businesses from A to Z. Its businesses encompassed investments in airlines, shipping, heavy machinery, energy, pharmaceuticals, real estate, and other profitable venues including zoological gardens.

The board of this giant conglomerate included well-known persons in the global business community: Mr. Simpson, CEO of Vouit Pharm in Europe; Mr. Nelson, CEO of the second largest biotech/pharm company in the US; Mr. Li, president of the Bank of Hong Kong, a semi-private institution with backing from Beijing; Mr. Fu, a financier/politician of Bangkok; Mrs. Biotti, wife of the president of the largest shipbuilding and shipping company in the world, based in Italy; and Mr. Lloyd of Kuala Lumpur. Mr. Lloyd was rumored to be one of the renegades of the Lloyd family insurance giant in England. These were the six core executive board members of the Phoenix Group.

There was an unusual non-voting member, a Mr. Hector L., a psychologist at the University of Hong Kong. His role on the board was unusual. When the Phoenix Group decided to have a new business in a certain locality, Hector L. and his staff would go to that location to evaluate the native cultural environment with regards to the start of a new business, including building a factory as well as an office building. Would the citizens be receptive to such an establishment? Their tasks even included the color of the buildings! After their assessment, Hector L. would give the board his opinion. The Phoenix board would make its business decision. No other conglomerate had such specialized professional involvement. That was part of the reason that the Phoenix Group literally controlled twenty to thirty percent of business enterprises worldwide.

There were also three silent board members. They held high positions in the People's Republic of China, the Republic of Germany, and the United States of America. Their involvement in the Phoenix Group was only known to the seven core board members. During board meetings, they were referred to as China, the US, and Germany. Their names were never used. Since they held high positions in their respective governments, they had the privilege of travelling incognito with only their most trusted associates, if necessary, to this top floor in the Phoenix Tower. And with the resources of the Phoenix Group, their comings and goings could be conducted in the utmost secrecy. Rarely, board meetings would include all three silent members. They had derived a means of communication only known to themselves and a few most trusted associates. The age of the board members ranged from thirty to fifty, with the youngest from China.

Every so often the Phoenix Group would host a worldwide open house for their stockholders, scientific/tech elites, educators, entertainers, public media personnel, authors, and many celebrities of one sort or another in the world. However, these events never included presidents or prime ministers or any government officials regardless if they were political knowns or unknowns.

With extensive holdings and hidden political power, the Phoenix Group was the largest financial institution in the world. For the ten board members, that was not enough. They wanted the rest, seventy percent, including military might.

As a form of opening statement, Mr. Nelson, who was chairing the meeting that day, said: "More than six years ago, an unknown group, still not known to us, developed a powerful bioweapon in the quest of world peace. Yes, we have had no wars since then because this unknown group gave the protocol to all. Like nuclear warheads, everyone has them and everyone knows their destructive force. This bioweapon is in some way similar to nuclear power."

"I heard that there is a US-China cooperation in science, a newly formed consortium. But I do not know its purpose or nature," Mr. Lloyd said.

Mr. Li, the banker from Hong Kong, added his comment. "Yes, indeed. I just learned that too. Our friends in China and the US told me that they are forming a consortium. It sounds innocent enough. However, I think their goal may concern us. I don't know for sure. Did they discover our objective? There are no clues at all, so far."

"Yes, I overheard the same by chance at the last United Nations Council on Health meeting," Mr. Nelson said.

"That is disturbing," Mrs. Biotti said.

"Indeed. I don't think they, the UN Health Council, or even the Security Council knows for sure yet. When two superpowers cooperate instead of trying to dominate or outdo each other, a particular third party, that is us here, must exercise extreme caution," Mr. Fu from Bangkok said with a cautious expression.

Mr. Li added. "I think the Chinese and American governments probably found out about the early retirements and disappearances of the ten top molecular biologists, those recruited by us. That may be their deduction of the fact of our task. I don't think they know it is us who recruited these scientists, or our goal."

"This Sino-American consortium, has its name been announced? This is the first time I have heard about it," Mrs. Biotti asked.

"No, not yet," Mr. Nelson said. "The whisper I heard is unfavorable and may be detrimental to our task. I heard, again it's not certain, the consortium not only involves scientists but also soldiers, I mean security departments, probably including the US Department of Defense and the Liberation Army of China."

"Have any of us heard from our friends?" Mrs. Biotti asked.

A phone rang, followed by an encrypted statement appearing on the monitors in front of all the members of the board.

"China and America are cooperating to set up a Sino-American Genetic Research Consortium as of yesterday, SAGRC. The core scientific members from China are Dr. Wang and Dr. Lee. Not yet known who from the US. Both sides may involve security personnel."

"Our suspicion is now confirmed," Mr. Fu said.

Another message arrived from America, encrypted as well.

"Core members from the US are Dr. Calvin of the University of Hawaii who is ex-FBI, Dr. Alex of the Interior, and Morrison, president of the US National Academy of Sciences."

"We'd better start checking in detail all these core members of SAGRC, their publications, responsibilities, expertise, and family backgrounds," Mr. Nelson said.

"And we shall ask our scientists their opinions of them, it may be important to our endeavor, our future," Fu of Thailand said.

Another encrypted email arrived, another message.

"Two additional scientists from the US are Dr. Somer from Sloan Kettering and a Dr. Robert, University of Tennessee."

Shortly after the joint announcement by China and the US, the Phoenix group was indeed surprised; it became cautious and alert. Did this rogue Phoenix Group believe what was said in the joint announcement on SAGRC?

Another confirmation email came from the US.

"Confirmed. Somers from Sloan Kettering and Robert, University of Tennessee. Calvin, marine products, University of Hawaii. Alex from the Interior and Caleb Morrison, National Academy of Sciences."

BIRD'S WING ISLAND

There was a cluster of islands along the eastern shore of the New Zealand archipelago called Paradise Islands, most of them uninhabitable because they were so small and subjected to the destructive force of the typhoons. However, some islands did have a small number of inhabitants. Some were even big enough to cater to a small number of tourists who preferred solitude or a quiet getaway. Some had a hundred or so residents who had been there for generations past. On these islands there were only primitive accommodations.

There were a few simple rules that all tourists must obey when they visited these islands. The rules were simple: whatever you brought in must be taken out, including waste, just as with the exploration and/or scientific investigations in Antarctica and at the North Pole. Those who violated the rules would be fined and were not allowed to go there again. These rules also applied to travel agencies who managed the tours. They would not be allowed to organize future tours to the archipelago.

Portable waste containers, aptly termed honey buckets, were provided for visitors. No pets were allowed on the islands. Transportation was provided by a few travel agencies sanctioned by the New Zealand government. After each visit, government officials would inspect the sites to make sure nothing was left behind.

Not every island was uninhabitable because of its size, elevation above sea level, or other environmental reasons dictated by the Archipelago Preservation Agency (APA) of New Zealand. To enforce the rules, these islands were patrolled almost daily, sometimes twice or more if necessary, from the air and/or by patrol boats. Since the establishment of the rules, there had been just a few violations. In the 1990s tourists had no consideration for nature or other tourists; nowadays their attitudes were changed.

Shangri-La did exist, albeit not perfect.

There were a few islands outside the jurisdiction of New Zealand that no one claimed, and no one knew who these territories belonged to. Once in a while they were visited by tourists who presumed they belonged to New Zealand. One of these had native islanders who had been living there for generations. New Zealand left it to the islanders. This particular island was called Bird's Wing. No one knew how this island got its name.

On Bird's Wing were a few well-kept buildings where some ten non-native people lived. The architecture was certainly not native. The buildings bore no names. The islanders accepted the foreigners as members of the island family. Occasionally, luxury yachts would anchor in the bay for a few days. One of them had visited this island more than a couple of times while others just came and never returned. These rich tourists enjoyed the clear blue water and the white sandy beach.

On this particular day, a 65-foot-long yacht, *Ocean Breeze,* arrived in the small cove. On the rear deck was a small helicopter. After it was anchored, an outboard ferried three couples to shore. There was nothing unusual except they were not tanned like most tourists. A couple of people who lived in one of the small modern houses went to greet the visitors. After a casual conversation, the three couples were invited into their home.

Lunch was set up in the veranda behind a house looking out over the blue water with waves no more than a foot high with small white heads.

A perfect day.

"Welcome to our humble abode," said Dr. White, a middle-aged gentleman with a slight midriff bulge.

"Thanks, Dr. White. You have met my friends," Lloyd, tall with blond hair, said.

"Of course, I remember them well. Our benefactors," Dr. White answered.

Mr. Lloyd was the CEO of a biotechnology company with a unique approach to artificial intelligence. It was a very futuristic venture. His company in Kuala Lumpur was small, with some ten young scientists as the core employees. And, of course, all Lloyd's research activities were proprietary, the information not open to the public or any government concern.

"Are your friends content and satisfied with the arrangements and their living conditions?" Mr. Lloyd asked.

Dr. White replied: "Well, as happy as they can be, Mr. Lloyd. This is certainly the best and most beautiful place to have their laboratory and to think. They like the isolation without interference. They like their freedom without their superiors in their home institutions looking over their shoulders. Mrs. White and Mrs. Stiff are very active and mix in extremely well with the islanders. They have learned their native tongue, songs, and dances. They teach them ours. Mrs. Nasatir has a school for teaching the kids. Nothing official. We have been fortunate that the APA of New Zealand leaves us alone. Well, they do come regularly although they don't have jurisdiction here. However, we and the islanders follow their rules. Except for the honey buckets, of course." There were a few chuckles from their guests.

"Dr. White, you are doing a great job keeping the island as pristine as others," Lloyd said.

"The credit is not mine," Dr. White replied. "Mrs. Stiff is more or less an overseer for all of us. She makes sure we behave and follow the rules of the APA. Mrs. Nasatir was trained as a sanitary engineer, luckily for us. She has built a sanitation facility, so that nothing, no waste, is released into the water around us. The facilities and the process of waste are better than that on the best cruise ship."

"Where is it?" A lady in a blue summer dress asked.

Dr. White pointed to a small rise some five hundred feet from where they were having lunch. "Over there, Rose."

"That? No door, no window, no roof?" asked Judy, the wife of one of the visitors.

"Mrs. Nasatir, do you want to answer that?" Dr. White looked over to where Mrs. Nasatir sat. "All credit to Mrs. Nasatir."

"Thanks, Dr. White, for the compliment. Yes, there is a door and a roof. You cannot see them from here. Later I will show you. We ladies are not shy about taking the credit. We did a great camouflage job with the native vegetation. It can handle the population of the whole island. However, we only handle our own waste, the ten of us, a few more if necessary. The islanders have their own method. We have also learned from them how not to pollute and to keep everything pristine." Mrs. Nasatir spoke proudly.

After lunch, Mrs. White led the group to the sanitation facility. As they approached the rise, they began to see the door which was covered with native vines. The rise was actually a dome-like structure which was also covered with native vegetation. There were no windows; no need.

After their visit to the sanitation facility, they walked about a quarter of a mile to the center of the town. It was not much of a town, just a few huts where some fresh fish was displayed and a hut with a few people drinking the native island tea. A bigger hut was the schoolhouse where Mrs. Stiff and Mrs. White taught the few local children and whoever wanted to come. Mrs. White was holding a class with some ten children of various ages and a few young adults. It was a storytelling time with a little song and dance, American style.

When the group approached, Mrs. White stopped. "I'd like to introduce to you our visitors. They just came a moment ago. Of course, you saw that big white yacht, too. We hope they will stay a few days to enjoy our beautiful island. Welcome."

"Lovely," Mrs. Simpson said.

Everyone agreed.

There was really not much to see other than the blue sky, clear blue water, white sandy beach like powdered sugar, and gentle waves with an occasional flying fish leaping into the air. At the center or close to the center of the island was a small hill about forty to fifty feet above sea level with a few rocky outcrops. Islanders called it the Crown. On top of the hill was a sturdy cement building the size of half a tennis court. It had a wooden floor like a gym for the small school on the island. It also served as a refuge center when typhoons hit.

This building was built some half a century ago by a philanthropist from New Zealand.

A typhoon equivalent to a hurricane in the Atlantic is an event that occurs at least twice a year in the Pacific Ocean affecting almost everywhere in Asia including Japan and as far north as Korea. Some islands that are just a few feet above sea level are hit hardest because there are no barriers, thus, no escape. The wind and rain just sweep from one side of the island to the other side. Each year a large number of persons would perish, and thousands of properties would be destroyed. Affected localities would rebound and lives would be back to normal in a week or two. Fortunately, buildings on some islands with modern construction technology with cement and steel saved a lot of lives on some of these flat islands with no hills.

On Bird's Wing Island, there were huts with roofs of palm leaves. These were the homes of the islanders. There were a number of small modern brick houses, a few of which were flying New Zealand flags. They could be used as guest houses. There were also a few cisterns for storing rain water, the only fresh water source in the island. With just over a hundred islanders and a few permanent foreigners, water from the few cisterns was sufficient for the population on the island.

There were a number of sheep and goat grazing around. No cattle. Chickens and ducks could be seen. One could easily discern that the main staple was fish. There were vegetable gardens some of which were as large as a basketball court. The island imported other foodstuffs and commodities from the mainland; that would be New Zealand.

Of course, there were satellite dishes. There was a small electricity-generating plant using natural gas to supplement the solar panels. There was a small desalting plant which was rarely needed.

It was mid-afternoon, one could see a few fishing boats on the horizon. They were homeward bound bringing the catch of the day.

Life on the island was simple but not backward. Almost everything one needed for modern living was available.

Yes, Bird's Wing Island was paradise on earth.

But there was something else hidden from the neighboring islands and the occasional visitors except those who were involved in this special something. This special something was a biotech laboratory with the latest equipment that housed several of the top molecular biologists in the world. Some of them had been missing or retired from their scientific activities for more than a year.

Drs. Nasatir and White were from the United States. Dr. Stiff was from Australia. There were occasional visitors to their laboratory.

The disappearance of a few scientists from the scientific circle was not noticed or considered unusual. After all, there were thousands of molecular biologists and molecular therapists in the world. Retirements and relocations were nothing unusual, especially in times of peace.

However, these scientists were the exception, with little in common with the norm.

Their identities had been changed.

Sino-American Conversation

At the first full member meeting of the Sino-American Genetic Research Consortium (SAGRC) in Beijing, in addition to the scientific aspect of the consortium, members were consulted about the early retirement of the ten top molecular biologists and molecular therapists in the world. All their retirements were legitimate. But their whereabouts were unknown. This concern was a hidden agenda built into the responsibility of the SAGRC.

Dr. Wang opened the meeting with a short greeting. "Welcome to Beijing. I am not sure how many of you have been here before. Welcome."

"Thank you. Dr. Wang," replied Dr. Somers of the Sloan Kettering Institute. "It is always a pleasure to visit Beijing again. With all the history and the art treasures, there is always something new for me. The last time for me was just last year during the Cell and Molecular Biology conference here."

Dr. Somers was one of the pioneers in the treatment of autoimmune diseases with molecular therapy techniques modifying the amino acid sequence of the gamma globulins, the antibodies. Her research effort had gained international attention. Some thought she might be a candidate for a Nobel Prize.

Dr. Wang took the floor. "Allow me to present some new information. Oh, yes, Dr. Lee had an urgent family problem. She will not be joining us.

"As you know we have been asked to ascertain if there are key scientists missing. Both our governments suspect that whatever the rogue group's intention may be, it will involve scientists, scientists with genetic expertise. I have undertaken the task of looking into this matter. We, our intel agencies, have found there are ten top molecular biologists who have retired, taking early retirement or due to family problems. All legitimate. I have collated the information for all of us. Please fill in the blanks. Ms. Mei Mei."

Ms. Mei Mei was a unique individual. She graduated with honors in biology from Beijing University. Afterward she attended Fudan University in Shanghai to earn another degree in computer science, software specialized in cybersecurity. She was recruited by the Chinese side of SAGRC as a secretary. In addition, she represented China in tennis at the Olympics although she did not win a medal.

"Thank you, Dr. Wang." She handed a list to all the participants.

Dr. Bishop – Harvard. Retired due to health reasons. He is now living on an island near New Zealand with his wife.
Dr. Chan – University of California, Berkeley. Retired, sold his house in Berkeley and moved to a small bungalow in Costa Rica.
Dr. Cliff – Singapore. Retired due to family reasons. He moved to Indonesia.
Dr. Jeng – Stanford University. Unknown whereabouts.
Dr. Nasatir – Toledo, Ohio. His whereabouts are not yet clear.
Dr. Stiff – Australia. He retired to take care his sick wife because he has no confidence in other caregivers. Unusual. He is somewhere in New Zealand.
Dr. White – Ohio State University. Retired due to health reasons. He moved to Acapulco, Mexico.
Dr. Trent – New Zealand. Marine ecologist. Retired, health related. Whereabouts unknown.
Dr. Wing – Singapore. Close friend and colleague of Dr. Cliff. Also moved to Indonesia. Retirement reason unknown.
Dr. Xavier – Rockefeller Science Center. Nuclear Medicine. Retired. Whereabouts unknown.

"That is all I have at this moment. Not much detail. Question marks on all their whereabouts. Some or all might have changed their names, taking on new identities," Mei Mei said.

"Thanks. Ms. Mei Mei. We know the persons and their presumed reasons of retirement from science, albeit suspicious. I think we need to look into this in more detail. I know some of these scientists by reputation. I remember Dr. Chan and Dr. White had short tenures, a few weeks, with the CDC when I was a director. I have to check into them." Caleb Morrison started to write notes on his iPad in caps for Chan and White.

"Agreed," said Dr. Robert. "We have the names. I don't believe their stated reasons for retiring from science. All of them had good jobs with reputable institutions. I know Dr. Bishop and Dr. Cliff personally but not well. I actually collaborated with them on a small project. I shared a podium with Dr. Bishop in a Developmental Biology meeting some years back. I know him slightly."

Dr. Robert, a newly added member to SAGRC, chaired the Department of Biotechnology at the University of Tennessee. In his department there were molecular geneticists, engineers, philosophy professors, and computer scientists. This inter-disciplinary institution was the brainchild of Dr. Robert who had inherited a large sum from his family. Since he had no need for the money and had no children, he convinced the University of Tennessee's board of governors to establish this department that resembled a marriage between the Carnegie Institution of Science and the Salk Institute. In time this department would play an important role in the sustenance of peace.

Dr. Calvin made a concise suggestion. "I suggest we start a background check—scientific background, their scientific activities, collaborators, and publications."

All the members agreed with that suggestion.

"Ms. Mei Mei, would you contact our security unit of the Liberation Army? And on US side, Mr. Morrison."

"On second thought," Dr. Wang said. "I think we had better not involve our respective security agencies at this time. Actually, as I remember, it was a mandate from our bosses not to involve us as well as our intelligent organizations. I believe we should first ascertain the scientific activities of the missing scientists. From their publications, including unpublished ones if we can find them. We will have some idea what they plan to develop."

"You are right, Dr. Wang," said Morrison. "I remember our President and Madam Ambassador both wanted the opposition, whoever they are, to think SAGRC is purely a scientific collaboration to fight cancer and other deadly diseases. If we ask our security agencies to get involved, there would be possible leaks. Let us concentrate on our task of the research and development of cancer and genetic diseases, our major primary goal. Of course we will analyze the science of these missing scientists. That too was a mandate."

"Good thing we thought about it. I had forgotten what our bosses decided earlier," Dr. Wang said.

Morrison nodded. "I have included Dr. Alex at our Department of Interior who is an associate director of our Environmental Protection Agency in our committee here. We will add others if needed later. At this moment, we will work in the manner of a think tank. As we agreed when our president and Madam Ambassador of China met in the Oval Office, SAGRC is just a scientific consortium with a purpose of pooling our resources to solve the most elusive medical issues and cancer. Later, we will form a clinical group to do the same."

"Yes. We shall let the public media know as such when asked," Dr. Wang continued. "My American colleagues, I have dreamed of such a day that two superpowers are brothers. I can speak for Premier Li."

"It is the same in the White House," Morrison said. "Maybe there will be other affairs, political or otherwise, for which we would develop such an amicable relationship. As I recall, our statesman Dr. Kissinger said that what is good for China is good for America, and vice versa."

"As to the whereabouts of the missing scientists and what their agenda may be, we should just let our respective bosses decide. Let them decide how to proceed. In the meantime, we shall concentrate our efforts in the research and development of the treatment protocols of several diseases. We, in short, are a pure and real scientific consortium," Dr. Wang said.

"Agreed," said all the members almost in unison.

"Mei Mei, would you give the list of the missing scientists to the ambassador of the United States? I am sure he knows what to do with it. No email and no phone. Walk it to the embassy." Dr. Wang was very wise to keep the information from leaking to the rogue group, whoever it might be.

With that said, they all went back to the discussions of how to proceed with the R and D of fighting certain diseases.

THE ASSIGNMENT

After a great dinner in one of the home-restaurants in San José, Costa Rica, the Tennessee friends went back to Harold's place. Since there were no other guests, they sat in the pavilion enjoying the cool evening breeze. June had entered into the computer an automatic reply to inquiries of renting: *"Sorry, no vacancies. Thank you for your interest."*

Sitting in the pavilion with a cup of decaffeinated coffee, John began to tell his friend the purpose of his visit.

"Friends, if you think our past work on peace without bullets, the so-called bioweapon, was clandestine, what I am about to tell you is more so. One twist, it is not private and not NGO; this comes directly from the horse's mouth, i.e. our president.

"Some background. You may or may not know that China and the US have formed a Sino-American Genetic Research Consortium, SAGRC. The purpose is to start searching for the means to annihilate or neutralize a possible new bioweapon.

"Both China and America have intelligence that there is a rogue group or a nation that has plans to develop a better bioweapon than ours. The conclusion was deduced from the early retirement of ten well-known molecular biologists, some of them known to us here. Their retirements were all legitimate. And they have disappeared.

"Our governments do not want them to know they are onto them. Therefore, the intelligence agencies are not to start looking into what their present activities may be or their whereabouts. To the public, SAGRC only concerns science; I mean, SAGRC will also evaluate the material of the work given to them. A mandate on top of R and D for fighting cancer, etc."

"Where do we fit in? I assume that is why we have our T-bones and California red, John?" June asked.

"Strange as it may sound, I was contacted by the White House out of the blue one day. Our president and I had a good talk over golf while he was on his golf vacation. He knows about me through his predecessor. Our meeting was not publicized but not secret either. Our surgeon general, Dr. Pei, was also present. He and I, and our families also, became great friends when we crossed paths at a meeting somewhere. We play golf about once a month. The president wants to know as much as we can give him on pharmaceuticals worldwide. And he wants Dr. Pei to predict what will be needed in the next four years. That was what the White House press gave the media. While we were teeing off at the third hole, the surgeon general was ahead in his golf cart while I rode with the president.

"Here is my conversation with the president as I remember it, not verbatim, of course."

"John, we know there is a rogue group or a nation doing unethical things to dominate, to control, or whatever I am sure may be harmful to the world. Like in the James Bond movies but with biotech. I am just thinking out loud. I want you to find out who they are and what they are doing. We know, probably you know too, that ten well-known molecular biologists took early retirement, all untimely and all legitimate, at least on paper. I think their retirements are related to the goal of this alleged group. China and the United States have formed SAGRC, as you know. I don't want SAGRC to do the detective work. I want it to concentrate on the medical sciences to fight diseases. In addition, I want it to analyze the work of these missing scientists. They will, with their collaborators, formulate agents to neutralize or to prep for the possible outcome of the work of the rogue group. I don't want this rogue group to know that we know about them. But I am sure they have some ideas that concern us. You will be my private eye. The only eye, so to speak. I trust you. I am not asking who your cohorts are or tell you how to do it. Would you?"

"Yes. Mr. President. You know I am no spy although I do have many contacts in molecular biology and molecular therapy both in the private and the public sectors. I have not paid attention to the missing biologists, however. There are many who retire or change jobs for one reason or another all the time. I and many of us think that SAGRC is immensely impressive and a historical undertaking by two superpowers. Of course, I don't know the dual responsibilities of the consortium. I could look around, talk with some of my friends. Is there funding?"

"Form a foundation. Or start a new business—a consultancy, for example. Whatever. I am not to know. Surgeon General Pei is your conduit to me. Funding will go through him. You don't need to know how. I know you two are good friends. Therefore, your golf outings will raise no suspicions for the opposition, whoever it is. And you are well known in both the private and public sectors, as you said. Aside from your scientific achievement, your past charity work with the Global Foundation is well publicized. In the context of intelligence, you are hiding in the open!"

"We were at the 8th tee; it was the end of the day. As usual, there were several reporters who were invited to this outing," John continued.

The president addressed the reporters. "We had a good golf outing. You know Dr. John, a recipient of a Medal of Freedom some years back. And, of course, you know our surgeon general, Dr. Pei. We golfed, talked about future medical needs, possible epidemics, pharmaceuticals, including health insurance and other things. I picked their brains. Both of them are pleased that we are cooperating with China to work on the elusive cancer cells. We will pool our resources, not compete. I took care of the green fee for Dr. John with my slush fund," the president said with a smile.

"Mr. President, what is the specific function of SAGRC?" a lady from the Washington Post asked.

"Marian, I guess you want to know more than what was released to the media."

"Yes, Mr. President."

"The core members, you know who they are, will recruit appropriate scientists to help. I just made a suggestion to Mr. Morrison to add a number of top-notch graduate students to the group. Young minds can do wonders."

"Mr. President, forgive me, sir, you are still a professor at heart," a New York Times reporter said jokingly with a smile.

"Probably, Will, no harm in that."

"Mr. President, is Dr. John involved in SAGRC?"

"No, Marian. Dr. John is my unofficial science adviser. He and Dr. Pei, you know, are great friends. Having them playing golf with me once a while is not only relaxing but productive as well. I need to know if we can predict forthcoming diseases. The goal is prevention. Proactive is better than reactive. This is the only way I can keep up with medical science for the health of our citizens. Thank you."

The president left with his security personnel. John and the surgeon general stayed and mingled with the few reporters.

"Dr. John and Dr. Pei, can you give us some specifics on your conversations with the president?" asked Marian, the Washington Post reporter.

"John, why don't you answer that?"

"Thanks. We told the president that our near-future prospect in healthcare should place emphasis on two fronts: cancer and genetic diseases. Actually, that is not new. And you all know that. However, we convinced the president that we should allocate some research funds to search for natural medicinal materials in the Amazon rain forest and other remote corners of the world. Merge ecology and medicine to train young 'explorers,' so to speak. And the president agreed."

"Dr. Pei?"

"I told our president that since we are cooperating with China on genetic research fighting several elusive deadly diseases, why not explore the content of the ancient Chinese scripts in medicine. Since the exponential climb in biotech and molecular biology, gene editing for example, we have forgotten that there is valuable information in ancient knowledge. SAGRC should look into that as well. The president agreed."

"Gentlemen, that is new to us, at least to me on these unusual topics," Will said with a surprised expression.

"Me too," echoed Marian.

"Ladies and gentlemen of the press, we need to get these good doctors back to their jobs." One of the White House staff signaled for a driver nearby.

Dr. John had the final word. "We will have a joint statement on these topics that the president has agreed to when we go back. To let you in on a secret, Dr. Pei and I actually talked about it before this golf outing. We talked our president into agreeing with us. It would not even make a small dent in the budget. But the payback may be great, we hope!"

"With that, Dr. Pei and I left the golf course in a standard-issue black Ford van."

"John, do you think the president knows about our bioweapon work with the Global Foundation?" Harold asked.

"No. I don't think so."

"Why you?" June asked.

"I am sort of a science diplomat, or PR person with the pharmaceutical industries. Since my retirement, you know, I have been going around the world to every corner more or less as a hobby looking for natural medicinal materials. I struck up a friendship with Dr. Pei who has an interest in medicinal history," John continued the conversation. "As soon as we told the president about our hobbies, he suddenly seemed to have a sort of a twinkle in his eye," John said.

"John, why don't you and Dr. Pei keep up your golf outings. Talk about things. Natural medicinal plants, for example. I will talk to Dr. Pei in our regular briefing as usual."

"The president did not elaborate. He just re-emphasized what he told me earlier," John said. "So here I am again to seek your advice and ask you to join me in this espionage adventure."

"Here I thought June and I would have the leisure to pursuit our writing and hobbies," Harold said.

"Harold, I think in about a year, two at the most, you would go a bit crazy with such a lazy life in this Shangri-La." John knew Harold pretty well.

"You are probably right, John. We know Harold."

"Our president mentioned a foundation or new business. He may be on the right track; a camouflage outfit, a front?" Harold queried.

"Let's get Jack down here. And Jerry too. June, do you still have their numbers?"

"Yes." June went to fetch her cell phone.

"Jack, June here ---- John and Rita are in my motel ---- Costa Rica --- we need you. Can you hang up your fishing poles for a few days? --- let us know the flight, you have my email and phone ---- we will pick you up at the airport, San José International, Costa Rica --- thanks, see you soon."

"Jack will take the next flight down. He will be here tomorrow evening."

"By the way, I am still pretty visible. I will be your conduit to the surgeon general who will be the conduit to the president," John said.

The next day Harold went to the airport to pick up Jack and more groceries.

"OK, you guys, you'd better have something good because I had to give up my fishing, the salmon run," Jack said as soon as he settled down with a cup of coffee.

John repeated what he told the others. "Jack, how should we proceed from here?"

"Let me think for a bit. Are there any of those good cookies that June used to bake for us?" Jack asked.

"How you remember! I just baked some yesterday."

"John, you should be in the background. You still work and are known by many. Although we gave up our research work, whoever wants to know can go to the computers, i.e. if there is any suspicion at all, however little it may be," Harold said.

"John, the president mentioned a foundation, a new business?" Jack asked.

"Yes, he did."

"Not a foundation. We don't have the funds, not yet at least until the president gives us something to start," June said.

"We will be funding through the surgeon general's office, through me. Secret funding. Just let me know how much and whatever you need."

"A new business, a business that will be our sort of intelligence organization. To find out where all these missing scientists are and what they are doing," Harold said.

"I think I've got it," Jack said. "How about a travel agency?"

"But we need some sort of headquarters," June said.

"No, we don't need physical headquarters. All we need is an email address," John said. "There are many businesses, not only in the cyberworld, that just use email addresses. All transactions are electronic, no paper. No need to have an office."

"But we do need space for the computers," Jack said.

"How about here?" June said.

"If someone wants to know, they may be able to trace the transactions here. Am I correct in that?" Harold voiced a thought.

There was silence for a few minutes. The Volunteer buddies were thinking.

"John, I remember a lady name Paz, a board member of the Global Foundation. Yes, she was VP of operations. Right?"

"Yes, Harold. She was in charge of all the travel, including all rescue missions to disaster places worldwide."

"Perfect," Jack continued, thinking out loud. "A travel agency. To go to places looking for these missing scientists."

John joined in. "Paz probably still has all the connections and the names of people who have helped us because of the Global Foundation. Let me call her."

John took out his cell phone and looked for the number for Paz.

"Hello, Paz? --- yes, John here --- how are you? --- great, got a minute? --- yes, some business --- are you free for the next few days? --- I am glad --- can you come down to Costa Rica? --- remember Harold and June? --- they have a small tourist hotel down here in San Jose --- yes, very nice and quiet. Rita and I, and Jack, remember him? --- let you know the details later --- email me your schedule and we will pick you up --- thanks, look forward to seeing you." John ended the conversation.

"Jack, great idea. Paz has the experience and contacts. She has such an admirable personality that, I believe, all her past coworkers and contacts around the world still remember her and will give her whatever assistance she needs."

The next day, Rita, John, and Harold went to fetch Paz from the airport.

"Paz, great to see you again. Thanks for coming down at such a short notice," John said and gave Paz a hug.

"I am glad you called, John. I have been doing charity work for the church, soup kitchens and the like in my community, senior centers, taking care of friends in need, etc. I will be glad to do something else. I came here for a couple of missions but never as a tourist to enjoy this paradise."

"We are here, our Shangri-La," Harold said as he was turning into the small street around the corner from the Bougainvillea Hotel.

As Paz stepped out, a gentle cool breeze welcomed them.

"Wow, what a view. And the cool breeze certainly cools off the heat. When I got off the plane, it was like entering a steam room without the steam."

"Paz," Rita said. "John and I are in #1 bungalow. June said that #2 is for you."

As Rita was informing Paz, June came out from the lobby and went over to Paz and gave her a good friendly hug. "Good to see you again. And work together again, per Sir John here. Go freshen up. Take your time. You must be a little tired, but may not be as you are still in such good shape. We will go out to dinner whenever. The bigger unit is our lobby."

"Thanks. Just give me a minute or two." Paz took her small suitcase and shoulder bag into unit #2.

Fifteen minutes later, Paz came out in a fresh dress. "I am ready."

"Paz, after dinner I will tell you what we have in mind. I hope you will join us for a new venture," John said.

"I am sure it will be good. I enjoyed working with you and others in the Global Foundation. I actually miss the excitement."

"Paz, wait, after you hear what John will tell you, you may change your mind," June said.

After another sumptuous dinner in a home-restaurant, they gathered in the pavilion overlooking the valleys and the lights in downtown San José.

"Paz, I will be brief," John said.

John proceeded to tell Paz what he told the others. "Jack, would you tell her what we have in mind since you have given us the idea?"

"OK. Paz, I think the best way to find out where the missing scientists claim they are is by looking, searching under the guise of a travel agency. Since you have the experience, we think you can help us. That is, of course, if you are available and willing. Our leader, John, told us it will be sort of clandestine in nature. You will take a group pretending to be tourists, real tourists, as a cover."

"Gentlemen, I actually had some notion that it would involve travel when John called. I had no idea why I thought so. I am in. The Global Foundation all over again!" Paz said enthusiastically. "I assume John will be in the background. I will need help. Arranging travel is not a simple matter. I will need computers and personal help too."

"You shall have it, everything you need," John said. "Paz, do you want Harrison?"

"Of course," Paz said without thinking for even a second. "Actually, I go to see him once in a while like old times. I make sure that kid, the geek, is healthy. Genius at times can lose sight of reality."

"Paz, would you please call him?" John said.

Paz went to her unit to fetch her cell phone.

"Harrison, this is Paz --- I am fine --- how are things, busy? --- good --- remember John and his Volunteer friends from the University of Tennessee? --- some of them are down here in Costa Rica --- yes --- we need you too, can you come down? --- don't worry about the expenses, it will be taken care of --- book the next flight and let me know --- look forward to seeing you down here." Paz ended the conversation. "He will be down tomorrow. He is a good kid. I may mother him too much though."

"No, Paz. You are doing the right thing for kids like that," Rita said.

The next day, Paz and Harold went to pick up Harrison at San José International airport.

"Here we are, Harrison. June and I retired down here after our work. To write and relax. But John came down and put us to work again."

"Harrison, we don't know how long our work will take. You may have to live down here with your toys," Harold continued. "You take one of these bungalows. Any one you wish. They are all pretty comfortable and have a view."

"No problem. It does not matter where I live. I don't even have a girlfriend. Don't need one. But I think I should keep the apartment in New York. The apartment building in Brooklyn is twelve stories with no less than five hundred units. Hardly anyone knows his neighbors. The doorman does recognize some regular eight-to-five people. I am not one of them. If I keep the apartment and the gadgets going, I can route all electronic communications from here to New York. It would be more difficult to trace anything to and from here. I assume it will be similar to what I did at the Global Foundation, clandestine and working in secrecy?"

"You are right," Jack said.

"What about the travel agency?" Paz asked.

"Yes," John continued. "Paz, you will be the front. You will lead the tours. Of course, you will have all the help you need. Our president and China want to keep the rogue group from knowing what our governments know although there is nothing solid, not yet. They want us to find out the facts: the missing scientists, their whereabouts; who may be supporting their research; what the projects may be. If and when we find out some facts, we will give them to the governments and let them do whatever is needed. We remain anonymous, just as we did with our bioweapon work. Rita and I will leave tomorrow. I will give our decision to open a travel agency to the proper channel. Harrison, will you program encrypted emails for us as you did before? Tell me what you need. I shall expedite the shipment secretly. You will get it in a few days after I get back home. From the time I leave San José airport, I will be out of the picture. We will communicate in encrypted emails when necessary."

"We understand."

John and Rita left for home the next day.

A few days later, a UPS truck delivered several boxes with no labels.

Harrison got busy setting up his toys.

So, another task confronted the Volunteer friends and two ex-Global Foundation board members.

THE COSTA RICA CONSPIRACY

An encrypted message appeared on Harrison's computer. Instead of transferring it to the computers housed in the lobby and the computers belonging to June, Harold, and Paz, Harrison printed it out.

Harrison handed copies of the message from SAGRC to Harold and June in the lobby. "I did not want to transfer this to your computers via Wi-Fi. Even in this remote location, I don't want to chance an intercept."

"Thanks. Good idea," Harold and June said simultaneously.

Names of the scientists and presumed last-known locations:
1. *Bishop – Harvard. New Zealand.*
2. *Chan – UC Berkeley, same as Bishop.*
3. *Bishop and Chan are very good friends. They retired to the same place and about the same time. Indonesia or New Zealand.*
4. *Cliff – Singapore University, Sidney, Australia.*
5. *Jeng – Immunology/pediatric. Retired? Unknown.*
6. *Nasatir – Artificial intelligence. University of Toledo, Ohio. Retired to Sydney, Australia.*
7. *Stiff – Neurologist. Australia. Retired, unknown location.*
8. *Trent – Marine Ecologist. University of New Zealand. Retired to Indonesia.*
9. *White – Bio-material scientist. Ohio State University. Retired to Indonesia.*
10. *Wing – Radiation physiologist. University of Singapore. Retired to Indonesia.*

11. *Xavier – Nuclear medicine. Rockefeller Science Center, NYC. Retired. Unknown.*
12. *Names and identities may have changed.*

The list was essentially what SAGRC had but with just a little more information. It was not much.

"Paz needs to see it too," Harold said. "Where is she?"

"I think she is outside, cooking."

June went out to the pavilion and handed the information to Paz.

"Harrison gave us this information from SAGRC. You are the head emissary now, Paz. Smells good!"

"Thank you, June, for the promotion," Paz said. "I hope you like my cooking."

"I am sure we will."

"I smell food," Jack said.

After a sumptuous dinner and dessert, they stayed outside in the pavilion.

"Coffee is ready. It is good Costa Rican coffee," June said.

"Jack, why did we have to do this?" asked June. "We have the CIA, FBI, DHS, and others, plus more than ten security agencies. In addition, China has the best search techniques for people."

"The intelligence communities and our president think that this rogue organization has tremendous means. Most likely it has people inside our governments. If it hears a whisper, it will hibernate and wait. Wait for another opportune time. In other words, it will be more difficult to find out who they are and what their plans are."

"Sounds like the Global Foundation again," Harold said.

"Not exactly, it's a different nature or façade. Washington and Beijing think it has the ambition of controlling the whole world." Jack actually was answering for John who had left Costa Rica. "Our bioweapon could have done that, maybe."

"If we are going to get involved," Paz asked, "how do we keep them from knowing? There could be a leak or Wi-Fi interception. All they need is to go online and type in our names. Suspicion and red flags will sound the alarm. Although we are all retired, our past is still with us."

Harrison suddenly straightened up from his slouch. He said, "There is a way to get around that. I can just hack into the personal files, change your names, or even delete them. It has been years since you all were active."

"Can you do that right here?" Jack asked.

"Yes, here with my new toys," Harrison continued. "If this rogue group suspects our activities or the guests with our travel group, they will find nothing. I can also route their inquiries to Paz's travel agency whenever we decided to open it, or to some big travel agencies. I can program an automatic reply without the travel agencies knowing. It is not difficult. Of course, there is always a slim chance it may fail. You will have to take that chance since we don't have an East River reclamation site here! Or I can route them through my New York address."

"That will work," Jack said.

"Some of us will travel as Paz's paid guests. It's a good cover since we are all retired people. Retirees have the time to travel. Get Jerry and Ruth involved again. We still have good legs," Harold added his comments.

"But not together. Different times, different destinations. No repeats," Jack said.

Harold gave a sort of summation. "From this list, there appear to be three or four locations—Australia, Hong Kong, Indonesia, and New Zealand. Australia and New Zealand may be just one, close enough."

June added. "Their activities might be complementary, i.e. working actually together with labs in close proximity, similar to our system with the bioweapon. I am puzzled by the involvement of Nasatir, Xavier, and Wing. Radiation and artificial intelligence!"

"Not one of these June mentioned can be detected by ordinary means. For radiation we cannot poke around carrying a Geiger counter!" Harold said.

"One thing at a time," Jack said. "I know the Lawrence Livermore lab was working on a gadget to detect low-level radiation, such as low-intensity X-ray. I believe it is a fluorescein scintillation counter or something very sensitive. I think they may have a prototype. I don't know how big. Not much detail."

"How did you find that out, Jack?" June asked.

"I still have friends in the Pentagon. They frequently fish with me. For your information, I still have security clearance because of my fishing buddies."

"How nice, I wish I still received pay from my university," Harold said jokingly.

Harrison raised his hand with an empty cup. "I cannot change Jack's identity. It's too risky to play games with the Pentagon."

"Harrison, I just won't travel with Paz. But her clients can come to my fishing holes where there is no electricity and no eavesdropping either. It's perfectly safe to talk, like here," Jack continued. "As I recall, this gadget from the Lawrence Livermore lab was developed from a technology called resonance ionization mass spectrometry, RIMS, to detect small quantities of radioactive isotopes. I believe it also uses laser tech. If it is small enough, Paz can carry it in her purse or in a travel bag."

"Let us transfer that to John. He knows what to do," June said.

"Jack, let us see first how big this gadget is. See if it can fit into a Canon or Nikon camera. Carrying a camera is nothing unusual for a tour guide. It is part of our dress!" Paz said.

"Great idea," Harold said. "Paz or her associate tour director does not even have to hide the gadget. We need to know the effective range."

Taking a sip of coffee, Harold continued. "Just my intuition. A bioweapon with a brain?"

"Let us continue tomorrow. I don't know about you guys, I am a little tired from all these thinking games. Our hotel is booked for the whole week. Jack, when do you have to go back to your fishing holes?"

"No definitive time. I left my booking computer home. If someone inquires about fishing, there's no answer."

"How clever," Paz said.

With that said, they retired to their respective cabins.

Another great morning on the hilltop near the city of San José.

Harold was up early and started to be a KP again. He made waffles and toast. When all the friends were in the pavilion, Harold asked them: "I made waffles and toast only. I'm taking orders for eggs, bacon, or ham. Got some sausages too."

"Harold, how about a little or some of everything from your skillet? Surprise us," Jack said.

"Ok, the coffee is on. Juice in the refrigerator."

After a hearty breakfast, they pitched in to clean up and sat around in the pavilion to continue their discussions, their assignment, about these missing scientists.

"I am going to test the efficiency of the satellite feed of the Costa Rican internet here," Harrison said and returned to his cabin.

"These missing scientists are cooking up something dangerous," Jack said. "We probably know some of them personally or by reputation."

"I met Nasatir sometime ago," Harold said. "Very smart. Sort of daydreaming all the time. He was talking about how to replace all the hydrogen atoms in DNA with radioactive tritium and carbon-14. He mentioned that the radioactivity would not be strong enough to break the chemical bonds but strong enough to cause a mutation to other organisms under certain appropriate conditions. I remember that he and another fellow I did not know talked about the possibility of DNA being able to think. I was not involved in the conversation then. I was listening nearby. Making a DNA or other macromolecules that can think? And radioactive?"

"Jack, did any of your colleagues in the Pentagon give you any hint of their doing this or something related to artificial intelligence?" June asked.

"No. Not that specifically. They did mention that the Biowarfare Division is recruiting AI guys. One of the guys was from Hong Kong. The NSA had some difficulty giving him security clearance. I don't think he was hired."

"If they use our protocol to make a radioactive bioweapon, it's not good. Seriously not good indeed," Harold said.

"Agreed. SAGRC will most likely come up with a hypothesis and let us know. We need to start snooping around," June said.

Harold raised his hand. "We have decided Paz shall have a travel agency. She can take us to places we suspect to be the retirement locations of the missing scientists. There is one more task. We have to find out what these scientists are up to. That is, we need to know their recent activities. SAGRC and the government have decided not to do this for a good reason, i.e. keep the perpetrators from knowing that we know. We will have to take up the task."

"We can give Harrison key words and names. He probably will get what we need in a day or so," June said.

At that moment, Harrison returned with a smile. "The connection is better than I thought in Costa Rica. No problem, that is, most of the time. Mistakes happen even in New York." Harrison paused and said. "Did I hear that you need me to find out what those missing scientists have done or are doing?"

"Yes. Harrison," June said.

Harrison thought for a moment. "I can do that easily enough with just key words and names. Actually, names will do. However, if my assumption is correct from what you guys have said, this group or nation is very sophisticated. Neither the US nor Beijing security agencies know who they are. Whenever or whoever goes online to find out the stories behind these missing scientists, some computers will register a hit. I am sure this group has the means to record the hits and even from whom and from where."

Harold stopped halfway as he was putting a cookie in his mouth. "That is right. I am sure these people have supercomputers too. They have been able to keep others from finding out who they are. If Beijing cannot do it, no one can."

"Harold, you are right," Jack said.

"How do we find out their backgrounds then?" June asked.

"Not online," Harold answered and continued. "We have to go back to the basic outdated method. That is, go to libraries, into the stacks, look through the indexes of the journals; hard copies, not the electronic files. Read the articles and take notes."

"Harold is right," Jack said. "That is the only way not to arouse suspicion. Suspicion will curtail the investigation. Their activities would cease temporarily!"

"June, do you still have the numbers for Jerry and Ruth?" Harold asked.

"Yes. I will call them. How about Jim?"

"Jim is off the grid. I talked to him last month. I think it may be health-related," Jack said.

June fetched her phone. "Jerry, June here----how is Carol? --- great --- got a minute? ---John was here a while ago--- he and Rita left --- Jack, Harold and Paz are down here in Costa Rica --- yes, we are having a great time. By the way, can you and Carol come down for a vacation? --- yes, as soon as you can arrange it. Email me the details."

June then called Ruth. "Ruth, June here--- I am running a hotel with Harold, you know --- yes --- complimentary for you and other Vols --- can you come down? --- good, wrap up your church business --- email me the plane schedule."

"They will be here. What a reunion it will be!"

"I guess I have to clean up the rest of the bungalows!" Harold said and continued, "Do you remember the redhead Bonnie? Her dissertation was in radiation biology, the effect of radiation on the embryogenesis of sea urchins. I believe."

"Of course. I talked to her on and off," June said.

"Do you know much about what she has been doing since her graduation and marriage, June?" Jack asked.

"Yes. She never had a job. However, she has been helping her husband in the lab. Her husband, I think his name is John or Jack, a childhood friend, worked for a biotech instrument company in the research division. All the publications had just his name, not Bonnie's. That was the way she wanted it."

"Perfect. Guys, we should include Bonnie if she is available and willing. Are they retired?" Harold asked.

"I'll find out. I call her now. Hope she is home," June said.

June picked up her cell phone, "Bonnie, June here --- I am well, glad you are home --- yes, some business if you have time. But first, are you and John or Jack retired? --- sorry to hear that --- when? --- last year ---" June put her hand over the phone and mouthed, "Her husband passed away."

June continued the conversation. "I, actually we, are wondering if you can join us, the UT bunch, for an adventure --- yes, adventure, we need your talent --- it's not flattery, Bonnie. Here, I will put the phone on speaker, see if you can recognize who is who."

"Hi Bonnie. I am Jerry."

"I remember you, Jerry, the insect man. And your wife is Carol, right?"

"Right. You have good memory."

"It's me here, redhead."

"Harold, you never change."

"Bonnie, I am Ruth."

"Wow, June, you've got the whole bunch in Costa Rica?"

"Yes, Bonnie. Can you fly down ASAP for a reunion? And it's business too," June said.

"No, not ASAP. I have to go to Kennedy airport to hop on a plane. Is tomorrow ASAP enough?"

"Great. Email me and we will pick you up. It is San José, Costa Rica."

"I know. You and Harold's Shangri-La."

"See you tomorrow. Bonnie, who am I?" Jack asked.

"Of course, your East Tennessee baritone gives you away, Jack. See all of you tomorrow."

Jerry and Carol arrived the next day.

Jerry looked around. "Jack, you stay slim. Harold too. You two seem not to have aged much. And of course, June, you are just as beautiful. The few gray hairs actually accentuate the look!"

"Carol, did you hear that? Jerry tried to flirt with me."

"Good. He is still alive!"

Everyone had a great laugh.

"I am going to pick up Ruth in about an hour. Anyone want to ride along?"

"Harold, I will. I want to look around San José a bit more. Take a detour," Jerry said.

"No problem. Let's go now. I will go through downtown, passing by the University of Costa Rica campus and the market place."

"I want to see the market place," Carol said.

The next day, Bonnie flew in from Kennedy airport. Jack and Harold went to pick her up.

"We are almost there, Bonnie. The hotel here is called the Bougainvillea. We are up the hill. The rest of our gang is waiting for you." Harold pointed to the hotel while turning into the small street going up the hill.

As Bonnie stepped out of the Jeep, all the Vols came over. Hugs and more hugs.

"Long time!" Bonnie exclaimed.

"Yes. Bonnie. We have been sort of working together for a while. Just those here, plus John and Jim. Jim has really retired now. John will be in the background. I heard that you may be available. That is, to work. No pay," Jack said.

"Well, I have been working with no pay ever since I married John."

"How so?" Harold asked.

"John was working in a biotech instrument firm, the research division. John had to work overtime a lot. So I went to the lab after hours to help. John did not want me to get a job. So I stayed home and took care of our two kids. The kids have their own families now. One is in France and our younger daughter went to China with her husband. Doing I know not."

"Bonnie, you still keep up with your science, though. Am I correct?" Harold asked.

"Sort of. Just a little radiation biology and instrumentation because of John's work."

"Guys, Bonnie must be tired. Go to bungalow #5, Bonnie. Wash up. We will go to another home-restaurant whenever you are ready. We will be in the lobby over there." June pointed out the larger unit.

"Thanks. See you later."

Like all the other Vols, Bonnie admired the view. "June, it seems cooler up here."

"Yes, always, about five to ten degrees. At night, sometimes you may need to throw a cover on."

At the home-restaurant, Bonnie asked "What is the adventure you mentioned?"

"We will talk about it after dinner. Right now, we want to know what your plans are. Will you stay where you are?" June asked.

"No, I will move. The house is too big for one person. I don't know where or when yet. I want to move to a little granny house down south, maybe back to Georgia. It is warmer there."

"I don't know if you noticed when we came up the hill from the hotel in the corner, there is a little house for sale, probably a weekend home for someone. I have seen a middle-aged couple once in a while and a Mercedes in the driveway," Harold said.

"There are many Americans who have their retirement homes down here. Costa Rica is the best country in Central America. The US pays a lot attention to Costa Rica because it is at the crossroads to the north through Mexico from other Central and South American countries. Law and order are good. Housing is about fifty percent, on average, of the cost stateside. I am sure you can find a little granny house here," June said.

"Thanks. Something to think about. This is good food. I've never had this style of cooking. A home-restaurant you said, June?"

"Yes, this is home of the owner. A little larger than most. You see three tables here and two out in the back. The owner's wife cooks. Her husband works for UPS. There are many like this in San José."

"Paz, are you a scientist too? How do you fit in with this bunch?" Bonnie asked.

"I worked with your buddies. I will give you the details later."

After a sumptuous dinner, they took the desserts back to June's place.

Sitting in the pavilion sipping the great Costa Rican coffee, Harold started the conversation.

"Bonnie, first a little background. We are sort of a clandestine group. Paz and John were board members of a charity foundation, the Global Foundation, based in New York City. Heard of it?"

"Yes, but I'm not familiar with it. Something like the Red Cross?"

"Yes, but much smaller. They did a lot of what the Red Cross does and other things."

"What other things?"

"Oh, yes, Harrison, our computer wizard, was also with the Global Foundation. Do you remember some years back some group developed a bioweapon, gene based, CRISPR-Cas 9 tech, to force the fighting nations to quit the killings? For a new world order, peace, a peaceful world as of now. Remember that?" Jack said.

"Of course. No, maybe yes. *You guys*?" Bonnie looked at each of her friends and exclaimed incredulously.

"It was the Global Foundation. That was why we did not want to discuss it with you at the restaurant. We here, plus John and Jim, were the culprits with support from the Global Foundation. John was our leader, just like in grad school. We were the guilty ones," Jack said. "In time, Bonnie, we will tell you all the details. You may not believe it."

"I believe it. I also understand the protocol for making that bioweapon. John and I discussed it too. Our firm was going to write a 3-D program for it. But the president, being a conscientious and peaceful minded person, said no." Bonnie continued, "Now what?"

Paz began to describe the Global Foundation and its rescue missions, other charity work, the support of the laboratory in Siberia, the Siberian Railroad and the means of communication, the board members, etc.

"What a noble act! And you are able to keep that secret all this time!"

"Yes, so far so good," Paz said.

"What now. Another bioweapon?" Bonnie asked.

"Yes and no. But now we are on the defense," Harold said.

"Carol, do you want to go to the market? I am sure it stays open until late, eleven or twelve, like market places everywhere. Let the scientists talk," Paz asked.

"Let us go. Let them talk." Carol got up and started walking to the Jeep.

"Don't forget to bargain," June said.

PHOENIX BOARD MEETING

All the core board members of the Phoenix Group were gathering, sitting, or standing around the beautiful mahogany conference table. The sideboard was loaded with snacks with international flavors prepared by the best chefs in Hong Kong.

After the servers left, board chairman Li of Hong Kong signaled the others to take their seats.

Mr. Li, wasting no time, started the meeting. "I asked for this urgent meeting for two reasons. One, the establishment of SAGRC, which we know already. It is very suspicious not because of what SAGRC presumably does, according to the public announcement by both China and the US; it is what it does not do. Two, there has been no action, activity, not even a whisper, apparently no concern about our scientists. These are not 'nobodies' in their fields of expertise. They are not even missed, it seems."

"I did not pay much attention to that. Maybe no news is good news?" Mrs. Biotti of Italy said.

"Academicians are notoriously complacent about their colleagues. Their whereabouts, retirements, etc. are not their concern. No talk about their absence in the scientific circle is not unusual." Nelson of the US expressed his opinion.

"I don't have an opinion. Just an intuition," Fu of Bangkok said.

"Mr. Fu, what is your intuition?" Lloyd of Kuala Lumpur asked.

"In this context, no news may be bad news. What I mean is that governments like China and the US do not appear to care. And yet, China and America formed this SAGRC whose purpose, so they announced, is to work on cancer and genetic diseases. It is honorable enough and should have been done long time ago for this dreadful human issue. But the timing? Our world has been at peace since whoever, we still don't know, invented this particular powerful bioweapon and blackmailed, which may not be the proper word, the fighting nations to lay down their arms. On the surface at this moment, things are calm. We have taken advantage of the situation and our plan is progressing very nicely. My intuition is that both China and America know about us. Not us. I mean 'us' in quotes." Fu finished his relatively lengthy explanation.

Nelson, CEO of the second largest pharmaceutical/biotech company in America, went to the sideboard, picked up some snacks, and said, "I don't have the same intuition as Mr. Fu. But I do have a tinge, just a micro-tinge of suspicion. I took a look at the composition of the SAGRC group. Yes, they are the best of the best. But there two people who stand out. One of them is Ms. Mei Mei of Shanghai. Her major scientific endeavor appears to be just at the periphery of cancer research. She is the secretary of SAGRC. I am sure she is very competent in biotech. She also has a background in counterintelligence, cybersecurity. Calvin of Hawaii and the Pentagon? He is another person with a security background. Ex-FBI!"

"Quite an observation," Mr. Simpson said. "How about other members? I have not taken as good a look at them as you did, Mr. Nelson."

"I asked my computer guy to check all the members of SAGRC before I came here. Other members may be appropriate. Maybe too much so, or not so, an unusual combination. For example, Alex of the US Environmental Protection Agency is a genius. Her approach to environmental protection is unusual, a genetic approach. Unusual. I would have thought she would be more theoretical than practical. An environmentalist to fight cancer? I now understand Mr. Fu's intuition. There are some points and factors missing in this SAGRC group. Plus, China and America both appear to have absolutely no concerns over and no interest in our missing scientists as Mr. Li alluded to. These are good scientists, not just some common academicians."

"What do you mean by 'no concerns'? Retirement and relocation are not unusual," Mrs. Biotti said.

"Maybe it is still early for us to concentrate on their absence from the scientific arena," Hector L. said as he took a sip of tea. He continued. "I am more inclined to think that SAGRC may spell trouble. The composition of the group is unusual, I agree with Mr. Nelson. I remember this genius Alex. Having her in the group will certainly help. She does not have to do the lab work. She certainly can interpret the results of others. I am sure she can interject ideas."

"At this moment, we need to really keep our eyes open and ears tuned," Mr. Li said. "We shall notify our friends in the US, China, and Germany to keep a close watch. There are no Germans on our board and among the missing scientists. Our German friends can help us."

"How so, Mr. Li?" Hector L. asked.

"Back to our 'no news may be bad news' notion. If our friends in China and the US start to inquire or just casually look into the activities of SAGRC, they may, just maybe, set off an alarm about us. They may not want us to know. That is, I still have an inkling that SAGRC is a cover to counter our effort. That means the US and China know about 'us,' albeit not by name. We are still well hidden from the world."

"In that case, we should tell our friends not to do anything," Hector L. said. "Maybe our German friend can covertly make some inquiries?"

The Phoenix board was quiet for a moment. An encrypted message appeared on the monitor in front of each board member:

We are dark. Waiting to see what SAGRC will do.

That was from China.
Not a minute later came a similar message from the US.
Another encrypted message from Germany.

Begin to indirectly, covertly monitor SAGRC.

"Lady and gentlemen, I am glad we are all on the same page," Mr. Li said.

"We still have to be vigilant. So, we shall instruct our staff to monitor for inquiries about the missing scientists, such as who—and when and from where—is searching for their publications and their whereabouts. If there are more than the usual amount of academic and scientific inquiries, that means they, China and the US, are suspicious. If none, I will feel better." Mr. Nelson gave the board a sort of logical deduction concerning the matter of the missing scientists.

Mr. Fu added his comment. "Business as usual. Our vigilance includes not only monitoring the activities of SAGRC, it should include the research activities of their outsourced researchers too. I don't think the members, although they are the best, can do all the lab work themselves. They must contract it out to various institutions. We can find out easily enough. After all, SAGRC said all findings and developments would be transparent and in public domain. In fact, Mr. Nelson, your firm can use them too."

"That goes for all our business. It is very generous of SAGRC, if that is its real purpose." Mr. Li was suspicious, the same as everybody else.

The meeting was adjourned with very cautious mindfulness.

None of the members was a scientist. But they all knew what science/technology can accomplish, especially for them, for their ambitious undertaking.

Global domination.

THE VOLUNTEER CONSPIRACY

While Paz and Carol went to the market place, Jack continued to give Bonnie the background, the latest from the White House, the SAGRC, and other details. When the ladies came back around 1.00 AM, they were still talking.

No one seemed to be tired.

"Guys, it is late. Let's continue tomorrow. How about it? I am sure Bonnie is tired from the long trip," Carol said.

"We are just getting started!" Harold said jokingly.

"I am intrigued, surprised, flabbergasted would be the right word," Bonnie said. "Although I do want to know the whole story, a tired mind jams up the white matter. Maybe we should continue tomorrow."

"Breakfast is any time after seven. Earlier, you cook your own!" Harold said. "Good night everyone."

"Harold, your Chinese-Southern accent has not changed," Bonnie said and gave Harold a big hug.

Next morning, Paz was up first. She made the batter for waffles and pancakes, beat a dozen eggs, brewed the coffee, and put sausages and bacon on the grill.

Soon after, everyone was in the pavilion.

"Harold and June, you two picked the ideal retirement spot. Well, not really. John put you to work again," Bonnie said.

"Harold, do you need me today?" Paz asked.

"Not really, we will try to work out the science in the morning. After lunch we will have to include you in the game plan. Carol too."

"All right. Let us go downtown," Paz was talking to Carol.

"Be careful of the potholes. By the way, the exchange rate is higher in Chinese restaurants. People in the street can also change money for you. But don't deal with them. Do not go to the bank; you need to have passports and wait; and the rate is lower," Harold said.

"Why Chinese restaurants?" Bonnie asked.

"My ex-compatriots have good sense with money."

"Legal or illegal?"

"Both!"

The ladies took the Jeep and left.

Over coffee in the pavilion, the Volunteer friends continued their discussion.

"Let's get started. I need just a minute to clear the dishes and put them in the washer. It's one way to keep the flies away," Harold said.

Jerry started the conversation. "I think Harrison is correct. Once we search for the work of the missing scientists online, whoever is behind the development of this bioweaponry will find out who is searching and from where. One or two inquiries are OK. But we need more. I believe we have to search the literature using old-fashioned legwork."

"Right, Jerry. We need to go through the indexes of journals in which these scientists may have published their work," Ruth said.

"We shall divide the labor. The University of Costa Rica and the Technology Institute in San José have good libraries. We go there once in a while. They are very good at giving courtesy library privileges to retired academicians. We go to the lectures once in a while too." June and Harold were frequent visitors to these institutions.

"That should not take long, a few days maybe," Ruth said.

Jack got up to fill his coffee cup. "No, sorry. We should not just show up and start to search. Not a bunch of old gringos, an unusual scene. I am just thinking what may be in the minds of this rogue group. I am sure they are monitoring by whom and how often the work of the missing scientists is being searched. Just like Harrison said. I would if I was them."

"Jack is right. I would have eyes and ears in all major libraries. They must have vast resources, a lot more than the Global Foundation," June added.

"So, we have to go back home and do the legwork there. That will not be so obvious. University libraries are full of gray hair," Jerry said. "June and Harold can go to the libraries in San José but not together and not to the same place at the same time."

"Harrison has set up encrypted email accounts like he did for us in the past with the Global Foundation so we can communicate," June said.

"Forgive me, what did Harrison do?" Bonnie asked.

"Sorry, Bonnie," Jack answered. "When we were doing the bioweapon project, Harrison set up special encrypted accounts for each of us and the board members of the Global Foundation. That was how we communicated and exchanged data. For the science part, June was the dorm mother in charge of supplies and data etc. John was the conduit to the Global Foundation."

"Thanks. How ingenious!" Bonnie again exclaimed incredulously.

"That was Harrison, not us," Jack said.

"John cannot even get close to any library. He just plays golf with Dr. Pei. He looks for exotic medicinal plants in the Amazon. We will give whatever we have to him," Jack said. "He knows what to do with it."

"We don't want to know what John does with all the information and material. Not knowing is the best way to keep it secret," Jerry added from his experience in army intelligence.

"I don't know when the ladies will come back. It is about lunchtime. Let us go to the restaurant in the hotel down the hill for lunch. They have great food too. And we will not be out of place because there are many American tourists there. Ready when you are." June started to put away the dishes and cups. "And, Bonnie, you can take a look at the granny house on the way down. We'll walk."

The six Vols—Bonnie, June, Ruth, Jerry, Jack, and Harold—started to walk toward the Hotel Bougainvillea.

"Bonnie, here is your granny house," June said.

"Not so fast, June," Bonnie said. "It is neat. It appears to have no more than two bedrooms. The windows are clean. There is no trash and apparently no pets. The owner keeps it in good condition."

"These little houses are weekend homes for the well-to-do people in San José, I think," Harold said.

"Harold, can you find out who the owner is? There is a For Sale sign in Spanish, but no phone number. Why not?" Bonnie took a closer look and walked around the house since there was no one there.

"Will do. I believe these well-to-do people probably have the mindset to keep up the environment and the neighborhood. It's good for our little hideaway too."

There were a couple of tourist groups and other guests in the restaurant; but it was not crowded. The maître d' saw June and came over and gave her a friendly hug.

"Welcome, Señora June and your friends." She led them to a table by the window overlooking the manicured garden. There was only one season in San José, spring/summer year around.

"Our special lunch menu is lamb marinated in red wine and herbs, and shrimp salad, Costa Rica style. Of course, whatever is on the menu is good. Señora June and Señor Harold know."

"We have tasted just about all the excellent dishes at both lunch and dinner. They are all great for your palate!" June complimented.

"Except," Harold looked at the maître d' jokingly, "no congee!"

"Señor Harold, you will have to be our congee chef!"

Harold and June frequently brought guests to the Bougainvillea. When their little hideaway was full, they would recommend their selected guests to this hotel.

The next day, Harold gave Bonnie the information on the house down the hill from his hideaway.

"Bonnie, the owner of the house is moving to the south. He asked for $300,000, including all the furniture and appliances."

"It is a great granny house," Bonnie said.

"I have the key. Want to go down to look at it?"

"Sure."

A few days later, Bonnie bought the granny house in Costa Rica.

She kept her old house in upstate New York, at least for a while longer.

First Announcement from SAGRC

Eight months after the inception of SAGRC, China and the US made a joint announcement in twenty languages online and on television.

We are pleased to inform the world that our consortium and its collaborators have accomplished the following:
1. *Early detection of breast cancer.*
2. *Non-surgical removal of adrenal tumors.*

The procedures of both will be reported in the next issue of the New England Journal of Medicine. All procedures are in the public domain. All medical institutions in both public and private sectors are welcome to practice or adapt the procedures.

We also welcome feedback. Please send your comments to the following address [a phone number and an email address were included in this announcement].

To express their gratitude for this accomplishment merely eight months after its inception, the president of the United States together with the Chinese ambassador jointly invited the members of SAGRC, their associates, collaborators, and their spouses for a celebration dinner at the new Chinese embassy in Washington, D.C.

"Ladies and gentlemen of SAGRC and all the collaborative scientists, many thanks for such an accomplishment in such a short time. The people of the United States and China, indeed of the whole world, cannot find the proper words to express our gratitude. SAGRC has shown that scientific cooperation is far better than competition for the good of the world.

"And welcome to our new embassy. The gallery is on your left and the sculpture garden is on your right. Please feel free to browse around. Dinner will be served down the hall." Madam Ambassador from China pointed out the direction to the guests.

"Ladies and gentlemen, here is the Vice President of the United States." The Chinese ambassador went over to greet him.

An average-sized, middle-aged gentleman walked over to the podium. "Ladies and gentlemen, I bring an apology from our president who is not able to come to this event. Because of the bad weather in London, his plane was grounded. Needless to say, the United States of America and China, and the world, are very appreciative of your effort and accomplishment in such a short time. I am sure there will be more of the same in the near future. We are grateful also to Madam Ambassador for her generosity for this event held in this brand new and beautiful embassy."

A sumptuous dinner was served while a quartet played in the background.

After the main course was served, Morrison stood up. He spoke without using a microphone. "All of us at SAGRC thank our hosts, the White House and the Chinese embassy, for this wonderful evening. Without your support and our collaborators, we would not be able to be here tonight. Briefly, our next priority is working on the deadly pancreatic cancer, to do research on early detection and treatment. We also hope to be able to reduce the occurrence of sickle cell anemia by genetic manipulation before the fetus is born. For the ladies and gentlemen of the press, we will have a short Q and A after dinner over there [he pointed to a door behind the dining room]. I represent all SAGRC members and associates in thanking Madam Ambassador from China and our vice president for your appreciation of our effort. We will continue to do our best for the health of the citizens of the world."

DIVISION OF LABOR

The six Tennessee Volunteer friends decided to divide the labor to ascertain what the intention of this unknown rogue group could be by looking into the work of the missing scientists. The intelligence communities of China and the US were pretty convinced, albeit not one hundred percent yet, that there was a link between the still unknown rogue group and the missing scientists. Familiar with the work of the scientists, both governments might be able to connect the dots to find out the nature of the project, the intention, and who was backing the work.

"Thanks for inviting me to be a spy with you guys," Bonnie said. "I will go back and settle whatever is needed and move down here later. I never thought I would have this kind of retirement. To be a spy, of all things!"

"Bonnie, you are right. We, too, never thought we would be involved again in bioweaponry in our retirement. That's all John's fault. He will have to pay for it later," Harold said.

"I don't know science. But I have no regrets about having a role in what you scientists have done. It was a noble act to bring peace to the world," Paz said with sincerity.

"No, Paz. You were one of the noble actors too, more so. Without the support of the Global Foundation we would not be able to keep the fighting near zero for many years," June put her arm around Paz.

"I am glad Jerry was part of it too," Carol said.

"Now, let us get down to the nitty gritty," Jack said. "As we said, we should not descend on the libraries here in Costa Rica at the same time. I talked to Jerry a while ago while walking back up after lunch. Here is what we should do.

"Since our governments of China and the United States have only recently known about the conspiracy or whatever it may be and the missing scientists, it will take at least a year to develop the bioweapon, assuming that's what it is. It took us a little over two years. We don't have to rush into our planned library work. Jerry, why don't you tell us the detail of the scheme."

"Ok, Jack. We'll go home and go to libraries near us, preferably university libraries because there is always a lot of gray hair there and a lot of students. It is more difficult to monitor who goes in, what information they search for, etc. In addition, there are a lot more scientific journals than in the public libraries.

"Point one, no online searching. Harrison is right. This group is certainly able to monitor who and how often and when someone is searching for the work of the missing scientists. A simple task like keeping track of who is searching for what merchandise, social networks, etc.

"Point two, we divide our labor. That is, each of us is responsible for two scientists' work.

"Point three, although we are responsible for two, we are to look into others at random.

"Point four, we give ourselves three weeks. Spread around the time spent searching. It is less obvious that way. Take notes, write down your comments and ideas.

"Point five, we will compare notes via encrypted emails.

"That is about it. Jack, anything missing?"

"No, Jerry. That is about it. Do it in your leisure time."

"Not all libraries have the same journals. Scientists publish their work in different journals. We may have to change our searching responsibilities," Harold said.

"Yes, you are right. Let us proceed as of now," Jack said. "June, have you got the lists?"

"Yes. I need to make copies. I'll be right back." June went to the office and was back within minutes with a list for everyone.

"Let us just go down alphabetically for ourselves and the missing scientists too. That is pretty random," Jerry said. "June, would you be our secretary and dorm mother again?"

"OK. Bonnie, you take Bishop and Chan. Jack, take Cliff and Jeng. Jerry, Nasatir, and Stiff; I will take Trent and White; Harold, Wing and Xavier. And Ruth, you just pick whoever you feel like. That should be random enough to start."

"One suggestion," Harold said. "We should note who sponsored the work, granting agencies, NGOs, industries, etc."

"Harold, great idea. From the supporting agencies we should be able to glean for whom these scientists worked," Jack said. "Anything else?"

"When do you want me to set up a travel agency?" Paz asked the group.

Harold replied. "Any time, Paz. Do the regular travel agency things. It will be a while before we find out what these missing scientists have done and will probably do. Then you will find them for us. Once you establish yourself as a bona fide agent, this rogue group will not be looking into your background, I hope. Your work with the Global Foundation will actually help."

"Paz, I assume you still have contacts in various places where you have visited or helped when there were disasters?" Jack asked.

"Yes, Jack, I do. I will contact them about my new job."

"Just a thought," Ruth said. "Should Paz's agency specialize in a certain niche? Like local flavor with Paz's local contacts?"

"Ruth, you mean I should take my group to somewhere and let local people show them around rather than the standard tourist fare?"

"Yes. Precisely. Like restaurants that don't cater to tour groups. Like those Harold and June took us to here, home-restaurants, for example."

"That is a great idea. Those who have helped us in the past will also benefit from it in some way," Carol said. "Your guests will enjoy this kind of tour. I would."

"Carol, I will need help. Maybe you can be my partner," Paz said with a big smile.

"Jerry, why don't I do that while you and your Vol friends do the science detective thing," Carol said, rather pleased with the thought.

"It may not be appropriate for Carol to participate because these people may check into the background of Paz's associates," Harold said. "An army wife may raise a red flag."

"Harold is right," Jack said.

"Well, I've lost my job before I have one!" Carol said with slight disappointment. But she understood the rationale.

"Small group. Selective. Like June's place here," Jack said.

"June and Harold, can I extend my rent here for an indefinite period so Harrison can help me too?" Paz eyed Harold and June.

"Of course," Harold and June answered almost in unison.

"Thanks. I will go back tomorrow to New York to wrap up a few things. Either sell or rent my condo out."

"Paz, keep your condo. I think John can secure a budget for your tax and other costs. Use that as your 'permanent' home/office but operate all the tours from down here. With Harrison next door our endeavor will go better. That is, we'll remain unknown to whoever our opponent may be," Jerry said.

"Ok, my fellow conspirators, let us go to work, but not too diligently. We shall compare notes in one week. Email first, then we'll meet here or elsewhere," Jack said.

"What about your fishing guests?" Harold asked.

"I shall have my doctor write an excuse letter, absent from classes!"

"Harold, June, can you take us to another home-restaurant this evening before we go our separate ways tomorrow?" Bonnie asked.

"Can we say no?"

"Yes. You can say whatever you like. But you have to take us there. My dear Confucius!"

Harold and June went to visit the University of Costa Rica and the Technology Institute of San José.

LIBRARY SEARCH

Harold took Jerry and Carol to San José International Airport early in the morning.

"Harold, I thought we had done our good deed, albeit not what we hoped for or expected. Now, we are on the defense," Jerry commented.

"It does seem that our work and good intentions have no end in sight."

"There is more than just bench science for your graduate student buddies," Carol said.

"We committed ourselves years back when John called," Harold said. "I have no regrets. Ever since I decided to be a scientist, I always thought there was more than just cleaning test tubes and collecting data. But I never thought that our science would be involved in this kind of science, cloak and dagger science if you want to call it that."

"You know, Harold, what we will be doing is like a literature search prior to our dissertation research," Jerry said.

"In certain way, yes."

"No staying up all night though," Carol added her comment. She knew what Jerry and others had gone through to earn their doctorates.

"I will go to the libraries of East Tennessee State University and Georgia Tech. There are a lot of gray-haired people there as you said, Harold."

"Great idea, Jerry. I want to visit Atlanta once in a while. Remember? My dad played football at Georgia Tech," Carol said.

"Yes, you still keep his helmet!"

Harold dropped Jerry and Carol off at the curb at the airport.

On the way back from the airport, Harold picked up a bunch of housing information brochures from one of the real-estate offices.

"Here, Bonnie, I got these for you, so you can have some idea what housing is like down here. Of course, these brochures here will not include the little granny house down the road."

"Harold, when did you learn all this spy business?"

"Bonnie, I think Harold is a natural, a natural spy. He has been writing international espionage novels. Come, look at his library. Here is a whole wall of mystery novels and thrillers. The six books in this big volume here are the originals in Chinese, and here is the translation of the famous Chinese classic *Journey to the West*, a fantasy novel."

"I was not a good student in high school in Hong Kong. I did not really want to study. Just enough to pass. My Chinese is worse than my English. That's not saying much, Bonnie."

"Good enough. Good enough to get us into this mess!"

"Hey, it's not my fault. Blame it on John."

"I have no regrets," June said. "Yes, John got us started. But we did not have to be in this mess. We did it willingly and with much pleasure although I did have some regrets with regards to the sacrifice of innocent people and animals, casualties of peace. Yet, I feel I have achieved more than just science. In fact, our ultimate goal in science is to make science to work for the good of all." Without getting too philosophical, June simply stated the truth.

"I am glad I am involved now," Bonnie said. "John, my husband, had this notion that I should just be a housewife. But then, he appreciated my help in the lab."

"Bonnie, your plane leaves in two hours. I will take you to the airport. Harold, you stay and clean up."

"Yes, June. Just like you told me to clean up my corner in the lab in Knoxville. See you, redhead. Have a good flight."

"I will visit NYU about an hour away, and the University of Long Island in the other direction."

They waved good bye.

"Harold, what a reunion again," Jack said.

"On the defense this time."

"Right," Jack said. "I am pretty far from civilization. I have a condo in Anchorage which I use in the winter. The University of Alaska is not like NYU or Georgia Tech. I hope its library has the right journals."

"Down where I live in the Florida Panhandle, I'm pretty far from civilization too, not much better than Jack's fishing hut. No snow, of course. It's a small southern town, not really a town, just a beach community, a small fishing village, an endangered species. It is a little over two hours east to Gainesville and about the same west to Mobile."

"The real boondocks?" Harold asked.

"Yes, more than the boondocks," Ruth said. "My excuse to go to the 'cities' is with my assignment."

"Ruth, your boondocks are worse than my fishing hut, so it seems, far away from civilization," Jack said.

"Yes, but warmer and the sea does not freeze! Florida State in Tallahassee has great facilities, but not so much at the University of South Alabama. But they should be adequate. Since my assignment is 'all of the above,' it actually gives me a lot of freedom."

"But the driving?" Harold asked with concern.

"My daughter is in Mobile. She and her children, four and eight, want me to visit them more often. I can always take a break from babysitting," Ruth said.

"How about Tallahassee?"

"It's the football season in two weeks. I have season tickets."

"Ruth, you have the worst draw," Harold said.

"I will manage. I still have good legs and my ticker still works fine."

June came back from the airport.

"Jack's plane leaves tomorrow morning, early. Ruth's is an hour later. We will have a relaxing evening," Harold said.

"Harold, June." Harrison came in. "I just got this email from John. I printed it out and deleted it from the computer."

Harrison handed a sheet to June. June laid it on the table so all eight eyes could see.

"Thanks, Harrison," June said.

Intelligence narrowed down the whereabouts of the missing scientists. Where they may be – South Asia, Australia, New Zealand, Hong Kong, Guangzhou, Hainan Island, and the Philippines. Excluding South America, India, Thailand, Sri Lanka, Cambodia, Vietnam, Myanmar, and Laos. Nothing definite.

"I'm glad they are snooping around before Paz has her travel agency," June said.

"China actually has the best intelligence for finding people, better than MI5 and our CIA especially in Asia and Australia," Jack said.

"Why don't they just do the work and let us retire?" Ruth said.

Jack made a brief summation of all the conversations in the past week. "They are on to it in a very covert way, I gather from John's conversation. If this rogue group hears a whisper or feels the breeze, it may 'disappear' and wait for the next opportune time. This outfit is very good, just as good as the Global Foundation, better, bigger, with more resources."

"I'm glad we already have the supporting agencies of the research of the missing scientists in mind when we peruse their work," Harold said.

The next day, Harold and June took Ruth and Jack to the airport.

On the way back, Harold said. "June, we have to be careful too. Jack thinks this organization is quite influential and resourceful. Maybe we should have Harrison change our identities. What do you think?"

"I think you are right. We were both in academia. It has been years since we left. I don't think we are listed in the current directories. They can, however, go back in time, they have the capability to do so. We can stay as their employees but change 'jobs.' For example, I would be just a clerk and you a mopper-upper! If anyone checks on us, we are still there but with altered personal files."

"June, you have become a good spy too."

As soon as they arrived at their hideaway, they called Harrison to change their past job identifications.

"Harrison, we will take up your suggestion to change our past. Stay with the same institutions but change our job titles."

"No problem. No one really cares too much when academicians retire. Just like these missing scientists. You guys did not care about them until John told us about their potential danger. But I would not touch Jack or Jerry, we don't want to play games with the Pentagon. They will have to be discreet in their part of the task. We are now on the defense as opposed to offense when we were with the Global Foundation."

"You are right, Harrison," June said.

PAZ EXOTIC TRAVEL

As soon as Paz arrived at her condo in upper Manhattan and had freshened up after the trip from Costa Rica, she got out her notebook with the people who had been her contacts while she was with the Global Foundation. By leading most of the rescues and emergency assistance efforts she had made many friends all over the world.

Paz selected thirty names from the list that were not in the regular popular tourist destinations and emailed them.

My dear friends. Since the termination of the Global Foundation, I have been doing charity work for my church and the community in which I live. I have decided to start a profession in which I have experience and with your help—a travel agency. My aim is to take tourists, small groups of less than ten, to exotic places where tourists hardly ever go. I want to include you in my tour as local guides. Show them your local flavor and sights. Of course, you will be compensated.

Please let me know if you are willing to be a part of this.

Within a week, Paz received over twenty positive replies. A simple, to-the-point ad appeared in all the major travel magazines:

A newly founded tourist agency, Paz Exotic Travel, will happily cater to healthy clients (eighteen and older) who want to visit non-touristy destinations. Small groups. Local guides may not be professional tour guides. Deposit required. No refunds. Itinerary may change. Travel light. Be willing to rough it. First come first served. Your experience is our future ad. If interested please email Pazexotictravel@travelnet.com.

Paz Exotic Travel was in business.

Within a week after the ad appeared, Paz received fifteen individual inquiries. She answered with the following message to all:

Thank you for your interest in Paz Exotic Travel. Our first trip will be to Costa Rica. The tour will be ten days. The itinerary includes, but is not limited to, mangrove forests, sandy beaches, private botanical gardens, a volcano, a rain forest walk, and other excursions. The itinerary may change at the last minute depending on the weather and other factors. Total cost approximately $5,000 per person. Deposit $500, non-refundable. Arrange your own round trip flight to arrive Monday next week at San José International Airport, Costa Rica. Send us your schedule and you will be met at the airport. Look for the sign "Paz Travel." There will be no more than ten in the group. First come first served as we said in our ad.

Just like this, an unusual travel agency was born. The first ten people responded and were met on the scheduled date in San José, Costa Rica.

This initiation of Paz Exotic Travel in Costa Rica had a hidden agenda.

The Volunteer conspirators selected Costa Rica because the intelligence information had excluded Costa Rica as a possible place where the missing scientists might be. This choice would not arouse suspicion in the mind of their opponent, the rogue group or nation.

"Thank you for placing your trust in our exotic travel group," Paz said to the group. "We will stay at the Hotel Bougainvillea tonight and the night of the conclusion of our tour. Other times other than on the tour, you are on your own, that is, if you want to extend your stay in Costa Rica. We can help, of course. Have a good rest. I will see you tomorrow morning around nine for a leisurely breakfast. When you are all ready, we will start. We don't adhere to a strict time like other tours. We are flexible. I am glad you are not carrying much. It is a small group, just eight of you, so no need to have name tags."

Paz took them to the Bougainvillea Hotel. After a good night's rest, the tourists gathered in the lobby waiting for Paz and her associate.

"Señora Paz," the proprietor of Bougainvillea Hotel said as Paz walked in the lobby. "Here is your group. I sort of assembled them here for you."

"Thank you, Señora," Paz gave her a hug.

"OK, let us go. Get your things. All of them. We will be staying in different places from now on."

Before the group got into the minibus, Paz introduced Daisy to the group.

"This is Daisy. She will be our host and our guide for the duration. Daisy is a retired marine biologist with the University of Costa Rica. She has collaborated on several research projects with a number of scientists in America, Japan, and France. She speaks all these languages in addition to Spanish. So, whichever language is comfortable for you, Daisy will be comfortable also."

Daisy was in her early sixties but had an athletic figure of a thirty-year-old. She just carried a medium-size backpack.

"Welcome to Costa Rica. I also am very glad that you have chosen, have faith in, and trust Paz Exotic Travel just from a simple ad. I am retired now. But I still have many contacts here and with many scientists abroad. I went to Toledo, Ohio, for a week to study fresh water clams, to Japan to study the mariculture of seaweeds, and to France, you would be surprised, for cooking!

"Today, we will drive to the Pacific Coast, stay overnight at the dormitory of the Marine Biology Station for one, maybe two, nights depending on the weather. I was actually a tour guide when I was a student at the university here. However, on this tour I will limit the narration to only what is necessary. You can ask me questions anytime, or just enjoy the scenery. There is plenty of water. Don't get dehydrated. We will introduce ourselves to each other as we go. Paz has the list. Ready?"

The tourists climbed into the minibus, a comfortable vehicle with AC and the necessary supplies. Daisy was also the driver.

After two hours driving on a two-lane highway dodging many potholes, they arrived at the University of Costa Rica Marine Biology Station.

Paz said to the group: "Here we are. It is vacation time, so there are only a few students and staff on site. There are many empty rooms, bunk beds. Take any room on the first floor. Some have two beds, some four. There are no locks, sorry. Toilets and showers to the right of this dorm. It's primitive compared to the Bougainvillea. Put your bags in any room you choose, then come and have a drink in the shade. Daisy should be back soon. When Daisy comes back from the office, she will have more instructions."

The tourists comprised four couples: a young couple from Hong Kong who appeared to be on their honeymoon, a retired couple who looked like marathon runners from San Diego, another retired couple from Ohio, and two ladies in their forties from France.

They seemed to be healthy and full of energy.

Daisy spread her arms. "Welcome to my paradise. I spent many days and nights here as you may have figured out. Just a simple directive: On top of the building where the toilets and showers are, see the aluminum corrugated tank? That is our water heater. If you want to take a warm shower, do it before sundown. In the morning, you will have a cold shower! In this heat of over thirty degrees Centigrade, or over eighty degrees Fahrenheit, a cold shower in my view is better, more refreshing. Please use the soap in the dispensers, it is biodegradable. Use the towels that I will give you. Keep them as we leave, use them later. They are the rapid-dry ones. Any questions?"

"I am starting to enjoy this trip already, Daisy and Paz," one of the French ladies said in English with a beautiful accent.

"Thanks."

"Put on your swimming gear. If you did not bring it, just put on something simple. Later you may want to take a dip somewhere. Hats, dark glasses, shoes too. You will need them to walk around. You can take them off on the beach if you wish. Cameras too. We will walk down this path to the boats," Daisy pointed in the direction of a trail going downhill to the shore. "Each dinghy will take four plus the boatman, me, or Paz. We will go into the mangrove forest. Keep your voices down. The motors are electric and we will paddle if necessary, so you may have to work too. Animals don't like loud noises. Watch the overhanging branches. Let's go."

The wind kicked up a bit, generating ripples on the otherwise mirror-like surface under a warm late-morning sun. The dinghies glided along the surface with a low humming noise from the electric motors. The experienced drivers were staff of the Marine Biology Laboratory. They knew the mangrove forests like the lines on their palms because they had been taking the marine biologists and students out here for many years. Like in ornithology, the amateur birdwatchers are the best ornithologists. Once in a while, the drivers would give some information to either Paz or Daisy in Spanish. Paz also spoke Spanish fluently.

One of the drivers pointed with his arm in a nine-o'clock direction, shutting off the motor. There sat a twelve-foot alligator and a slightly smaller one with their eyes just above the surface of the water in the mangrove vegetation. Unless one was an experienced observer, one would miss their presence. Above their heads in the dense branches were a couple of monkeys calmly munching their finds. The alligators appeared to be waiting for their lunch. The dinghies drifted with the gentle, hardly noticeable flow in the narrow channel. A couple of colorful snakes were hanging down from the branches no more than ten feet from the visitors. They, too, were waiting for their lunch. There were a couple of small birds on the tree branches and fish down below in the clear water. A small shark was swimming nearby.

The visitors spent a little over an hour in the mangrove forest, the bridge between the land and the sea. They came to a clearing with several species of birds foraging on the grassland.

"If you need the facilities, there are none," Daisy said. "But we have these special baggies. We need to carry the solid matter out. Find some bushes. Be careful, some snakes may not be friendly! Find a stick, your only protective weapon."

One of the two drivers told Daisy in Spanish, "Señora, tell your guests to walk to that rocky shore over there, they will see several kinds of crabs, very colorful."

Daisy transferred that information to her visitors.

"Wow, what is this?" the young lady from Hong Kong asked.

"That is a fiddler's crab. Over there, look, a sea turtle!" Daisy answered.

"The water is so clear. I can see schools of little fish, sea anemones, sea urchins, sea stars, many other animals and plants!" exclaimed one of the gentlemen in the group.

"What a treat!" one of the French young ladies said.

"Wait, there is more in the afternoon," Daisy told the group. She continued, "One of the drivers said that we will loop around this clearing. You can see the bottom of the sea about one to two meters deep. We will cruise slowly."

After looping around the clearing, they came to another mangrove forest. Even the amateur travelers noticed that the overall architecture differed from the one they just came from. The mangroves were denser and some of the branches almost touched the water. The trees and vegetation extended deeper, much like a rain forest on water. Some tree roots were as large as several inches in diameter and exposed above the water line.

"This is what we call a mangrove forest," Daisy explained. "You will notice that there are several four-legged animals. Look carefully. They are not hiding from us. They think we are just neighbors. We will take a walk on land. Put your shoes on. There are several pairs of shin guards in the boat. They are actually shin guards for football players. Wear them, pull them down to meet the top of your shoes. It's just a precaution; snakes bite below the knees."

The drivers found a good landing spot. They tied the boats to a tree trunk and the visitors went ashore. A couple of deer sensed visitors, raised their heads, and turned their ears toward the people. Noting no danger, they continued to graze.

A sudden whistle alerted the visitors.

"Over there, three o'clock," Daisy pointed. "A proboscis monkey. Very rare. We thought they were extinct until last year when these two drivers told us they were here"

"They looked at us," Paz said. "It's the first time I've seen them. Actually, Daisy, it's my first time to Costa Rica."

"Everyone pick up a stick, a good sized one," Daisy said to the group. "Stay with me and the drivers. Most animals, birds especially, will stay away or hide. For bigger animals, you see their droppings here and there. We just have to be observant; watch for snakes hanging down from the branches. They don't like to be disturbed. Wild boars are aggressive, but they are also afraid of us, we are bigger and more in number. There, three big ones! A big black snake, eleven o'clock, and left of the tree trunk is an ant's nest. These ants are as long as one centimeter. They bite and hurt!"

The group stopped their walk. They looked around; there was no sound, no movement, just the whisper of the breeze in the trees. Soon, several beautiful birds appeared from nowhere. Sounds came from under a small canopy formed by just a few trees. More birds. Bird songs. Movement on their right, deer.

For some ten minutes the group was part of the mangrove forest.

"We will take a walk around that big tree back to the boats," one of the drivers said to Daisy in Spanish.

Daisy translated that to the group.

As soon as they moved, the sound of the forest changed. People made a different noise that was foreign to the local residents.

"We will cruise again; it is about thirty minutes to that island," Daisy pointed to the west.

There was a small rise and white lapping waves at the fringe of the landmass that looked like beach.

"Relax, no more snakes now! You can see the bottom all the way to that island. It is about five meters at the deepest. I used to come here monthly to collect a special kind of seagrass. I tried to culture it in my lab. I failed. It tastes good and the nutritionists told me this seagrass is better than the seaweed you buy in the stores."

"And that seagrass only grows here?" a French lady asked.

"Yes, maybe in other places that we don't know about. And we don't know why. That was part of my research. I did not find the answer."

As they approached the island, one of the drivers pointed to his left, "Señoras and señores!"

It was a whale shark. A gentle giant.

The rise was actually pretty high with rocky outcrops. The white outline the visitors saw far away was in fact a white sandy beach. There were no pebbles where they landed.

Daisy made an announcement. "Please help bring water and the containers with food and the tents on shore. We will take a siesta here. The drivers need to rest before we go back. We will set up the tents. In about an hour, the outcrop over there will cast a shadow. You will feel the cool breeze."

"The temperature must be in the low nineties," one gentleman said out loud. "But the breeze is cool."

"Yes, this side of the isthmus facing the Pacific is cooler than the other side, the Gulf of Mexico. The Pacific breeze, we call it. With the shadows that will come later it will be even cooler. Now you have free time. Take a dip but don't go too far. The tide is coming in, so it's safer. If you see another whale shark, you can swim close, but don't touch it. Skates too. There aren't many sharks here."

Wasting no time, the two French ladies took their tops off and ran to the sea.

Paz and Daisy set up the tents and relaxed with their guests. The boatmen were taking a nap under another tent.

Paz asked the group, "What made you decide to take a risk with us?"

"Paz, we know you, but you don't know us," one of the ladies said. "Remember the fire many years back in San Diego? We were evacuated with just the clothes on our backs, literally. The Global Foundation gave us, some twenty people in our neighborhood, fifty dollars each. We went to Walmart to buy basic clothing and toiletries. My husband here, Raymond, and I and a few others did not even have our credit cards. We stayed in a motel nearby paid for by your Global Foundation. Paz, you were very kind and efficient. When we saw the ad for 'Paz Exotic Travel,' we figured it might be you. We took a chance. It is you! Now we are here. How fortunate! Wonderful!"

"I remember now. Your neighbors actually donated more money to the Global Foundation than we spent on you after the fire."

"This is my husband, Raymond, and I am Cynthia. Hubert and Rita are our close friends. They live in Ohio, as you know."

The young couple from Hong Kong introduced themselves. "As you may have guessed, we are on our honeymoon. We didn't want the usual honeymoon. We wanted a special one. When we saw your ad, Paz, we checked it out. There were no prior ads. But Paz Layug, VP of Operations of the Global Foundation came up. So here we are, just like Raymond and Cynthia."

"Thanks," Paz said. "I got bored after the Global Foundation closed up shop. Since I did most of the travel arrangements for our Foundation's rescue missions, I decided to have a travel agency, an unusual one. I knew Daisy because we came down here a couple of times to help. Daisy was very kind to arrange our exotic tour, it's just a start."

"My bride and I will take a walk around the rocks over there." The young honeymoon couple walked away holding hands.

"The water is great," one of the French ladies exclaimed while putting on her loose-fitting shirt. She was Gail.

"Gail and Marie, let me introduce to you your companions," Paz said. "They are Raymond and Cynthia from San Diego. And their friends Hubert and Rita from Ohio. The young couple from Hong Kong are on their honeymoon. They are Kirby and Sharon."

Marie was sort of drying herself putting on her T-shirt. She said, "The water is so clear, and the fish just swim around you like you are one of them. I stepped on a crab, sorry. I think I saw a whale shark, just a shadow far away. I've never been to such a paradise!"

"I am glad we have a good start," Paz said.

"When we leave here in about two hours, to give our boat drivers a good rest, we will collect some sea urchins and take them back to the Marine Biology Station. Tomorrow, I will run an experiment with them, with you," Daisy said.

"You did not tell me that," Paz said.

"The itinerary may change, right, Paz? According to your ad," Daisy laughed and put her arm around Paz.

A couple of hours before sunset, the group collected a couple of dozen sea urchins which were placed in a basket dangling in the sea from the gunwale of one of the boats. When they arrived at the marine biology lab, Daisy put them in of one of aquariums in the laboratory before addressing the group.

"Ladies and gentlemen, I think the water is still warm. Don't take a long shower. Share the water. Over there is the cafeteria. It is closed now because it is vacation time for the students. But we can cook ourselves. Paz and I will be there, probably at six. If we are not there, just help yourself. Eggs and bacon, etc. are in the refrigerators. There's no specific time or itinerary until tomorrow. You can walk around in the dark if you wish. Do take a stick and a flashlight with you. I hope the batteries are still working. Let us have our supper. One the cooks is my cousin. She has made some really good sandwiches for us. And great Costa Rican coffee from my garden!"

Everyone had a great time and was a little tired, except the young couple from Hong Kong. Some took warm showers while others showered with cool water later in the evening. They all were looking forward to the next exotic agenda.

No News May Be Bad News

The Phoenix Group in Hong Kong met again in the well decorated and very functional conference room on the top floor of the Phoenix Tower. Across from them in the leather chairs that could be adjusted to the comfort of the user by touching a couple of switches were monitors that were connected to all the business enterprises of this conglomerate. Their financial and top officials were kept up to date by five efficient computer experts. These five computer people were carefully selected for their jobs. In addition to their oath not to disclose what their duties were, a chip was implanted between their shoulder blades, much like those implanted into the prized puppies. Their whereabouts were monitored; and their salaries were more than three times that of equivalent jobs in other industries, plus year-end bonuses. A small, unintentional leak in casual conversation could lead to the consequence of losing dollars in the magnitude of millions; and the loss would extend to his or her personal wellbeing.

As usual, a sumptuous sideboard was prepared by the best chefs in Hong Kong. Many of these restaurants were part of the conglomerate. The owners might not even know who their real bosses were.

When all the seven members had settled down with their choice of drink in their hands, Mr. Li, the Hong Kong banker, started the conversation.

"Last time we met, we agreed that no news may be bad news. I have not heard a whisper or felt a breeze. Neither the US nor China appear to know about us, or do not want us to know they know. Any of you—?" There was no need for Mr. Li to finish what he intended to say.

"Nothing here," Mr. Nelson said. "The SAGRC group announced that it has accomplished the early diagnosis of breast cancer and a nonsurgical technique for the removal of adrenal tumors. In just eight months since the inception of the consortium! Certainly a great accomplishment in the history of medical science. We all know it is impossible for the members to accomplish this. They must contract the work or give grants to many investigators. Our firm has already formed a team to capitalize on the generosity of these two superpowers."

Mr. Nelson continued. "Having said that, my intuition tells me that there is more unsaid. With their vast resources both in capital and people, they can recruit others, NGOs, private detective agencies, camouflage outfits, and the like to look for us. I firmly believe that SAGRC is just a front. Double duty!"

"Mr. Nelson, I tend to agree with you," Mrs. Biotti from Italy said. "However, how would these entities know what our aim, our product is? Let me put it this way, how will they know we have assigned our scientists to produce a better bioweapon?"

"To follow Mrs. Biotti's notion, they don't even know who and where our scientists are. That might be just my assumption," said Mr. Simpson of Vouit Pharma.

"The retirement of a mere ten scientists from their institutions among thousands like them would not be missed." Mr. Fu of Thailand added his opinion with some optimism.

"Mr. Lloyd?" Mr. Li turned to Mr. Lloyd of Kuala Lumpur.

"Honestly, I don't know. Mr. Fu is right, thousands of academicians retire, die, quit, change jobs all the time."

"These scientists, our scientists, are not just common academicians," Mr. Li pointed out. "They are at the pinnacle of their field of research. Like in business, if anyone of us here were missing, I believe it would make the front page of the Wall Street Journal!"

"Forgive me if we are glorifying ourselves. We are the Nobel Laureates of business. Our scientists are good, very good indeed, but they are not Nobel Laureates although they are certainly of that quality or near it," Mr. Lloyd said.

"There is some parallelism, but it's comparing apples to oranges, Mr. Lloyd." Mr. Nelson interjected a bit of American humor into the seriousness of their meeting.

"Mr. Li, we do need to keep our ears and eyes tuned to this SAGRC group and their collaborators," Mr. Hector L. said. "In addition, we need to monitor the CIA, PRC Liberation Army, MI5, and all intelligence institutions of not only the superpowers but also major players like the UK, Germany, even South Africa, and others."

"If you type in the word 'undercover,' you will see the number of people we have placed in various institutions in different countries. Names too, but we don't need to know that," Mr. Li said.

"Mr. Li, what a marvelous job!" Mrs. Biotti exclaimed.

"Not all the credit goes to me, Mrs. Biotti. Before you joined us, we decided to place 'industrial spies' in our competitors' firms. We just extended them to organizations and public institutions that are imperative to our success."

Mr. Li continued. "Mrs. Biotti, you may remember that we did not ask your husband to be on the board. We asked you. And we told you the reason. Remember?"

"Yes. I do remember. And actually, I am honored that you gentlemen trust me and what I can do for the Phoenix group. I believe it is high time for me to be working the D.C. social circuit and walk the Great Wall."

"Yes, Mrs. Biotti. Your husband suggested to us to include you instead of himself. He is too visible, like us here," Mr. Lloyd said. "He is our silent partner."

With not too many words, Mrs. Biotti became a tentacle and an antenna of the Phoenix Group in Washington, D.C.

"I think we should add another task," Mr. Simpson said. "I believe we need to ask our computer guys to monitor major university libraries in the world to see if someone, anyone, is searching for the publications of our retired scientists. Like ad firms, they monitor how many hits, for what kind of products, and by whom."

"That should be easy to do. We do that too in Malaysia," Mr. Lloyd said. "If there are more than the normal number of hits, that would mean we are not unknown. At least someone is suspicious, especially from the US and China."

"Brilliant idea, Mr. Simpson," Mrs. Biotti said.

"By tracing those who search the literature for the work of our scientists, we can even find out with whom they may be associated. It's just a standard marketing technique," Hector L. said.

"We are, so far, unknown. Anything else, lady and gentlemen?" Mr. Li asked.

"Yes, we should monitor new businesses, start-ups, and mergers that may be of interest to us," Mr. Nelson said.

"We need to know not only their business focuses but also the background of the people, the proprietors, CEOs, everything." Hector L. added his comment.

"Yes. Certainly. Especially those subsidized by governments, not just China and the US, but also by European countries, Japan, India, and others," Mr. Fu of Thailand added.

"Such as?" Mr. Li asked.

"Banks, pharms, transportation, new hedge funds, new scientific institutions especially medical and biological, biodefense industries, travel agencies, etc.," Mr. Fu opined.

"Why travel agencies?" Mrs. Biotti asked.

"My question too," Mr. Nelson added.

"If you are searching for people, but you don't want people to know, you don't want to send out private eyes, for example, so what would be the best cover-up?" Mr. Fu said.

"Another great idea," Mr. Li said. "I shall instruct our computer geeks to include new travel agencies in their daily routine monitoring."

LITERATURE DETECTIVES

After their friends from Tennessee left, Harold and June cleaned up their Shangri-La and started to take in few guests. They began their literature search in the libraries of the University of Costa Rica and the San José Institute of Technology. Following Jerry's instruction, they went to the libraries with some sort of random visitations.

"Harold, I found something interesting today," June said after she came back from the UC library. "Wing of Singapore and Xavier of Rockefeller coauthored a review in the New England Journal of Medicine three years ago. It was a theoretical treatise rather than a research paper. No citation or granting agencies. They proposed that in the future, five to ten years, medical science in the area of radiation therapy will change. The biggest change will be the elimination of whole body radiation for the metastasis of various forms of cancer, breast, sarcoma, and others. What they proposed, in a nutshell, was the use of low-level radioactive isotopes incorporated into monoclonal antibodies against the cell surface antigens of cancer cells in an injectable medium."

"That is pretty ingenious. All the basic techniques are readily available. I don't keep up with this technology. We should look for something like this too."

"I will go to the medical school library tomorrow."

"While you are there, you can look up Jenny. She heads the radiology department. Maybe she can give us some updates."

Bonnie was pretty excited to reunite with her graduate school friends. Finding an ideal little granny house in Costa Rica was also a plus. As soon as she put down her one-piece carry-on, she went online to select three real estate agents to interview to sell her old house. Within two weeks she sold her house. Since she had thirty days before handing over the keys, she started to travel to NYU and the Long Island University. Bonnie's note:

Bishop at Harvard – with his graduate students, Cheong from China, Lee from Singapore – isolation of a short, repeated sequence upstream from one of the sequences for gamma globulin. This may be the control sequence for the immuno-proteins. Research supported by Immuno Inc. which is a subsidiary of Alpha Pharm, the second largest pharmaceutical company in the US. He also had Cancer Foundation support.

Chan at UC Berkeley – remote pacemakers and sensors. Travels to Kuala Lumpur frequently (deduced from his research papers using patients there as experimental subjects, which is not approved in the US). Co-owner of a high-tech company, Cardio-Tech, in Kuala Lumpur.

Jack went back to Alaska. Since the time was between the end of the fishing season in the summer and the beginning of a cold front, he moved to Anchorage where the University of Alaska called home. This institution far away from the mainland had the best fishery department among all the institutions of higher learning in the United States. Jack's note:

Cliff at Singapore – DNA sequence controlling cardiac muscle contraction. Chromosome #18. In vitro assay with cardiac muscle culture. Support from Singapore Medical Science, Inc. (from Med Business Review.) He also coauthored two recent papers with Wing of Singapore on the probability of incorporating or replacing carbon with carbon-14 in some cardiac muscle molecules. From the University of Singapore catalog. Wing's and Cliff's laboratories adjacent to each other. Good friends too, probably. There's a footnote with 'Assay done in collaboration with Singapore Medical Science, Inc.'

Jeng at Stanford – pediatric immunology/tumor biology. Publications on the genetics of fetal immunoglobulin, sequence and controlling sequence, exon and introns. Reactivate fetal immunoglobulin genes in adult cells. Support from various sources— US Department of Health, National Science Foundation, and private corporations in Singapore (Singapore Biotech, Inc.) and Hong Kong (Hong Kong Biomed Tech, Inc.). He has also a number of publications on fetal immunology and relation to tumorigenesis. No recent papers.

Jerry and Carol went back to their hundred-acre gentleman's farm/cattle ranch in East Tennessee.

Two weeks later, Jerry said to Carol. "I will visit Atlanta and go to the George Tech library to get some information on these two scientists, Nasatir and Stiff."

"Remember, don't be too obvious. No online searches."

"Don't worry. I still have a guest library card there. So I can go into the stacks where they put the older editions of journals."

Jerry on Nasatir and Stiff:

Nasatir and Stiff went to graduate schools at the University of Melbourne. Nasatir published three papers on the subject of artificial intelligence, one of them with Stiff. Stiff is basically a neurosurgeon but practices only enough to keep up his technical knowhow (my assumption). His major research concentrates on the region of the brain concerning logical thinking. He has isolated the DNA sequence associated with abstract thinking. He and one of his graduate students from Africa tried to use the CRISPR technique to change the sequence and incorporated it into newborn mice with limited success. This African student has graduated and went back to Ethiopia where Stiff used a number of people as experimental subjects.

Ruth went to three Florida State football games and stayed overnight the day before the game. On these game days, Ruth stopped by the library of the Florida State University Medical School. She randomly selected one of the ten missing scientists. On the first visit, she drew Bishop of Harvard.

Bishop, with support from the second largest pharm in the US, isolated the gamma globulin genes from patients in Boston General. He also isolated the same genes from Africans in Ethiopia with support from the United Nations, UNESCO. He and Stiff of Australia are comparing the sequence complementarity of the immune globulins of Africans and white Caucasians.

Wing of Singapore wrote a theoretical treatise with Nasatir on AI and the effect of low-dose radiation. Interesting combination.

Trent is a marine ecologist. He and Stiff started a study on the intelligence of dolphins and the possibility of injecting AI minicomputers, microchips, into their brains. They published a paper three years ago presenting negative results. Last year at the International Conference of AI in Hong Kong, Trent suggested using stingrays and seals instead as experimental subjects. The detail was not published, just a title.

After June's visits to the library of the University of Costa Rica, Harold made several visits to the library at the San José Institute of Technology.

A surprise find, Trent was born on an island in the New Zealand archipelago which is not under the control of New Zealand. However, New Zealand extends its courtesy to monitor tourists there under New Zealand's regulations. Got this from a footnote about the authors in a popular science magazine. Trent also published a couple of papers with Wing and Xavier on the radioactive isotopes retention in dolphins, seals and stingrays. Trent went to the lab of Chan in Singapore during his sabbatical leave last year (a note expressed support from Singapore Biotech, Inc. and the University of Singapore visiting professor program).

White of Ohio State was hosting a conference on using DNA-like or RNA-like macromolecules embedded into micro-drones with degradable proteins as skeleton, a modification of the process developed by us. The modification includes low-level gamma or X-ray from the molecules. Stiff, Cliff, Trent and Xavier were in the audience, not participants. White has published three papers, all theoretical, with an interpretation of research papers by his peers.

A month after these Volunteer friends went to read hard copies of work by the missing or retired scientists, Harold sent John an encrypted email:

John, we have gathered enough information for a discussion. Should we send it to you or should we peruse it prior?

John replied – Discuss, I will also hand your info to SAGRC. The more input the better. Have a mini-reunion again. Then contact me again.

Harold showed John's reply to June. "We will have to be 'fully booked' for next month again."

"Or we could have them as Paz's guests."

"Oh, no. Whoever these people are, they might monitor new emerging businesses, including travel agencies."

"Yes, but not travel agencies! High-tech pharm, AI, and such. Not travel agencies!"

"June, if I were them, I would include travel agencies because travelers or the agencies could be a camouflage for snooping around. Jack has the same idea also."

"Man, you are treating this project like the espionage stories you have been writing."

"Well, that is part of it. And I am not publishing it until our work is done. Just in case I become a best seller!"

"You and your wild imagination. You must have been born with a wicked mind. Like your Confucius!"

"You and a few friends like me for that."

"The cleaning lady is sick today. Go clean up the stove."

"I don't do stoves. I do lab benches!"

"Treat that stove top as your lab bench!"

June went to Harrison's bungalow. "Harrison, would you send emails to Jack, Bonnie, Ruth, and Jerry telling them we need to discuss what we have found in our literature searches. A mini-reunion. Copy John."

"Ok, June. I like this bungalow. This place beats New York City."

"Glad you like it. We all enjoy the hospitality of the people down here. A bit slow, but kind and friendly. They don't treat us like 'gringos' as other South Americans do."

Within a few minutes, Harrison came to the pavilion where Harold was doing his kitchen duty.

"Harold, I just got an email from Jack. Here it is," Harrison handed a copy to Harold.

No reunion in Costa Rica. Have John arrange for us to meet in Boston, Orchid Hotel. Harold and June close up shop, vacation in America.

Several days later, encrypted emails arrived from John to all his Vol friends.

Arrangements made. Orchid Hotel. Boston. Mr. Shum retired. His son took over. Same as before. Next week. Just walk in. Bonnie too.

No Compelling Evidence?

Mr. Li, the Hong Kong banker, was travelling to Singapore. Prior to his trip, he sent an encrypted email to all the board members.

Can we meet? Singapore. Ritz-Carlton, Singapore Millennia. Two days. Suite of my bank.

The reply was affirmative from everyone except Mrs. Biotti who was attending the Kennedy Center Honors celebration of the arts in America. She had started to be a socialite on the Washington political scene, a socialite detective or a lobbying spy socialite.

"Mr. Li, what a suite you have. Right underneath the famous swimming pool. Have you ever taken a dip in it?" Simpson asked with admiration.

"No, Mr. Simpson. I am not a swimmer. Besides, I am not comfortable with heights. My grandsons aged ten and twelve loved it. My daughter, like me, stayed way back on a chair!"

"I think Mr. Lloyd stayed here a couple of times," Mr. Fu of Thailand said.

"Yes. Three times. Each time on a different floor. It's great service. Of course, we pay for it. The Waldorf Astoria cannot even come close."

"There is an old-world charm in Waldorf," Hector L. said. "I heard there are a couple of 'carpet guards' constantly monitoring the wear and tear."

"There is something similar here too," Mr. Li said. "The manager here, a friend of my son, told him that there are about ten of these kinds of people, watching the pool, carpet, steps, wall marks, etc."

"No wonder they charge an arm and a leg," said Mr. Nelson using American slang.

"Shall we get started?" Mr. Li said.

The servers left after placing sumptuous snacks on the sideboard.

"There are two items. First our financials. With sanctions on North Korea and Ethiopia, we should be concerned with our business there. Coal from Korea; bone meal, i.e. fertilizer, from Ethiopia."

"Yes, Mr. Li," Mr. Nelson replied. "I have instructed our fertilizer producer in Addis Ababa to shut down production and give all the workers a week off. If we can convince the United States to exclude bone products in their sanction, we are back in business. In addition, it's not so easy to do business in Africa. They started to learn about labor unions five years ago. We have to have special training for the supervisors, locals."

"I know," Mr. Lloyd said. "Our Chinese associates in the diamond field had to import a number of Chinese skilled laborers in critical positions in the production line."

"How about North Korea?" Mr. Simpson asked the group.

"I talked to our Chinese contact yesterday," Mr. Li answered. "China is pressuring the US to exclude coal exports from Korea because China needs the coal. China is using the leverage of not buying soybeans from the US to lift the sanction."

"Interestingly, soybeans originated from China and the US is now the biggest producer in the world," Hector L. said.

"Likewise rice," Mr. Nelson said.

"Breeding and genetic engineering sure have done much good," Mr. Fu said.

An encrypted email arrived from Mrs. Biotti:

Had dinner with the US agriculture couples. They mentioned sanctions or China's not buying. Need instructions.

"She is good, better than good," Mr. Simpson said. "Let her talk about soybean, corn, and other cash crops. Tell her that the US really does not want all those corn and soybean crops to rot in the field if China does not buy."

"Good idea," Mr. Li said. "A word or two to the right persons, even unintentionally, can result in unintentional benefits."

"Some unexpected," Mr. Nelson added his comment.

"Shall we instruct her to just express her sympathy to the farmers?" Mr. Li asked.

"Yes. Mrs. Biotti came from a farm, not a big one. There are no big farms in Italy. Americans don't know that," Mr. Fu said.

"Americans are great people. However, many of them are enjoying their great life at the bottom of a well, including some politicians. I remember a VP who did not even know where Korea was. The New York Times did almost half a page on many people similarly 'not knowing' or being 'uninformed' or 'ignorant,' including the names of the members in the House," Mr. Simpson said.

With that said, Mr. Li emailed Mrs. Biotti:

Express sympathetic concerns to soybean, rice, corn farmers in the US.

There had been no outright wars between nations. However, trade wars still were used as political leverage.

Mr. Li continued after eating a crab leg and taking a sip of hot tea. "Our next concern is what we talked about in our last full board meeting in Hong Kong. That is, no news may be bad news."

"Is there any evidence that people are checking the work of our scientists or looking for them?" Mr. Simpson asked.

"No, no unusual number of searches from our routine monitoring of major university libraries worldwide. A few, but no unusual increase in frequency. But that does not mean no one is searching. We may miss some minor university libraries. I did not instruct our computer people to monitor public libraries which have only limited scientific literature other than general ones like Scientific America, Discovery or Current Sciences, etc."

"What is your concern, exactly?" Mr. Fu asked.

"Same question here," Mr. Lloyd said.

"What concerns me is if the Chinese and the US governments find out the specialties of our scientists, they may be able to deduce from their research the nature of our planned bioweapon," Mr. Li answered.

"Mr. Li, our scientists are public figures. I mean their expertise is listed in the catalogs of respective universities. It is an easy way to find out. No need to go to the libraries." A comment from Mr. Nelson.

"Yes and no. Mr. Nelson. Their backgrounds and training are no secret. However, it is their current research and that of the last few years that is important to us. And remember, we have decided with our silent partners what products or weapons we should concentrate on, militarily as well as politically, including health, like genes, etc."

"Yes, Mr. Nelson. Mr. Li has reminded us," Mr. Lloyd said. "We had many discussions. The gene-editing protocol CRISPR-Cas9, with which people can be euthanized without suffering, is a powerful biotech that was given to us by someone still unknown to us. However, every nation with a biotech or a molecular biology lab can duplicate the work."

"Right. We decided to find the right scientists to extend this powerful biotech, gene editing, and more. We did. And our scientists have changed their research emphases to fit our aim," Hector L. said. "Thanks to Mr. Simpson's research staff we found them and they agreed to join us. It is a great challenge for them, scientifically, not politically or financially for them."

"I cannot take all the credit. Mr. Nelson's research director, Dr. Carl, contributed just as much. It is unfortunate he passed away. Otherwise he would be a great leader of our effort," Mr. Simpson said with much regret.

"We are also fortunate to have Dr. Jeng of Stanford to take over the coordination effort. And he is doing a great job as well," Mr. Nelson said.

"I talked to our scientific team last month. They are actually very enthusiastic. They wanted to take up the challenge. One plus point is they all know each other. Some of them are good friends and have done research and published papers together. They met informally after I talked to them. They are now at the last stage of their research. They are ready to proceed to make the final product for us. We have a laboratory on Bird's Wing Island, outside of New Zealand's jurisdiction. And we will also have a laboratory in Melbourne. They are close enough. We have been able to change their identities, gave them new passports, etc." Mr. Li said.

"We can't change their faces!" Mr. Fu said.

"True," Mr. Li said. "We always take that chance. So far, we have done well."

A message appeared on the monitor of the laptop that Mr. Li carried with him.

Information about new travel agencies.
Paz Exotic Travel; pazexotictravel@travelnet.net
Proprietor: Paz Layug. Ex-VP of Global Foundation, defunct.
First trip, Costa Rica. Clients: newly-wed couple from Hong Kong,
retired couple from San Diego, retired couple from Ohio, two French
ladies, thirtyish, no info.

Mr. Li read the message to the rest of the board members.

"That seems to be innocent enough," Mr. Nelson said. "I know the Global Foundation and one of their board members, a John Jones, VP of AZ Pharm Inc. John retired right after the Global Foundation ceased their activities. He had a stroke. I think he is now a golf partner of our surgeon general. We need to watch them closely."

Mr. Nelson continued. "Paz Layug was in charge of all the travel arrangements and rescue matters. She must know and have worked with a lot of people around the world. Her exotic travel agency is right up her alley."

"Who was the local contact on her first tour and where?" Mr. Fu asked.

Mr. Li hit a few keys and said. "Costa Rica. Local guide a retired marine biologist name Daisy. She took the clients to places like isolated islands, mangrove forests, and the University of Costa Rica Botanical Garden and Research Center which is not open to the public. And other places she knows that no tourists have gone. Probably her research areas or collection locales in the past were not accessible to tourists."

"That must be a great tour for Paz's clients. I would have liked that too," Hector L. said. "Probably Mrs. Biotti also. Next tour?"

"No information."

"I am more inclined to concentrate our efforts on the financial sector and start-ups rather than travel agencies," Mr. Lloyd said.

"I am glad to know that our scientific team is content and willing. In two years?" Mr. Fu asked.

Mr. Li explained some of the detail. "Probably, maybe less. We have to ship the equipment, more or less, incognito. Some of it will come from our own companies. That poses no problems, we need to buy some. As we know, everything we do must be legitimate, except the project in the laboratories which must be hidden." Li was chairing this particular bioweapon project.

The Phoenix board had a good meeting. Another board member, Mrs. Biotti, was doing her social clandestine part in Washington, D.C.

Everything appeared to be on track as planned as long as their scientific team did not divulge what they were doing and for whom to any of their many acquaintances in the scientific arena.

"Gentlemen, it appears as of now there is no compelling evidence that our task is known to the US and China, or any other countries. I am sure our silent partners will raise a red flag if otherwise.

"Oh yes, I forgot. I have reserved several suites for you. If you wish to ask your spouses or friends to come over for a week in Singapore, feel free. We all need a vacation sometime," Mr. Li said with cheerful optimism.

FAMILY VACATION IN DISGUISE

After a great afternoon of eighteen holes, Dr. Pei and John sat in the shady coffee shop in the club house.

"John, there is an indication that they are doing something in Australia, Melbourne, and maybe New Zealand. Just a fine thread of evidence. We may have to check it out."

"That can be done easily enough. Want me to contact my friends? How do you know that?"

"Actually, it's just my own suspicion. Our satellites monitor all traffic on land and at sea, you know, yachts, cruise ships, etc. There is a yacht that has visited an island called Bird's Wing outside of the jurisdiction of New Zealand but within the archipelago of New Zealand. It is from Melbourne and it has visited this particular island more often than usual for normal rich men's vacation outings."

"Dr. Pei, why don't we, your family and mine, take a vacation together? We have not done so since our grandchildren were pre-teens. I bet they will enjoy each other's company."

"Great idea."

"Would you make a reservation at this resort, Paradise Resort, on an island in the Indian Ocean? One week. Let me know when and we will fly there either together or separately."

There was a hidden understanding between these two gentlemen in their conversation at their golf club.

Two weeks later.

"John, Rita and kids. It's good to be here with you again. It has been three, four years?" Dr. Pei walked with a fast pace toward John's family as soon as they got off the small inter-island prop plane.

Hugs and more hugs.

"Wow, John, your grandson has grown. Six feet and one-eighty? Jeff?"

"Yes, Dr. Pei. Almost six feet and almost one-eighty," said Jeff, John's grandson. He looked over to Dr. Pei's party. "And that must be Gloria."

"Jeff, you remember me! I have grown too, but I'm not one-eighty pounds!"

"Gloria, if you reach even close to one-fifty, you can go jet skiing by yourself." Jeff went over and gave Gloria a good hug and a playful pat on her behind.

"Jeff, behave," Gloria said with a pleasant smile.

"John, we have two suites, bungalows, next to each other. We're in luck."

"Rita, Dr. Pei and Vivian are great organizers." John was holding Rita's hand.

A couple of golf carts came over.

"Ladies and gentlemen, we will take you to your bungalows," one of the drivers said.

Ten minutes later, they arrived at their bungalows and started their family vacation on this tropical island in the Indian Ocean.

One of the drivers said to them when they arrived at their bungalows: "Here are the keys. Actually, you don't need to use them. Over there on your far right is the pier for jet skis, pedal boats, kayaks, and other water sports. On your right that gravel path will lead you down to the beach. Everything is close by. Over there behind the bungalows are the restaurants, a ten or fifteen-minute walk. If you don't want to walk, just call and we will come and drive you there. Yes, downtown is a thirty-minute walk. You may want to use us. There are up and downs in the narrow streets. Enjoy your stay. For anything you need, just pick up the phone."

Gloria and Jeff wasted no time changing into their beachwear. They started jogging to where the jet skis were.

"Young people, full of energy. They don't even need to adjust to the time change," Dr. Pei said.

"Meet you guys in thirty minutes in the coffee shop," Rita said.

"OK."

Two days later, while the Pei and the Jones families were walking around the resort, a golf cart slowly approached the paved walkway. When it came close, John stopped; so did the cart.

An elderly gentleman was waving a cane. "Dr. John?"

"Mr. Shum, what a surprise," John said taking two steps at a time to the golf cart.

"What a coincidence. John, are you on vacation here?"

"Yes, Mr. Shum, with my family and friends. Let me introduce them to you.

"This is Dr. and Mrs. Pei, our surgeon general," John put his arm around Dr. and Mrs. Pei. "And this is his son and daughter-in-law, Donald and Marsha. And this is my daughter Patty and her husband Rick."

They shook hands.

"My grandson Jeff and Dr. Pei's granddaughter are over there somewhere, jet skiing. You will meet them later."

"When did you get here?" Mr. Shum asked.

"Two days ago. Great place."

"This is Bertha, my wife. Where is my phone?"

Bertha handed Mr. Shum his cell phone. He dialed a number.

"Susan, Shum here. I just arrived. I've met some friends unexpectedly. Dr. Pei and Dr. John's families."

"Yes, Mr. Shum. They are our guests for this week," Susan answered on the other end via the ether space.

"Susan, wait, let me ask them." Mr. Shum turned to John and Dr. Pei. "Would your families have dinner with me?"

John and Dr. Pei looked at each other and their families.

John said, "Of course. We will cancel our reservations."

"No need. I'll just tell Susan."

"Mr. Shum, let me guess," John asked. "Is this Paradise Resort one of yours?"

"You guessed right, Dr. John."

Mr. Shum dialed another number. "Bran, how many people can our Gulfstream carry?"

Bran on the other end answered, "Twelve with our present configuration, plus Mary and myself."

"Thanks." Shum turned to his friends. "Bran is my pilot and Mary the flight attendant. Let us say 7.00 PM in the main restaurant. OK with you?"

"Yes, Mr. Shum," Dr. Pei said.

"See you later, Mr. Shum," John added.

As Mr. and Mrs. Shum drove away toward their bungalow, John told the others. "Mr. Shum is in his nineties. Still healthy and wealthy. Mrs. Shum has some health issue but they're under control. I know he owns maybe a dozen or so hotels around the world. He owns the famous Orchid Garden in Boston. He and I served on the board of the Global Foundation. He was the largest contributor to our functions."

"A good friend to know," Mrs. Pei said with admiration.

After a sumptuous dinner, they all went out to the patio, joining a number of guests. A cool breeze came off the ocean, making the awnings flutter.

"Ladies and gentlemen," Mr. Shum said to his guests, "I will be just a minute. Dr. John, would you walk with me, on my left side, just in case. I don't want to fall again. I need to stretch once in a while to get the circulation going."

"My pleasure."

"John, I got your email several days ago. What is up your sleeve this time?"

"Mr. Shum, we are on the defense this time."

"Yes? Meaning?"

"Remember our bioweapon? We gave the world the protocol. And now there is an echo bouncing off a distant wall. A rogue nation, group, or another Global Foundation."

"Does Dr. Pei know about our bioweapon?"

"No. No one yet."

"What can I do?"

"Can we use your Orchid Garden Hotel again, maybe other places if needed?"

"Of course. Any time. Just email me. I will make the arrangements. My son, Bob, is handling the day to day business. I will just call him. And I will not tell him why. He does not know about our conspiracy, the Global Foundation and your Volunteer friends. By the way, does this involve your friends from the Knoxville days?"

"Yes. You've heard about SAGRC, the Sino-American Genetic Research Consortium?"

"Yes. But I don't really pay much attention to medical matters. Just my own health and my wife's."

John proceeded to tell Mr. Shum the real reason for SAGRC.

"Both China and the US don't want to let this rogue group, perpetrators if you will, know we know. We must find out who they are and what they plan to do. So, I have engaged my Vol friends again. This time they, and we, are on the defense."

"I understand. John, do you still have Harrison?"

"Yes. Paz Layug too. Paz is operating a travel agency as a façade to hunt down the missing scientists. My Vol friends are studying the work of the missing scientists in order to find out what they may be developing, or plan to do."

"Scientists vs. scientists, like intelligence and counter-intelligence. Interesting indeed!"

"Great parallelism, Mr. Shum."

"Let us go back,"

"Sorry, Dr. Pei and all," Shum said. "I need to stretch my legs once in a while."

"No need to apologize. We don't want you to fall again and we want to keep you healthy too," Dr. Pei said.

"Dr. Pei, I am in good hands. I have the 'first doctor' here!"

"Thanks, Mr. Shum. I do my best. By the way, when you go back, if you can come to D.C. with Mrs. Shum, I will introduce her to one of my associates. I think he can resolve her health issue. Just don't tell anyone, it's your tax dollars at work!"

Everyone had a good laugh, including Jeff and Gloria.

"Gloria, it's a good thing we have yet to pay tax!"

"Dr. Pei, I just told Susan that we will charge you and Dr. John the government rate. And for you two young people, Gloria and Jeff, there is no charge for using all the jet skis, kayaks, scuba diving gear, and whatever. Just return them in the same condition as you check them out. Watch out for sharks. That is no joke down here. Follow the instructions of my experts. Sharks like the warm water on the Tropic of Cancer."

"Thank you, Mr. Shum," Gloria said and went over to give him a hug and a kiss on his cheek.

"It's our bedtime now. Bertha and I go to bed early. See you tomorrow," Mr. Shum continued. "When will you go home?"

"At the end of this week. That makes six days already," John said.

"That will be our departure day too. I just asked my pilot how many he can carry on his Gulfstream, he said twelve plus him and Mary, the flight attendant. Why don't you cancel your flight and fly with us back to Los Angeles? I will stay in L.A. You can use the plane back to D.C. I assume that is where your homes are."

"Mr. Shum, what a treat!" Gloria went over and planted another kiss on his cheek.

"Gloria, behave," Mrs. Pei said looking at her lovely granddaughter.

"Now, Gloria. How about walking me back to my bungalow. On my left side."

"That will cost you another free flight, Mr. Shum."

On the social page in the Washington Post was a short report on the family vacation of Dr. Pei and John on an island in the Indian Ocean. There was no mention of Mr. Shum on the island at the same time or his owning the resort.

BOSTON REUNION

It was the first time for Bonnie at the Orchid Garden Hotel in Boston. As she walked into the spacious and well decorated lobby, she stopped and looked around, like a country girl who went to town!

"Miss Bonnie. Please follow me to the penthouse, Mr. Shum's instructions," said one of the twin brothers, longtime associates of Mr. Shum.

"Yes. Thanks. How did you recognize me?"

"Mr. Shum sent over a recent picture of you with several of your friends."

"Oh."

Bonnie was led to a private elevator to the penthouse. As she stepped out the elevator, Jack was there waiting.

"Bonnie, you made it," Jack gave Bonnie a good friendly hug.

"Some hotel!"

"Bonnie, I am Shum. I know all your Volunteer friends," Mr. Shum shook hands with Bonnie. "Welcome to my hotel. This is Bob, my son. He manages this hotel."

"Good to know you, Miss Bonnie. Whatever you need, just call. Dad, I need to go back downstairs now. Good to meet all of you."

"I will go down with you." Mr. Shum walked with a cane, but his eyes still sparkled and he showed no signs of senility.

"John will not be with us. In fact, he will not be seen with us anywhere. He is too visible. And he is hiding in broad daylight!" Jack opened their meeting/reunion.

"Jack, you need to fill me in on some details as we go. I may have to ask questions. I don't know how you guys pulled off this bioweapon tech euthanizing people without suffering! June showed me the picture of a nursing mother who died with a smile on her face," Bonnie said.

"Please feel free. John is a good friend of our surgeon general, Dr. Pei. They play golf about once a month, sometimes with the president. They have interesting hobbies. Dr. Pei is interested in ancient Chinese medicine. He actually learned enough Chinese to read the old literature with the help of a linguistic expert. John is doing his Amazon thing, which is public knowledge in his circle of friends and colleagues. I am sure this rogue group is watching them closely all the time."

The elevator door opened. Two servers, the twin brothers, came in with a table full of food. "Dr. Jack, Mr. Shum told me to tell you that you can use this penthouse as long as you like. He and his family will not be using it for a while. Here are the keys for your suites with your names on them. Use them as long as you need to. When you leave, please give them back to us. They are sort of special for our special guests. Just call if you need anything. There are cold drinks and spirits behind the bar. A microwave oven too. Have a good day."

Bonnie, like all the Vols, asked with amazement in her voice. "How did Mr. Shum get involved with you guys, or was it the other way around?"

"Bonnie," Harold said, "Mr. Shum was a board member of the Global Foundation with John and others, including Paz. He has got more money than God! And he is very generous. Shall we?"

They took out their notes. For fear of intercept by using email, the Vols had mailed each other their notes via the ordinary postal service.

"Jack, why don't you sort of summarize them since you probably have perused them on the long trip down here," Harold said.

"Sure. As you know, these ten scientists, or at least eight of them, appear to have completely different topics of research. That is, from what is said in their respective institutions' description and background training. Bishop and Cliff are two molecular biologists; they have similar topics, maybe. If you look at their coauthored publications, many of them have collaborated with each other. They are virtually working together. My brief conclusion, based on our protocol, is that they may be trying to create a gene weapon that is able to think with artificial intelligence conscribed into the DNA sequence, maybe other macromolecules, the nanobots like ours, maybe more. With a material scientist, White of Singapore, the vector or vectors could be biodegradable. I don't think the bioweapon, which I assume it is, will euthanize people like ours. Their product would just play hell with our brains, thus the two medical doctors, Chan and Stiff, the neurologists."

"Jack, how about the radiation part?" Bonnie asked.

"Harold, your turn." Jack looked at his notes.

"My guess is low-level radioactive isotopes incorporated into the DNA molecules or other macromolecules including the carrier molecules of the drones. A sort of a double-dip. If the edited gene does not work, the radiation takes over because of AI conscription into the bioweapon, a dirty weapon."

"And Dr. Trent, a marine ecologist?" June asked.

"Here is a double-dip too," Harold said. "Trent published with Xavier and Wing on the retention of various radioactive isotopes, their biological half-life, in dolphins, seals and stingrays. And just by chance I saw a footnote that says Trent was born on one of the islands in the New Zealand archipelago."

Jack got up. "I forgot this." He reached in this back pocket and took out a folded sheet. "I sketched this interaction, a connection chart from their coauthored publications. Let me make some copies."

Jack went over to the copying machine to make copies.

"Well, they are all connected," June said. "Someone has to have had a thoroughly thought-out plan to recruit these scientists."

"Let us try to start with what we have. That may not be their starting point," Harold said. "But we have to start somewhere."

"I have no doubt that these people have used our protocol and modified it. No other gene-editing technique that I know of is appropriate," Jerry added his comment.

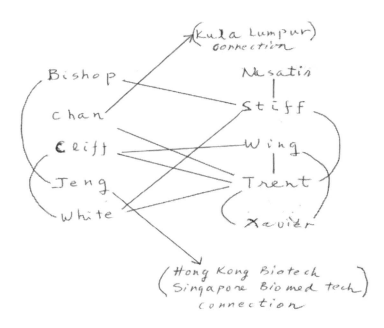

"Let us start with DNA," Ruth said. "A synthetic sequence of a certain function can be inserted anywhere into the genome with CRISPR-Cas-9 tech. Maybe even more than one chromosome."

"If that is the case, it will mean more than one action, reaction, and interaction on or with other genomic information. A cascade or a domino effect?" June queried.

"That certainly can be done. And done easily enough even with the possible incorporation of isotopes with low-level radioactivity. We mentioned that earlier," Jack said.

"Jack, what is in your mind?" June asked. "Hydrogen, carbon, nitrogen?"

"I don't know, even phosphorus or oxygen in the backbone, not the bases, A, T, G, or C, or U."

"Possibly," Harold said. "If they take my triple-stranded DNA and cleave one off, that could be done. I just thought of that."

"I wish John, my husband, had not been so insistent that I remained a non-scientist; then I could have joined your conspiracy,"

Bonnie said with some admiration and a little regret to her Vol friends. "I read your protocol. It's amazing how you guys formulated such a feat!"

"Bonnie, we put our heads together and had almost unlimited support, financial as well as personnel," June said.

"Don't forget," Harold added, "psychological support too."

"Psychological? I don't understand," Bonnie said.

"Bonnie, actually, it was the Global Foundation. Other than financial support we had Paz, remember meeting her in Costa Rica? She is the most talented judge of personal character I know," Harold said. "With its vast resources, Global Foundation hired the best psychologists to vet in much detail all our associates, their backgrounds, mentality, etc., all the bio-parameters. Paz and the psychologists constructed profiles of everyone involved in our project. We, of course, knew our own laboratory associates. We used only those we trusted. They all received extraordinary compensation."

"That must have involved quite a lot of different people," Bonnie said. "Tell me later. Let us go back to the interaction chart that Jack has drawn. Sorry, Jack, but you are not an artist!"

"We were talking about inserting a synthetic DNA, a functional one. Assuming that can be done, we may ask what function or functions." Ruth added her comment.

"I think it might be related to immunotherapy. Jeng of Stanford is a pediatric immunologist. That seems to be out of place, according to Jack's chart. He has not published or worked with the others. Not as much as other scientists in the group. But why? Why him?" Harold was thinking out loud.

"Not one function, multiple functions, multiple nucleotides with different functions?" Bonnie also was thinking out loud.

"Let's see. We have here molecular biologists, neurologists and neuroscientist, cardiologist, a biomaterial guy, a radiation physiologist, a nuclear medicine man, a biophysicist, and an artificial intelligent fellow." Jack pointed out the expertise of the missing scientists. "Bonnie's multiplicity!"

"Bonnie, would you elaborate a bit more?" Jack said.

"OK. I think they, whoever they are, are developing some gene-related weapon that will not just affect one set of genes or one phenotype. What I mean is that the bioweapon will have the ability to exert more than one effect. For example, immunity and tissue degeneration, but not necessarily just these two."

"How did you come about that?" Harold asked.

"AI, artificial intelligence."

"You mean that this bioweapon can alter or change their intended aim or target, or effects?" June asked.

"This bioweapon can think?" Ruth said.

"Yes," Bonnie answered with affirmation.

"I believe redhead is right on the money," Harold said and reached over to hold Bonnie's hand. "Thanks for joining us."

"More than glad to, Confucius!"

"Now," Jerry picked up the thread of thought. "We have here ten scientists who on paper may have unrelated research endeavors. But they have a common goal. A bioweapon that can think, a lot more potent than what we created. Off the top of my head, I think they may be onto the immunological angle. Genes for immunity, from fetus to toddlers to adults. They will be able to edit the genes with our protocol, it's not hard, to fit what they want. That includes cancer too."

Harold expressed his thought. "Jerry is probably correct since there are two missing scientists whose work is related. And neurologists on neuropathies like Guillain Barré Syndrome? It may be farfetched, but I would venture to say that they may be working on turning on and off immune-related genes depending on what they wish to be beneficial to them—money or power or both."

"Harold, was that close to or similar to what you guys did?" Bonnie asked.

"Yes and no, Bonnie," Jack said. "Our endpoint differed. We wanted peace. We got it. For now, at least. I don't think these guys, who have to be plural, want more or less peace—my philosopher professor probably would give me an F for that more or less peace! I think they want control, power, both business and political, maybe more."

"Jack, that is a huge, huge ambition," Ruth said. "It's unbelievable even just thinking about it."

"The science, the gene-editing part, immunity genes, the neurological angle, it is not difficult. But why and how do these two radiation physiologists and nuclear medicine men fit in?" June raised the question.

"And a cardiologist," Ruth said.

"I don't think Dr. Chan is just one of those cardiologists doing stress tests and stent implantation routines," June commented.

"From what I read, their research papers don't really represent their professional titles. They are interdisciplinary, so it seems, multidisciplinary even," Ruth said.

"And low-level radiation, isotopes?" Harold said. "Jack, remember we talked about a gadget that can detect low-level radiation? Sorry, I just changed the subject."

"That is fine. I did check with my friends at the Pentagon, they knew about the machine too. Maybe it is good time to see if John is able to contact the Lawrence Livermore Lab since Paz has got her travel agency up and running," Jack said. "I will contact John later. Let us take a lunch break. I will email John on this."

"Good idea," Harold agreed. "We don't need much. Mr. Shum's staff gave us a great breakfast. But a little fresh fruit and a light lunch will be good. And we can talk about the old times in Knoxville. I will call them."

Harold picked up the phone.

"Yes, Doctor?" said the voice at the other end.

"Would you prepare a light and refreshing lunch for us? Fresh fruit, coffee, both regular and decaf. Thanks."

Thirty minutes later, the servers wheeled in two carts with a variety of small sandwiches, finger food, and drinks.

"Just give us a call when you have finished. We will come and clear the table."

"Thank you so much," Harold said to the two Orchid Garden Hotel staff, Mr. Shum's trusted hires.

GENTLEMEN TRAILBLAZERS

There is no other place in America that can be compared to springtime in Georgia. The fragrance of the blooming crabapple trees along with the new flower buds of the cherry blossoms and peaches can mesmerize anyone who is just sitting there. If one walks the Appalachian Trail, one can see many wild flowers beginning to bloom.

"Hey, Bob, good to see you again." A young trailblazer, Mary, *in her boots and backpack greeted a young man going in the opposite direction.*

"Mary, good to see you too," Bob said. "What was it like in Georgia?"

"Just great, greater than great. Sweet onions are not yet poking their heads out the soil. The flower buds on the peach trees are beautiful. In a few days, you should smell the fragrance," Mary said.

"Are you stopping at Elizabethton to take a shower?" Bob asked Mary.

"Yes, I think I will. Maybe we can have lunch. Then you can go south and I'll go north."

Mary and Bob were not their real names. They were their "trail names." Trailblazers have their own culture when they are on the trail.

Dr. Pei and John were also walking the trail for a couple of miles before they went to the golf club for their eighteen holes.

There were several young men and women who did not look like trailblazers following Dr. Pei and John twenty or thirty feet behind, out of hearing range. They were protective personnel assigned by the White House. It was not really necessary. The protective personnel did not know why.

"John, any news from your contacts? Whoever they are. I don't want to know." Dr. Pei asked.

"Yes. They formed a travel agency, 'Paz Exotic Travel.' Paz was a fellow Global Foundation board member. She was in charge of the travel arrangements for our rescue missions. With her personality, she has remained friends with numerous persons all over the world where Global Foundation provided assistance in the past. We think that her contacts are her local guides taking guests to where no tourists have gone. Our combined intuition tells us that these scientists are hiding somewhere. They might have even changed their identities. Paz may be able to give us some assistance in finding them instead of sending CIA people. My friends have their pictures and public info lifted from university catalogs."

"That is ingenious! Has Paz taken any groups yet?"

"Yes, a first group with eight people touring Costa Rica. They just ended the tour a week ago. And these people have written fantastic reviews and comments to travel magazines. Paz Exotic Travel came through with flying colors, double A!"

"Why Costa Rica?"

"My friends thought based on our intelligence that the scientists are not in Costa Rica or any countries in Central or South America. Going there would not raise suspicion that Paz Exotic Travel is our eyes and ears."

"How and who I am not going to ask! Can they handle all the clients? I am just thinking, a small agency like this."

"Paz is very selective. First come first served, i.e. with selective 'firsts.'"

"What else do they need other than what we have provided for them?"

"A very technical item. A low-level radiation detector. Not a Geiger counter."

"What is it?"

"A prototype from the Lawrence Livermore Laboratory. A fluorescein spectrophotometer or something like that. My contact asked if Paz can carry one around like a camera. Or better yet, make it into a camera or video camera-like instrument. The reason is, my contacts have studied the work of these missing scientists. From their reading, some of these scientists have published research papers together. They came to a preliminary conclusion that their work involved low level radioactive isotopes, probably inserted into the DNA or other macromolecules of their bioweapon. If Paz is in the neighborhood, she may be able to actually pinpoint the location of the laboratory. Here is the description." John handed Dr. Pei a handwritten note.

Dr. Pei read it and put it in his pocket. "Let us go play golf."

They went off the trail, got in a black standard-issue Ford SUV and headed to the golf club. John and Dr. Pei did not have trail names because they were not regular trailblazers.

A note in the Washington Post, page C6:

Dr. Pei, our surgeon general, and Dr. John, retired VP of AZ Pharm, did a short trailblaze along the Appalachian Trail before their golf game at a local golf club. These two gentlemen and their families are good friends.

A BIOWEAPON THAT CAN THINK?

Bonnie was looking out from a floor-to-ceiling glass window in the penthouse of the Orchid Garden Hotel. She said to no one in particular, "What a view! Looks like every window in this hotel has a complete or partial view of the Boston Harbor. I see the tall ship, the sailing ship. What is its name?"

"I think it is the USS Constitution," Jack said. "One can take a tour around it. I think it has been completely restored to almost the original form."

"I have always wanted to sail on one of these tall ships. Right now, let us see if we can sail through the maze, the scientific maze," June said. "Let me see if I can make a sort of preliminary summary, OK, guys?"

"Go ahead, June," Ruth said.

"From reading the papers of these missing scientists, it seems that:

"One, even before their retirement or hiding, or whatever, they colluded with a certain group. Their basic approach is just like ours but with a different goal.

"Two, based on our protocol they may have selected at least two DNA stretches, possibly sequences for immunity.

"Three, they may have programed a DNA sequence, or other macromolecules, to have artificial intelligence.

"Four, they probably use drones, vectors, and other media or vehicles. That is what I think although we have not discussed it yet. I said this because there is a material scientist involved, Dr. White.

"Five, they are using radioisotope in DNA which is radiation-resistant and at the same time radiates their target or targets."

"Good summary, June," Jerry said. "Let's take your points one at a time. Number one, it means that they are further into the development than their papers imply. That is, they had that idea and proceeded to work on it even before their disappearance. Before the Chinese and Americans knew about the conspiracy."

"Although Dr. Jeng at Stanford did not publish or did not appear to have collaborated extensively with anyone on the list, he may actually be the main man," June gave her hypothesis.

Jack added to June's comment. "June has a point. Dr. Jeng does not have a long list of publications compared to others. But whatever I read, he is not just a pediatric cancer guy. I went back a few years. He actually did some work with CRISPR tech. He did a partial amino acid sequence of fetal immunoglobulin. Somehow, no further work on the DNA or mRNA sequence has been in print, as far as my reading went."

"Interesting, very interesting," Harold exclaimed. "Research on pediatric cancer and immunological reaction to it, pediatric cancer or tumor, is a sort of a niche area."

"Allow me to back up a bit," Bonnie said. "Harold's reading of marine ecologist Dr. Trent's research concerning the retention of radioisotopes in dolphins and stingrays told me that there was collusion before their disappearance. Jerry mentioned that too. Timing?"

"You guys are right," Jack agreed. "I think we need to alert John on this. Maybe SAGRC can ascertain that."

"Harold, in your studies on embryonic and adult hemoglobin, did you run into anything on immunoglobulin genes?" Ruth asked.

"I have to think about it. We know the sequence relationship of fetal and adult hemoglobin. Maybe, just maybe, or as a working hypothesis, we could say these two groups of proteins, hemoglobin and immunoglobulins, may share some common characteristics, like on the same chromosomes. However, immunoglobulin consists of two heavy chains and two light chains. As the cell responds to incoming antigens, there are variable stretches in both the heavy and light chains' reaction to them, depending on the characters of the incoming antigens. Those variable stretches make the immunoglobulin specific to various antigens. No, right offhand I don't think the controls at the DNA level of hemoglobin and immunoglobulin are the same."

"Could the turning on and off of the respective genes for hemoglobin, like fetal versus adult, have something in common with immunoglobulins?" Jerry asked.

"I don't know. But certainly the on and off signals may be the same with a similar but not identical sequence upstream," Harold answered.

"So, June, you think this Dr. Jeng at Stanford might just be working on the 'on and off' of fetal and adult genes for immunoglobulins?" Jack asked.

"Harold, maybe you can answer that," June said.

"That is certainly very complicated because fetal immunity is closely related to maternal immunity," Harold said. "I have to look into the immunoglobulin, the antibody, story to see if there is some parallelism of antibody to hemoglobin."

"We'd better tell John about the timing," Jack said. He proceeded to email John.

John, the program may have been in place before the retirement of the scientists. How long, we don't know. We just gleaned this from their published work and made an educated guess. Check it out if you can. Will inform you of our thoughts in a day or two.

A SECRET LABORATORY

From the top floor of the Phoenix building on a clear day, one could not only see Shenzhen but also part of the new bridge/tunnel linking Macao and Hong Kong. The primary builder was Chan Brothers Engineering, Inc. The Chan brothers were twins educated in England. The Phoenix Group was part owner of that company.

The Chan brothers were invited to take part in this particular board meeting. One of the twins, Robert, was there, but not his twin brother, Joe.

"Sorry, gentlemen, my brother Joe came down with a fever. He did not want to spread his germs to us. I am pleased to be invited. Anything we can do for Phoenix, we shall give it our best effort."

"Thanks for coming, Robert," Mr. Li of Hong Kong said. "To make it brief so we don't waste your time, I will convey the board's wishes right now.

"Robert, we want to build a simple but practical laboratory in Melbourne. After a year, maybe two, we will dismantle this lab. We don't want to use local builders."

"We do have connections in Melbourne," Robert informed the board. "Since you don't want to use locals, I will need details as to the function of the lab. Our firm owns a couple of warehouses on the waterfront in Melbourne."

"Robert, that is perfect. Can we rent the warehouse, say for two years?" Mr. Li asked.

"Robert," Mr. Nelson cut in the conversation. "May I add that since we are partners in a certain way, therefore our venture will not have a paper trail. Will that be possible on your end?"

"I don't see why not. We actually appreciate it very much that the Phoenix Group helped us to land the contract of this Hong Kong-

Macao linkage. We do it the Chinese way, handshakes over a cup of tea!"

All the Phoenix Group board members shook hands with Robert. Mrs. Biotti was in Washington, D.C., doing her socialite/spy/lobbying tasks.

"Thanks, Robert," Mr. Li said. "Mr. Simpson will address what we need."

"Thanks, Mr. Li, and Robert," Mr. Simpson said. "Mr. Nelson, would you fill in any information that I may have missed?"

Without waiting for an answer from Mr. Nelson, Mr. Simpson continued the conversation. "Our plan for the laboratory is as follows:

"One, house five to six scientists with their assistants, about ten to fifteen people.

"Two, we will lease the warehouse without a written contract as we have shaken hands on it.

"Three, since we don't want local builders involved, that means you need to use your own employees from Hong Kong. You will find housing for them for whatever length of time you need. I assume it probably will take no more than a couple of months. The sooner the better. The work must be discreet, if not secret. Mr. Nelson, anything to add?"

"Yes. It is a temporary laboratory. We covered that already. Materials should be easily dismantled, but yet good enough for experiments with infectious agents like viruses." Mr. Nelson added his comments.

"Robert," Mr. Fu from Thailand asked. "Your warehouses, what is their location? Would you tell us how your warehouses are related to those owned by others? For example, would the increase in traffic raise questions from your neighbors?"

"One of our units is at the edge of the water. Actually, it has a private landing. One has access to our unit from land or sea. There is another warehouse owned by someone else about an eighth of a mile from ours. They have a private landing too. These are the only two warehouses with access to the bay. By the way, one cannot see the other because of the bend in the shoreline. Pretty private."

"Perfect," Mr. Li said with much pleasure.

"How soon do you want your laboratory?"

"In a month or two, three at the most." Mr. Li said. "Can it be done?"

"Expenses? Costs? Any limit?" Robert asked.

"Efficiency and discretion are our principal concerns. The sooner the better." Mr. Li said.

"I understand."

There was no need for these top business people to discuss in detail the financial matters. They would not take advantage of each other or dare to. Too much at stake for both. Besides, they were in a certain way partners.

"We have confidence in your work, Robert. I hope your brother gets better soon," Mr. Lloyd said.

"Robert, I forgot to mention to you," Mr. Nelson said. "We have purchased the necessary equipment already. It is all in boxes and ready to go. We just need space and lab benches, good ventilation, hot and cold water lines, electrical outlets, constant temperature control, etc."

"Would you email me as to the space needed for these instruments? I will place the lab benches accordingly," Robert said.

"No email and no written correspondence. Robert. You or your brother will converse with me orally," Mr. Li said. "For whatever you need."

"I understand."

The next day, Robert and Joe were in their office. Robert conveyed the discussion with the Phoenix Group on the construction of a laboratory in one of their warehouses in Melbourne.

"Joe, it's not easy. What do you think? How do we accomplish this handshake contract?"

"That is fine. Actually, I like it. I like the challenge."

They were identical monozygotic twins. One left-handed and one right-handed. Mentality wise, Joe would take more risks and be more daring in their business venture.

"How can we be discreet, secret more appropriately, and efficient in such a short time?"

"First, we will divert some of our existing business to the other warehouse. However, we will keep the same schedule and about the same volume. Instead of transporting merchandise to warehouse number One, the one with the landing, we will transport the general merchandise to number Two and transfer the necessary equipment and building materials for the lab to warehouse One. We may have to send 'regrets' to some companies because of a shortage in space or some other excuse."

"On the surface, we are still doing our regular business."

"Have you got a list of whatever is needed by the Phoenix Group?

"Yes, here it is," Robert handed Joe a couple pieces of paper.

"Robert, we are in luck. We have just about thirty percent of these items in our warehouse number Two. We can start to transfer them almost immediately. For the rest, either you or I will go to our friends' shops. We'll pick them up, no deliveries."

"The Phoenix Group does not want to use local builders. That means we need to send our own people to Melbourne."

"We will pay them extra and charge that to the Phoenix Group. Better select those who speak good English."

"How about Willard? He is a good super. Let him pick his workers based on our conditions and our agreement with the Phoenix Group."

"Good idea. Willard is married but has no children. His wife, Henri, is a good organizer too. How long have they been with us, Robert?" Joe asked.

"Fifteen years, at least. He worked for Dad before we took over. He is loyal, we can trust him."

Robert picked up his cell phone. "Willard, are you on the floor or out in the field?"

"I am on my way back. Ten minutes." Willard answered on his car phone.

"Please stop by. Thanks," Robert said.

Ten minutes later, Willard came into the office. Willard was Eurasian, five ten or eleven with light brown hair and broad shoulders. He had studied engineering technology at the Hong Kong

Technology Institute. He actually could be an engineer hovering over a desk with blueprints or doing computer graphics and designs for whatever was needed. But he liked field work; he liked to have callouses on his hands.

"Willard, how was the field work?" Robert asked.

"The guys were a bit relaxed after the holiday. But they are back to their good work. The foundation is almost finished. We will let the cement cure for a few days. Oh, yes. We need to remind our suppliers of steel beams that we will need them in two weeks. We cannot let them hold up our schedule."

"OK. Thanks. I will give them a call. I will tell them also there are two new steel beam suppliers," Robert said.

"Got a new assignment, Robert?" Willard asked.

"Yes. Overseas, Australia. A month or two."

Robert proceeded to tell Willard what the Phoenix Group had in mind.

"It shouldn't be difficult. Three or four workers will do. I will be there myself. I guess you want it that way."

"Yes, Willard. It has to be discreet, in fact, secret. We will figure out a way to move the materials needed and the equipment that the Phoenix Group has purchased into warehouse number One without our neighbor casting any suspicious glances."

"Warehouse One is the one with the landing, right, Robert?"

"Yes. We plan to use it as well as the street entrance, as usual, same schedule. But we will need to use the landing more. I have called our Melbourne side. The boat is working fine. The pilot told me he had to buy a new water pump. A minor matter."

"How about the equipment that the Phoenix Group needs?"

"That is the real easy part. They will just ship it to us as routine storage or transit merchandise. When we receive it, we just transfer it to warehouse number One. It is building the laboratory that has to be done in secrecy."

"Robert, we need to find housing for the workers. I will take those without families. We need to pay them extra."

"That is fine. No problem with money. I will see if I can find some B&Bs for them. Four persons? Wives?"

"I will let you know tomorrow."

"Joe, Willard needs three to four people to go with him to Melbourne. We need to find housing for them for a month or two, maybe longer."

"Robert, that can be done easily. Dad still owns an apartment building there. Mom and Dad always keep a couple of furnished units vacant for us and for their vacation. I will call them later. It's still too early. I hope they have not gone on a cruise. They went to Melbourne last week."

"I forgot about that. We shall tell Dad our plan. Do you remember if Dad had dealings with the Phoenix Group?" Robert said.

"I don't know. We can ask him."

BIOWEAPON WITH AI

The next day the six Volunteer friends had their breakfast again in the penthouse of the Orchid Garden Hotel. After the servers cleared the tables and brought in fresh coffee, they started to discuss the possible planned bioweapon by the missing scientists.

"You guys are at the defense end this time," Bonnie said.

"Yes. More or less. And we have to think like them," Jack said.

Harold picked up the trend of thought. "I believe their objective has an immunological angle. Starting with editing genes for immune reactions. I was thinking last night that they may want to switch on or off the genes, like fetal and adult hemoglobin genes. If that is the case, they can pretty much play a role in any kind of illness in a population."

"Harold, I don't get it. What did you mean by sickness in a population?" Ruth asked.

"How will that be related to pharm business?" Jerry asked.

"Both," Harold answered. "What I mean is, hypothetically, if there is an epidemic, or even an annual flu outbreak, they can manipulate the immune systems to fit their products," Harold shared his hypothetical thought.

"Wow, Harold. Are you thinking what I am thinking?" Jack said. "The reverse of immunotherapy?"

"Or anti-immunotherapy?" June said.

"Or, they can make people sick at will, spread the germs, and trigger mass biological warfare across populations rather than individuals. However, it could be at an individual level, it's the same principle, but deadlier than what you guys did." Bonnie was thinking out loud.

"Well said, Bonnie," June said.

"We edited the DNA for individuals in a population. They are manipulating the DNA of a population. Since there are individual variations, they need to create a program to consider the variables. Therefore, artificial intelligence! Built into the bioweapon, the genes, and probably the drones too!" Harold postulated.

"And with low-level internal radiation as insurance!" Jack added his assertion.

"That is deadly!" Bonnie exclaimed.

"June, can you do a summary again?" Ruth asked.

"Let me do some thinking first. After lunch?"

"Let us go to the marketplace. I don't think we are being monitored. But we should be just like other people in the crowd. The marketplace is not easy to monitor. We will leave separately, sort of hang around the fountain, then find a place to eat," Harold suggested.

Harold called downstairs. "We will go out for lunch. Would you bring some fresh coffee and fruit for us for the afternoon? Thank you."

The marketplace was crowded as usual with the lunch crowd. The Vol friends managed to find two tables close by to have their Boston clam chowder and Boston cream pie. After a brief walk along the pier they went back to the penthouse in the Orchid Garden Hotel.

June sat down and started to scribble some notes while the others were getting their fruit or coffee.

"You guys did this kind of reunion while you were developing the bioweapon?" Bonnie asked no one in particular.

"Yes, we did, at various places," Ruth answered. "The only time we were out in the open was when we were at the homecoming game against Alabama."

"We all went to the game, sitting together like we used to, but not in the student section any more. We did discuss our work, before and after," Jack said.

"I missed all the fun," Bonnie said. "But John, my husband, needed me in the lab as well as at home."

"You are one of us now, a member of our defense team," Harold said. "By the way, redhead, does your hair ever turn gray like ours?"

"No, Confucius, redheads stay red forever and ever!"

"Guys, I have sort of made a summary of what we have discussed. And you have to fill in some blanks in the summation," June said looking over her notes. "I'll get some coffee."

June was about to get up, but a cup of coffee appeared right in front of her on the coffee table.

"Thanks. Let me see:

"One, based on our protocol they—I shall refer to the missing scientists and whoever is behind their work as 'they'—are developing or attempting to develop a deadly bioweapon.

"Two, they are targeting a population rather than specific individuals in a population.

"Three, they are editing the genes responsible for immunity. They may want to be able to switch on/off the genes to achieve their ultimate purpose to manipulate the nature of the disease to fit their drugs.

"Four, using low-level radioactive isotopes as an insurance if the switch does not work, the intended targets will gradually regress in health due to the long biological half-life of C^{14}, tritium or P^{32}, or other isotopes not easily detectable.

"Five, here is the salient point: Artificial intelligence is being built into the bioweapon, in the DNA most likely, and even in the drones or nanobots which deliver the product. Another fail-safe mechanism.

"Six, in two of the papers, the authors mentioned using a RNA virus that has caused an epidemic in the past. What would that be?

"With that, they can actually create an epidemic and manipulate the health of a population. Additionally, they can monopolize the drug market!"

"Thanks, June," Harold said. "We may want to see how they could do all these, especially artificial intelligence. The replacement of elements with radioactive isotopes as well as radiation-resistant macromolecules in the bioweapon would be other characteristics of the bioweapon."

"I think we may venture to say that they will concentrate their efforts on two fronts, the heart and the immune system," Jerry said.

"How would they build in artificial intelligence?" Bonnie asked.

"I may be able to answer that," Jack said. "From my fishing friends in Pentagon, the Biowarfare Division is working with computer programmers and cybersecurity experts. They are trying to take the DNA triplet codes and turn them into digital codes. They would modify the digital codes, then back-translate them into DNA triplet codes. Then insert the changed DNA back into the genes using CRISPR tech."

"I don't see the advantage in doing this versus direct CRISPR tech," Jerry asked.

"One can interpret the digitizing codes more easily than DNA triplets. All it takes is one nucleotide substitution to jumble up the whole DNA sequence. But not digitalization. Correcting the digital codes is much easier than the correction for the DNA triplet codes," Harold explained to Jerry.

"Do you think these guys can make the drones or the medium, nanobots, monitor algorithms too?" June asked.

"Hold on, I just remembered something I read. Actually, it was a footnote. I did not think about it at the time," Harold said.

"What did you miss, or what did we miss?" June asked.

"In one of the papers, it mentioned something about radiation-resistant DNA. I correlated it to the incorporation of isotopes into some molecules."

Harold continued. "If the bioweapon can think, they can certainly process and monitor algorithms in their quote work unquote. These molecules are radioactive and yet resistant to radiation. Logical?"

"Is there another radiation-resistant organism other than cockroaches?" Jerry asked. "Microbes?"

"Yes, *Deinococcus radiodurans*. But I did not read anything related to it," Bonnie said.

Other Vols said they too did not read about it in the papers of the missing scientists.

"That is deadly, more than deadly. Downright immoral!" Bonnie exclaimed.

"I think we'd better let John have our thoughts," Harold said. "It's too long for even encrypted email. I think we'd better let Bonnie hand-deliver to him since she was not one of us conspirators. But how?"

"I am sure these people are keeping track of our surgeon general and all the SAGRC members and their collaborators as well, including John," Jerry said.

"Or let Paz do it," Jack suggested. "Arrange an 'accidental meeting' with the two of them. Chat about their Global Foundation days. John will know what to do."

CHANCE ENCOUNTER

Paz received an encrypted email from John, her fellow Global Foundation board member in the early days.

Paz, please go to Atlanta to attend the Conference on World Travel next week. I will be presenting my trips to the Amazon hunting rare medicinal plants.

The Conference on World Travel was the biggest travel show in the United States. Unlike other industrial conferences, it only took place once every two years in a certain major city. Other than booths and workshops, it included several specialized, usually exotic talks by people not related to travel agencies but maybe of interest to travelers.

This year, one of the specialized talks was by Dr. John Jones, VP (retired) of AZ Pharm, Inc. The title was "Hunting exotic medicinal plants in the Amazon."

John, one of the Vol conspirators, showed many unusual photographs including one aerial picture of a small tribe not yet exposed to the outside world. The flyby was brief, but it was long enough to show the surprised facial expression of a small number of native people looking up.

"Ladies and gentlemen, thank you for attending my Amazon talk. I have made a list of possible medicinal plants for our modern world. Please take a copy if you wish. In conclusion, I wish to make two requests. That is, please do not just venture into the Amazon without a local guide. And please do not go in with a large number of people. We all need to keep this amazing rain forest and its indigenous people, animals, and plants as they are. It is good for them and good for us. Thank you again."

As John was stepping off the podium, he heard a familiar voice, "John, Dr. John, over here!"

John looked over to where the voice came from.

"Paz, is that you?"

"Of course, you don't recognize me?"

"Yes, I do. I was just surprised to see you here. We need to catch up on old times. Have you got time to have a chat now? I have finished my duty here."

"John, of course. By the way, it was a good presentation. It brings back some memories of when we did a couple of rescue missions in the Amazon, near Manaus. Remember?"

"Yes, Paz, you were leading the team. Now, tell me what you are doing here?"

"John, I am running a travel agency, Paz Exotic Travel." Paz told John with much enthusiasm. "I took my first group to Costa Rica."

"Let me guess, you used the people you met during our work for the Global Foundation as local guides. I met only a few since you were the one who arranged all the travel arrangements. Who was helping you in Costa Rica?"

"You may not know her. It was Dr. Daisy, a marine biologist whom I met when there was an unexpected eruption of a presumed-dead volcano."

"I remember the incident. But I don't remember meeting Dr. Daisy. You know, I rarely participated in your excellent and efficient rescue missions."

"Thanks, John," Paz said.

"Let's go to the Pittypat's Porch Restaurant down the street. Have you been there? A real southern treat, just like the book *Gone with the Wind* describes."

"I read the book, required reading in American lit in my high school in the Philippines. But I did not see the movie. Clark Gable and Vivian Leigh?"

"Yes. Good movie. You still can pick up a video. It is still a classic."

After they were seated, Paz reached in her canvas bag and took out a few sheets of paper. "John, here are my ads. Please do some promotion for me if you have a chance."

John took a casual look and put them in his briefcase. "Thanks, I will. Maybe I will even take a tour with you."

Those few sheets were not ads for Paz's travel agency. They were the summary and comments distilled from the published papers by the missing scientists who were suspected to be working for some rogue group with an ill and unethical purpose.

"I am going back to D.C. this evening," John said. "Paz, are you staying for the duration of the conference?"

"Yes, I don't have a booth. But I do have a lot to learn. Taking a group is not like what we did when we were with the Global Foundation."

"Where are you staying?" John asked.

"The Omni."

"Good. Me too. There is just enough time for me to go back to the hotel, check out, and head to the airport."

As they walked back to the Omni from the Pittypat's Porch, Paz told John that his Volunteer friends read the hard copies of the publications. They did not go online for fear of whoever was monitoring everything related to the goal the rogue group had in mind.

"Great idea. Paz, there is probably a tail on me now and all the time."

"That was why I hand-delivered my ads to you," Paz said. "Jack and Jerry thought this group must be very resourceful. Much more so than our Global Foundation."

As they entered the lobby of the Omni, John said. "I will go up to fetch my bags. Paz, it was good to bump into you. I am glad you are well and doing this exotic travel. Good luck."

They gave each other a good friendly hug as they said goodbye.

Just as John reached the elevator, he turned around. "Paz."

Paz turned around and headed to where John was.

"Paz," John said. "Just a thought. If you take people to the Amazon, be sure to call Professor Alvarado. She is most likely still active and not yet retired like most of us. You know, she is probably the person most knowledgeable about the Amazon."

"Thanks, John. I will," Paz said.

"I may even take that tour with you."

They said goodbye again.

A man with a similar ID tag for the travel conference was casually reading the program not far from where John and Paz were saying goodbye to each other. He recorded every word of the conversation, including when they met at the foot of the stage where John gave a talk. But he could not record their conversation in the restaurant or while they were walking to the hotel from Pittypat's Porch.

ANOTHER BREAKTHROUGH

In the auditorium of the US National Academy of Sciences, a jubilant mood again filled the air.

Chairing the SAGRC, Caleb Morrison opened the meeting with much pleasure.

"Ladies and gentlemen, the press included [a little good-natured laughing was heard], our Sino-American Genetic Research Consortium is pleased to announce another accomplishment. Many thanks to our colleagues around the world. A preliminary clinical test has confirmed that the procedure for the early detection of adenocarcinoma is very encouraging," Caleb paused a few seconds to let the audience absorb the good news.

"In addition, the cause of the rare neuropathy Guillain Barré Syndrome has been elucidated. Briefly, during the flu season when the swine flu virus is prevalent, the number of cases of Guillain Barré Syndrome always increases. But we did not know why. We do now." Caleb again paused a few seconds while the press wrote furiously in their notepads.

Caleb continued. "As most of you know, this rare although not deadly disease, unlike some forms of cancer, affects one out of some three hundred thousand people. The result is paralysis from which there is eventually a recovery, but not necessarily one hundred percent. We know now that it is caused by the swine flu viral infection first to the motor neurons at the lower extremities, the ankles. Our consortium, with the assistance of several laboratories and their medical scientists, can now block the upward spread with immunotherapeutic technology. As soon as a patient feels a little numbness in the toes, he should immediately go to see his or her primary care physician. Without going into the detail, which is now released to the public, antibodies to the swine flu virus plus activation of genes for autoimmune reaction are the salient procedures for treatment. As I said, the detailed method of diagnosis and treatment is now in public domain."

With that short statement, the house erupted into applause with cheers and a few whistles.

"The president is not able to join us. But he sent his congratulatory note. I will read it to you:

We, China and the United States, realize that if we pool our talents and resources, we will be able to cure some diseases, some more deadly than others, in a shorter timeframe. This, as you know, is why SAGRC was formed. I sincerely congratulate the success of the consortium and those institutions whose scientists have rendered their expertise and time.

China and America have been at odds from time to time. But not this time. Our collaboration has borne fruit.

I am confident that many other previously incurable illnesses, including cancer, will be defeated.

Ladies and gentlemen, and everyone involved, again, congratulations from the Oval Office."

More enthusiastic applause from the audience could be heard in the building of the National Academy of Sciences in Washington, D.C., near the Reflecting Pool.

Caleb continued. "Please feel free to take the protocols. Members of the consortium will be around to chat with you for a while. Then they have to meet in about thirty minutes, to work. The progress of the consortium will be announced from time to time. Hopefully, the duration between announcements will get shorter and shorter!"

With that, Caleb and the members of the consortium stepped down from the podium to mingle with the audience.

After many handshakes and informal chatting over wine and hors d'oeuvres, the audience left.

Members of the consortium, except Mei Mei of the Shanghai Institute of Cell Biology, went to the conference room on the second floor of the building. From the windows of the conference room one can see the bronze statue of Einstein on the front lawn.

Caleb opened the meeting. "Ladies and gentlemen, thank you for coming. Ms. Mei Mei is not able to come because of family business.

"We may not have enough time today to talk about what I will give you. We can convene again at a later time. I don't think we should have conference calls or even send encrypted emails. These people must be very resourceful due to the fact that neither of our security departments, China and the CIA here, have any idea who they are. However, we do know there are scientists missing or retired, with unusual and untimely retirement. I cannot tell you how we make that connection because I myself don't know. It's way over my head!

"The recent activities of these ten missing scientists are in this folder."

Caleb reached into his thick briefcase, pulled out the materials and handed them to each of the committee members.

"The reviewers, that would be the right designation, have summarized the activities of the missing scientists. We gave them the names and they studied their publications. We don't want to do it because of our 'clandestine' assignment. Here is their summation. I understand they read the hard copies of the journals in which the works were published. Not online because they were cautious. They think these people may monitor who is reading the publications and from where. Just like Fifth Avenue ad companies. Take a moment to peruse them. Then we should discuss what to do and how to do whatever is necessary." Caleb went to the sideboard to get a soda, sat back down, and again read his copy of the summation by the Volunteer friends.

There were no names on the folder other than those of the missing scientists. It did not take long for these top-notch scientists to comprehend what was in the folder.

"Our silent scientific partners did a great job," Robert of the University of Tennessee said. "I agree with them that the research of these missing scientists appears to have no connection and be unrelated."

Lee from Beijing added her comments. "I agree. I also agree with their assessment that these missing scientists must have been working or interacting prior to our governments' suspicions. They must have done the preliminary experiments based on the protocols given to us by another unknown entity some years back."

"Does it seem out of place for a marine ecologist, Trent, to play a role?" Calvin asked no one in particular.

"No," Alex of the US Environmental Protection Agency said. "As we delve deeper into the genetic changes in all living things, it has become clear to us that gene interactions, not only within a species but also between species, play a more important role than what we use to think and knew about our environment."

"Good point," Lee from Beijing agreed. "Maybe they use marine vertebrates as a model system. One of the reports was on the retention of radioisotopes in dolphins, stingrays—"

Before Lee finished her comment, Dr. Robert of the University of Tennessee suddenly had a thought. "Excuse me. Dolphins have been trained to be carriers of weapons by our navy in the past, I believe. Mr. Morrison, do you have any information on that? Sorry to interrupt, Dr. Lee."

"Not at all, Dr. Robert."

"Yes. The navy did carry out some research using dolphins as carriers for weapons. The experiments were not well designed. Therefore, the results were useless. Besides, using animals resulted in having to sacrifice them. The project was terminated. I don't know why this group would assay the biological half-lives of certain isotopes in these marine animals."

"Our reviewers put the emphasis on the area of immunotherapy. Dr. Somers, what is your thought on this?" Caleb turned to where Somers of the Sloan Kettering Institute sat.

"After reading the summaries by our reviewers, I, too, agree with their opinion. I believe the goal of this rogue group is to have control of a certain disease or diseases, to create an epidemic, maybe. They may attempt to manipulate the DNA sequence for immune responses, including allergy reactions, to fit their products. It is like designing fertilizers for certain plants and insecticides for certain insects. In the seventies it was the profitable ventures with cash crops and seed productions, for example. They used genetic engineering to develop seeds compatible with the fertilizers and herbicides of their design. In time, the plants of subsequent generations will invade farms that never used their seeds. In time the farmers will have to use the designer fertilizers and herbicides." Somers took a sip of soda and continued. "I am trying to draw a parallel between diseases and drugs, and plants and fertilizers. I don't know if this makes any sense."

"I agree with Dr. Somer," Calvin said. "They will try to manipulate a certain disease or diseases. The Ebola and Zika viruses immediately come to my mind. Both of these viral diseases are in part related to environmental variants, humidity, temperature and vectors. The last element, vectors, like the mosquito for Zika virus, has certainly environmental connotations."

"That is most likely why Trent is involved," Caleb said.

"If Dr. Somers' notion that these scientists have attempted to manipulate certain disease or diseases, that means we have to look at the pharmaceutical angle. Who maybe benefits politically as well as economically." Wang of Beijing theorized from the discussion at SAGRC as well as their consultants' summary.

"And, I may add, biotech too," Dr. Robert said.

"Will there be serious geopolitical implications?" Caleb asked.

"Good question," Wang said. "I think there will be."

"Dr. Wang, please elaborate," Caleb said.

"Developments in Africa, South America, and the Amazon come to mind," Wang answered.

"Related to the Ebola and Zika viruses?" Calvin asked.

"Maybe even parasitic diseases, like schistosomiasis, for example," Alex said.

"Maybe they will even attempt to edit the pathogenic genes," Robert of Tennessee hypothesized.

"To adapt to the properties of the drugs? Produce drugs effective for the edited virus while existing drugs will be ineffective against them." Lee of Beijing followed the trend of thought.

"That would be just like GMP, genetically modified plants, well said," Alex said.

"This is worse, much worse, than the 'die in good health' bioweapon. We still don't know who these guys were," Wang said.

"Not to be more pessimistic," Alex added, "in addition, they will incorporate artificial intelligence into their products!"

"Into the DNA or RNA, or the vector, the carriers?" Somers raised the question.

Alex mentally said to herself that she had to be very careful about what she said because she was one of the perpetrators while she was just in her teens although she was not directly involved with the development of the protocol. Her suggestions to edit mitochondria DNA in the Krebs cycle and 3-D printing were significant inputs to the successful project of the now-defunct Global Foundation.

"Other than the angle of immunity, the bullets and the carrier, the drone, are just as important. Notice there is a biomaterial scientist, Dr. White, in the group," Robert said. He continued his narration. "Our consultants mentioned immunotherapy and anti-immunotherapy. Could that mean they will attempt to change the immunity of the affected people by editing the immunoglobulin DNA, or the synthesis of it?"

"Could be, Dr. Robert. Or they could change the mRNA too," Somers answered.

"And insert radioactive isotopes into the products. Why?" Lee said.

The SAGRC had a tall order to fill because they had to fulfill their task of fighting diseases which was their cover for neutralizing or countering the forthcoming bioterrorism. And they still did not know what the bioweapons might be. Yes, they had a good idea from the reviewers, the Volunteer friends. Both China and America knew of the existence of the bioterrorists. But they did not know who they were or who was behind the work. They only knew the scientists and possibly their work and interaction. They had not yet connected the dots or did not have enough dots to be connected. Where was the laboratory?

"It has been a long day, with the reception and everything. Let us arrange to meet within the next week. Peruse whatever we have on hand. If you do want to know more about these missing scientists, do remember, don't go online. Go to the stacks," Caleb suggested to the members as a reminder.

"Good idea," Calvin said.

"I will email you early next week to arrange for us to meet again. We cannot wait too long. These guys are good and have vast resources. We know there are ten missing scientists. There may be more. Just not knowing who they are tells me that," Caleb said in a very serious manner.

As the members started to leave the conference room, Caleb suddenly remembered something.

"Hold on, ladies and gentlemen, I've just remembered something," Caleb said. "Our president will be visiting Asia, including China, next week. Maybe we Americans can hitch a ride to Beijing. We will meet in Beijing then. I will check it out with the White House and email you."

"Caleb, that will be great. A chance to ride on Air Force One!" Alex, the youngest member in the group, was excited already.

Secret Laboratory

"Congratulations, Robert and Joe, on the completion of the bridge-tunnel from Hong Kong to Macao in record time," Mr. Li said to the twin-brother engineers. "It now only takes thirty minutes or less from here to Macao."

"Thank you," Robert answered. "And thank you for the financial backing from the Phoenix Group; most importantly of all, the political aspect. That is, for us to be the lead engineering firm instead of someone from Europe."

"Mr. Li," the other twin, Joe, said. "We are about to finish the laboratory in Melbourne. Just a few more days and your staff can move in. We have received several shipments from a tech instrument company, Hi-Tech, Inc. They are in the laboratory now. If you wish, we can fly down there today or tomorrow. We want to be sure we have built everything you need to your specifications."

"Thank you, Joe," Mr. Li said. "Let me see what my schedule looks like."

Mr. Li pushed a button on a panel on his table. "Jan, please bring my appointment schedule here."

A tall, attractive Caucasian lady, conservatively dressed, entered the office of Mr. Li with a laptop and an ordinary appointment book. She handed both to Mr. Li.

Mr. Li looked at both and said, "Jan, please cancel my appointments for tomorrow and the day after." Li then turned to Robert. "Robert, will we be back by tomorrow afternoon?"

"We can come back the same day if you wish," Robert said. "Our Gulfstream has reclining seats for sleeping. Comfortable, nothing luxurious, just practical. It is a nine-hour-forty-minute flight time from here to Melbourne."

"Jan," Mr. Li said to his secretary. "Can you come with us tomorrow to Melbourne? Bring a camera also."

"I think so, but I have to call my mother to take care of my cat and my daughter. I'll be back in a few minutes." Jan left the office.

A few minutes later, Jan came back. "Yes, Mr. Li. I can go with you."

"Very good. Thanks, and thank your mother as well. My chauffeur will fetch you in the morning." Mr. Li then turned to the twins. "What time?"

"Early is better. Less traffic. Eight o'clock at the gate of the private hangar area. Give your name to the guard and he will direct you to our hangar. Pack an overnight bag just in case. We cannot fight Mother Nature."

Paz Exotic Travel, Trip #2

You've got mail.
> Paz clicked on her email app.
> An email from Wendy.

> *To whom it may concern.*
> *I read with interest about your travel agenda to exotic, non-touristy places. My friends and I, our tai chi group, take a trip once a year. We have been to just about every corner of the world except New Zealand and the North Pole. I also noticed in your ad that it says small groups. We usually have ten to twelve healthy seniors. We would like to go to New Zealand, including islands in the archipelago. Would you consider catering to us?*

> Paz read that email with a lot of interest. The reason was that John told his Volunteer friends that some of the missing scientists might have gone to New Zealand, Australia, Singapore, or the Philippines. And a yacht had visited repeatedly one particular island, Bird's Wing, in the New Zealand archipelago.
> Paz sent John an encrypted email.

> *A tai chi exercise group wishes to go to New Zealand including islands in its archipelago. We should take advantage of their wishes.*
> John replied, *"By all means. Do you have contact there?"*
> Paz replied. *"Yes. Pastor David Fung. I shall contact him before I reply to the tai chi group."*

Paz looked at her notebook which had all the contacts from her Global Foundation days. She found Pastor Fung in Auckland, New Zealand.

Paz dialed the number. "Pastor Fung, please --- glad to find you. Do you remember me, Paz Layug of the Global Foundation? --- no, no longer the Foundation --- I am running a travel agency --- yes, a small one --- let me give you some information about our travel agency [Paz proceeded to tell Pastor Fung about her specialized travel itinerary] --- yes, small groups, ten persons plus my assistant and me --- can you take us around New Zealand? --- great, are you retired already? --- I remember you are a sailing enthusiast, an expert --- I'm in luck. I will give you the dates and details later. Thank you very much."

Paz had ended her tour in Costa Rica two weeks earlier. There were five-star comments from her clients. The tai chi group was just one of several curious inquirers that occasionally flipped through travel magazines. They read the comments from the Costa Rica travelers.

"Harold, June." Paz was sipping her decaf coffee. "A tai chi group in California just called. They want me to lead them on a tour to New Zealand and the islands in the archipelago."

"Didn't John say some of the scientists may have retired to Australia, New Zealand, Singapore, or the Philippines?" Harold asked.

"Yes. I remember he mentioned that," June said.

"And I remember John told me in Atlanta at the travel conference that there was a suspicious yacht, one that only multibillionaires could own. Satellite monitoring by a certain American agency revealed that it has visited a small island along the eastern shore of New Zealand with more than the usual frequency for rich people's vacations. The island is called Bird's Wing. Unfortunately, the satellite could not read the name of the yacht or take a clear photo of it."

"That is very interesting," Harold said, sipping his favorite ginger ale with a piece of lime. "Which country does this Bird's Wing Island belong to?"

"No one really knows. And no island nations in the Pacific claim it either. It is not under the jurisdiction of New Zealand. But New Zealand does patrol it regularly and see to it that the visitors follow the rules of the Archipelago Preservation Agency. It's a courtesy to its neighbors. It is not like many of the islands in South China Sea. Many of them are claimed by China, Indonesia, the Philippines, Vietnam, and even India because they are in the midst of a very busy shipping lane." June was very knowledgeable about this part of the world.

"A good hiding place, Bird's Wing Island," Paz said.

"Like our lab in Siberia when we were creating our secret weapon with the Global Foundation," Harold said.

"Paz, I think you are spearheading the hunt," June said.

"Paz, there is the package from an unknown origin, you know what I mean," Harold said.

"Yes," Paz said.

Harold went to the lobby and fetched a package delivered by a private transport service. In the package was a camera with a Kodak label. There were also instructions.

"Let me see if Bonnie is in." Paz called her on her cell phone. "Bonnie, good you are home. Can you come up for a minute?"

"Of course. I'll be there shortly."

"Hah, here is my special camera," Bonnie said. "I shall read the instructions and get familiar with it."

"Bonnie, we have a tour in two weeks. New Zealand and its islands with a tai chi group from California," Paz told Bonnie.

"What is tai chi, I've heard of it, some Chinese exercise?" Bonnie asked.

"Yes, Bonnie. I do that too, almost every morning before breakfast," Harold told Bonnie. "I made a tape of myself performing!"

Harold went to fetch a tape of tai chi for Bonnie that he made.

"Thanks, Harold. I am surprised how much and what you guys can do and have done," Bonnie said with admiration.

"I will email John and then arrange things with Pastor Fung in New Zealand," Paz said.

"Paz, is this Pastor Fung one of your contacts, one of the people you worked with in the past?" June asked.

"Yes. He was the local contact when we participated in a rescue mission when a dormant volcano suddenly came alive and caused a tsunami north of Auckland. He let us use his church as headquarters for our rescue mission. We left when the Red Cross came. Pastor Fung and his congregation helped a lot. The Global Foundation later donated some money to his church. I think he used it for the renovation of the main chapel."

"Will he be willing to be your local guide?" June asked.

"Yes. Indeed. And there's a plus; he is an experienced sailor and owns a big sailboat. He used to take his congregation to the islands. He knows the waters around New Zealand well. I actually asked him to take my group to islands that are rarely visited by tourists. Some of them are so small that no one ever sets foot on them."

"That will be your second exotic tour!" Harold said. "Wish I could go."

"Me too," June said.

Paz emailed the tai chi group.

Wendy, I have made contact with New Zealand about your group's wish. A retired pastor, Pastor Fung, said he is willing to take your group to some sites in New Zealand rarely visited by ordinary tourists. In addition, he is willing to take your group in his sailboat to visit some of the islands in the archipelago. However, his boat can only take ten people. That means eight of your group, my associate and myself. His son might be able to be the first mate. He said we all have to pitch in to help too. I will do all the prep and organize provisions according to the APA, the Archipelago Preservation Agency of New Zealand. We will leave two weeks from now. Travel light. The weather will be warm "down under." No set itinerary as we advertised. Get back to me if this is OK with your group. It is tentatively a ten-day tour, US$4,000 per person. Please arrange your own flights to and from Auckland. Paz.

A few hours later, Paz received a reply from Wendy, the organizer of the tai chi group in California.

Paz, perfect. We all have our passports. We will email you the time of our arrival in Auckland for a ten-day tour. We look forward to it.

Paz immediately called Pastor Fung in Auckland.

"Pastor Fung, it's all set with my clients, eight people. All healthy seniors in a tai chi group from California. I told them about sailing with you in your boat. They are excited, but I don't know how many can take the waves. My associate, Bonnie, and I are fine." Paz said.

"Sounds good, Ms. Paz. My son may be able to be my first mate. If not, we all have to help to sail my boat."

Pastor Fung was glad to be doing some serious sailing again with this "congregation," a.k.a. Paz Exotic Travel and her clients.

"Thank you so much, Pastor Fung," Paz said. "I will do all the prep and organize provisions according to the APA of New Zealand."

"Yes. Just make sure you follow the rules. If not, they may not even let me sail in these waters again."

Paz had her second exotic tour, her first hunt, in New Zealand waters.

Wendy's tai chi group arrived in Auckland. Paz and Bonnie were there to greet them.

"Welcome to New Zealand," Paz said to Wendy's group. "Who is Wendy, please?"

"I am Wendy." An attractive middle-aged Chinese lady extended her hand to Paz. "I assume you are Paz."

"Yes, Wendy," Paz said. "And this is Bonnie, my associate. We always travel together. Bonnie also takes pictures and videos for us."

"This is us." Wendy waved her arm toward her group of two men and six women. "This is our tai chi group. As you can see, my friends are all seniors. But we are pretty healthy. This gentleman, Lonnie, is eighty-three but looks twenty years younger! He is our tai chi friend and instructor."

Paz and Bonnie shook hands with the tai chi people.

"We will stay in a good hotel, although not five star, tonight. Tomorrow, we will have breakfast there. Pastor Fung will drive the van to wherever he takes us, in fact, he won't tell me. That will be our itinerary the first day!" Paz told the group. "I talked to Pastor Fung about our ten-day tour. He said it will be pretty tight to sail around the north tip of New Zealand to Auckland. I hope we will make it back for your return flight."

"Paz, I did not tell you earlier. We have actually booked the return flight four more days after our ten-day tour. We also want to go to some touristy places."

"That works out fine." Paz was relieved to hear this.

The next morning, Pastor Fung came with a van by himself.

"Here is our guide," Paz said to the group. "May I introduce Pastor Fung. He was born and raised in New Zealand!"

They all shook hands.

"I did not tell Paz where we will be going today. I wanted to surprise her," Pastor continued. "We will drive about an hour to a little town called Waiuku. We will visit a Buddhist monastery. Have any of you visited a Buddhist monastery before?"

"No," -- "Not me," --"No," --

The tai chi group, Paz, and Bonnie got into the van which was more like a small bus capable of holding sixteen adults plus room for luggage.

As Pastor was driving. He started to tell the group about the monastery. "The abbot at the monastery is a friend of mine. Actually, we went to theological seminary together in Sydney, a Baptist institution. After we graduated, I came here to Auckland. He wanted to study other religions, so he went to India to study Hindu. A year later, he went to China to study Buddhism. Guess where, I think you will have a pleasant surprise. Shaolin Temple!"

A chorus of surprised exclamation was heard.

Wendy said. "I bet the abbot knows martial arts too."

"I don't know," Pastor Fung said. "He's never mentioned it. In fact, I did not know what Shaolin Temple was until one of my congregation members went there and came back with a video of the monks doing all sorts of unusual movements.

"This next forty-five-minute stretch is a winding road that rarely has traffic. It is to me the most scenic drive in this region. I shall shut up and let you enjoy the scenery. Keep my eyes on the curves!" Pastor Fung spoke to the group, then turned off the speaker and put on a CD with soft music, almost like chanting but with more notes.

"We are about there," Pastor Fung said shortly. "Keep the windows closed and your elbows inside. The road is narrow and we may scrape some tree branches. Hardly anyone comes here except a small number of devoted Buddhist followers. They come pretty regularly to do maintenance work for the monks. There are six monks, I last heard, including the abbot."

After a pretty rough twenty minutes going uphill on a dirt road, they arrived at the monastery.

There was a sort of parking lot with patches of grass. Up ahead was a small chapel or temple with a green roof, black sidings, and a faded yellow door. On the left was a dormitory-looking building with faded black sidings and windows on all four sides with curtains drawn. There was a red tile roof and a fan at one end that one usually finds spinning slowly in warehouses. This was where the monks lived and meditated. They rarely came out. One of them would be in the chapel every morning to preside over the morning chant and meditation for the public. Off to the left of the dormitory/meditation building was a kitchen. The monks lived simply and ate simple meals; no meat, no spicy vegetables like onions or garlic or hot peppers. They had mainly water, vegetables, fruit, and rice.

On this hilltop, the summer was cool. But winter was just as severe as the rest of the island. There were heaters in the monastery. There was a phone, but no television.

As the bus stopped, the abbot came out to greet his guests.

"Welcome to our monastery. I am afraid we have nothing with which to welcome you. We do have water." He put his palms together and bowed slightly to the group. After this traditional Buddhist greeting gesture, he and Pastor Fung hugged each other warmly.

"Pastor Fung, good to see you again. When was the last time? Three years ago. You came up after a big storm to make sure we were OK. We lost part of the roof of our chapel."

"My dear Abbot, here is the tai chi group I told you about on the phone." Pastor Fung proceeded to introduce Paz, Bonnie, Wendy and other travelers.

"Abbot, I remember you went to the Shaolin Temple. Did you learn martial arts? You never mentioned it," Pastor Fung asked.

"Yes, that was part of the routine study. Contrary to rumors about Shaolin martial arts, we practice them as physical exercise to keep healthy. We do tai chi too."

The abbot looked over at Wendy's friends, eyeing them with a warm smile. "Let me show you our chapel, our meditation and study hall for the public. Over there."

Inside the chapel it was very neat and very orderly. There were no chairs. Cushions were arranged in rows of five or six. In front of the cushions were smaller cushions upon which foreheads were placed, part of the ritual. The altar had a gold-plated Buddha in the meditation posture. There were four fearsome-looking guardians, two on each side, to protect the Buddha. Above the Buddha were two flying figures with subtle feminist physical forms. One was playing a string instrument while the other carried peaches on a plate in her hands. They are more or less equivalent to angels in the Christian world. Other ornaments, paintings, incense holders, scrolls, etc. were traditional Buddhist. The décor had a harmonious impression of serenity. Although the chapel was small with a capacity of no more than thirty people, it had a feel of openness.

A couple of the tai chi friends were Buddhists. Upon entering the chapel, they immediately kneeled in front of the altar, lit incense sticks, and placed their donations in a receptacle with red and yellow silk fabric.

The abbot gestured to the rest of the group to come forward. He sprinkled water over the group, a blessing.

After a relaxed visit inside the chapel, they went to a covered pavilion where there were chairs and a long picnic table.

"Please join us for a simple lunch," the abbot said. "The food has been prepared by these two ladies [he pointed to two middle-aged ladies, one Caucasian and one Asian] for us."

Under a cool cloudy sky, the travelers sat down at the table. At one end was the abbot and at the other end was Pastor Fung. While they were having their delicious vegetarian lunch, a young Caucasian monk with a yellow gown came out to fetch a case of bottled water and promptly returned to the dormitory.

After taking a leisurely walk around the grounds which were not manicured but clean, the abbot said to the group, "Shall we do a set of tai chi? Mine is traditional Yang form."

"Ours too. With a little Wu thrown in," Lonnie said.

"That is fine."

Paz and Bonnie went back into the pavilion to watch.

Twenty minutes later, they all bowed to each other with their palms together, the Buddhist greeting.

"Pastor Fung. Thank you for bringing your friends here. Other than our fellow Buddhist believers, we hardly ever have tourists. Only very special tourists. Your friends are very special. I have to go back now." He put his palm together, bowed slightly, and returned to the dormitory/meditation building.

The two lay ladies who prepared the food came out after they had cleaned up the tables and put away the washed dishes while the group was doing tai chi.

One of them said to Pastor Fung. "Pastor Fung, would you give us a ride to town? My husband brought us up here this morning and he had to go back to work. The abbot told us that you would come up in a minibus. Have you room for us?"

"We will be glad to. Just tell me where to drop you off," Pastor Fung said.

"Who cooks for the monks?" Wendy asked.

"They do it themselves in their own kitchen." One of the ladies pointed out a small building to the group.

"Our next stop will be Thames where I have my boat. We will stay in a lodge, fairly basic. Actually, it is my son's ranch. There are a few horses, a lot of sheep, chickens too," Pastor told the group after dropping off the ladies in Waiuku. "He was a scoutmaster. That was for his troops. In the morning we will sail north through many small islands."

The tai chi group had a great day and did their exercise with a real Shaolin Temple monk.

EVACUATION

While flying from Hong Kong to Melbourne to look over the laboratory, Mr. Li received an email from his computer people.

Mr. Li, I am tracking Paz Exotic Travel. The travel agency is taking a group of tai chi practitioners from California to tour New Zealand. According to their itinerary, after two days in Thames they will sail north in a boat owned by a Pastor David Fung from Thames, through the archipelago, around Cape Reinga, and to Auckland in the Tasman Sea. There are eight in the tai chi group, two men and six women, all senior citizens, plus Paz the tour director and her associate, Bonnie, and Pastor Fung, the captain.

Mr. Li forwarded the email on Paz Exotic Travel to Mr. Lloyd in Kuala Lumpur.

I am on my way to Melbourne on the Chan Brothers Engineering's Gulfstream. Can you go to Auckland and hire a yacht to evacuate our scientists and their wives on Bird's Wing? We don't want them to be seen on the island in case the group goes there.

Mr. Lloyd called Mr. Li.

"Mr. Li, do you think this Paz Exotic Travel is working for the government?"

"No. Just in case. Travelers take pictures. I don't think we should let anyone know we have a base there. The locals don't know.

They just know that these American couples retired there to get away from the cities in America."

"Good idea, Mr. Li. Travel agencies like to flash their photos as ads for their businesses. I will get to it right away. I will go to Auckland myself. I think our yacht will get to Bird's Wing before the sailboat. I will email them and arrange the evacuation right away."

"Thank you, Mr. Lloyd. I am on my way to look at our new laboratory. The Chan Brothers were kind enough to let us use their plane."

Two days later, a beautiful yacht, *Trade Wind*, arrived at Bird's Wing Island. The scientists—White, Nasatir, and Stiff—, their wives, and their associates told the local islanders that they would be visiting their families in the United States for a few days.

GOOD SAILING

Wendy and her tai chi friends had another treat upon arriving at the ranch of Pastor Fung's son. The lodge was nothing special, rustic but comfortable with ordinary amenities.

"Wendy," Paz said. "If your friends want to do a couple miles of horseback riding, it can be arranged. Pastor Fung said these horses are for hire to walk or trot. I did not know this either."

"As you said, Paz, the itinerary could change. This is a good change. I will ask them. I have ridden before. I don't know about the others."

A few minutes later, Wendy came back. "Paz, we would like to go riding. When?"

"I'll go to see Larry, Pastor's son."

A few minutes later, Paz came back to the group.

"Wendy, see that barn over there at the end of this dirt road? We will saddle up there. Wear long pants. Hats. If you have gloves, use them. Larry will lead, Pastor will bring up the rear. By the time you come back, supper will be ready. Bonnie and I will make a simple meal."

Off went the tai chi friends on horseback.

"Since New Zealand has more sheep than people, you have a choice of lamb or lamb!" Bonnie said to the tai chi people upon their return.

"Lamb chops, lamb stew, or roast leg of lamb," Paz added.

"Any form of lamb will do, it smells great," Lonnie said.

"There is no big hurry to leave tomorrow," Pastor Fung said. "I checked the marine weather, we are in luck. There's a good wind for the next few days. Larry will not be able to be my first mate. That means we all have to be sailors. Anyone have sailing experience?"

One of the ladies raised her hand. "I do, or I did. I used to sail with my husband in his small sailboat, just around Dana Point, California. Not much really. I've never been on a big boat like yours."

"Pastor Fung, I did some sailing," another lady said. "I think it was a forty-footer."

"Good enough," Pastor said. "You all will learn on the job. If everything goes well and the weather cooperates, we should be at the Three Kings Islands in three or four days. That depends also on how long we want to stay on some no-man's island overnight. If we like it, we will stay longer."

"Sounds good to me, Pastor Fung," Wendy said.

After a hearty breakfast, Paz Exotic Travel's clients were ready to cast off.

"Dad," Larry said to Pastor Fung. "I talked to Liam last night. He finished his exams early and will be home later today. If you can wait, he can sail with you."

"Paz, Wendy, and friends," Pastor said to the group. "My grandson, Liam, will be home for the school break in about three hours. He can be my first mate. He is very good. Should we wait?"

Without any discussion, Wendy said, "Let's wait."

"Anyone want to ride again?" Pastor asked. "We will select the good trotting horses. We just walked yesterday. A warning, your back may feel a little stiff afterward. And we will go up that hill and down the other side."

"Any special instructions?" One of the members of the group asked.

"You are all very healthy. Don't fight the ups and downs. Follow the rhythm of the horse. Use your legs. Relax your waist. Drop your shoulders. I think your tai chi will help too."

"Let us warm up, do one set," Lonnie said.

Pastor and his son went to prep the horses while the tai chi people did their thing. Paz and Bonnie continued to prepare sandwiches. They even brought along fishing poles.

After trotting for almost an hour, the tai chi group came back exhilarated and energetic.

"Liam is on his way. About twenty minutes," Pastor Fung said. "Maybe we can have our lunch now."

A clunker was heard. "Here is Liam," Pastor Fung said.

"Grandpa, good to see you," Liam came over and gave Pastor a great bear hug. Liam was over six feet and built like a lumberjack.

"Liam, get ready to set sail. I hope you have a week at least," Pastor said to Liam.

"Grandpa, I have more than a week. My exams came the first two days of the final exam week. And we have a break for a week before next semester."

"Liam, I am Wendy." She shook hands with Liam. "Do you play sports?"

"No, Wendy, I am clumsy. Just big. No sports genes. I love to sail with Grandpa. He is a hell of a sailor."

"Let us go. Any of you have motion sickness?" Pastor Fung asked.

"We don't know yet. We brought along ginger," Lonnie said.

With their light luggage, they boarded the forty-foot ocean sailboat with an auxiliary motor, *Four Seas*.

"Have a good sail, Dad and friends." Larry waved after he dropped them off at the yacht club.

Liam and Pastor did not even need to use the auxiliary motor to get out of the narrow inlet. They did it with a reefed mainsail. When they got out to sea, the boat started to rock a little on a couple of feet of swell. The full sail was deployed.

Pastor gave his first instruction. "We're sailing north heading into the wind. So we will zigzag. Watch the boom which will swing. When the boat lists to the left, go to the right. Lean against the gunwale. Follow Liam. That is to provide balance. The boat sails better when it is not listing. Also, note where the closest life preservers are."

"For those who don't want to move around, just sit where you are. Duck when the boom comes across. The clearance is high enough. But sometimes the wind plays tricks," Liam said to the group.

They sailed crisscross across the eastern shore of New Zealand through many small islands. Two days later, just before reaching the north tip of the island, Liam called out to his grandpa.

"Grandpa, I was looking at the marine weather forecast. There may be a small storm heading this way in about six or seven hours."

"Thanks," Pastor said. "I think there is a fairly good-sized island with a few inhabitants around here. I think it is called Bird's Wing. I was there a couple of times to shelter from small storms. It has a pretty good small protective cove."

"Yes. I remember that too. I think it is just over there on the near horizon," Liam pointed his hand in a northwesterly direction. Less than two hours away."

"Let's go there for the night."

Paz and Bonnie looked at each other for a fraction of a second with a subtle, undetectable nod to each other.

Two hours later, they reached Bird's Wing. After dropping anchor, the travelers took a dinghy to shore. Several children welcomed them, jumping up and down and clapping. A couple of adults also came along.

Pastor Fung was first one on shore.

"Hello, everyone. I was here a couple of times before. I am Pastor Fung. With me are my friends from America. There appears to be a storm coming in about six hours or so. We would like to stay here for the night. We will leave tomorrow when the storm is gone. Or we hope so."

"Welcome. We don't have any kind of hotel here, but we do have modest accommodation for your group. Some may have to sleep on the boat. The cove is pretty well protected unless there is a typhoon. Over there is our small schoolhouse. It can take you all, but you will need to sleep on the ground. We don't have enough beds for twelve."

"That is perfectly alright," Pastor said. "We will manage."

Pastor Fung introduced the group to the islanders.

"Where are you sailing to?"

"We will sail around the Three Kings Islands and down to Auckland. A leisurely sail," Pastor told their host.

Children were active, happy to carry the bags of their visitors to their schoolhouse with some thirty chairs and tables and a blackboard on the wall. It was functional and practical; it even had a piano and a TV. There was a small power generator in the back which was rarely used.

After the evening meal, the dark clouds could be seen not far offshore. The tai chi group did a set of tai chi before the storm hit. The children were awed and many of them imitated the moves, having a lot of fun. Afterward, they showed off their dancing and singing that they learned from Mrs. White.

Wendy said to the host, "Those houses on the other side of the island, do they belong to you too?

"No, they are not ours. They belong to three couples from America. They built the houses for their retirement to get away from the city. They are good friends. These songs and dances were taught by one of the ladies. They have just left for America to visit their folks."

"Will they be gone long?" Paz asked.

"I don't know."

"They look nice and comfortable, modern too," Bonnie said.

"Do they mingle or socialize much, like fishing together with you folks?" Paz asked.

"No, other than the ladies, the gentlemen stay busy with whatever they do. We get along really well. They follow the APA rules although we are not under the jurisdiction of New Zealand. You can look around if you wish. They are not here."

"No, we will stay on this side. We will respect their privacy even though they are not here," Paz said.

The wind started to come ashore with over ten-foot swells in the sea. Everyone started to go home or seek shelter.

It was not a severe storm. It lasted about an hour. The sea was calm again and the sky was clear with a beautiful sunset.

"How many people are living on this island?" Paz asked one of the ladies who were preparing dinner for them.

"We have twenty houses. All you see here. Some young men and women don't want to stay, so they go to work on the mainland. We fish and grow our own vegetables. New Zealand is very kind to us. They treat us just like their own citizens. They take care of us if we need medical care. Frankly, we don't know to which little nation we belong. It has been that way for as long as I remember. Some of us have three generations under one roof," one of the resident ladies said.

It was a perfect, relaxing evening. The tai chi group was elated.

Around 2.00 AM, Paz woke up Bonnie. She whispered, "Bonnie, let us go quietly to check out the Americans' houses."

"Ok. Let me get my radiation-detection instrument."

There was enough ambient light even though all the lights were off in all the houses on the island.

As they approached the houses, Bonnie turned on the instrument. The machine gave a beeping sound when it came near to one of the houses. Bonnie at once turned it off but kept her eyes on the dial.

The indicator needle oscillated between the green and red zones. There was low-level radiation coming from one of the houses!

"Let us go back," Bonnie said. "This house is hot. Others are not, probably residences."

Paz and Bonnie went back to their sleeping bags in the schoolhouse.

The next morning started out beautifully. The wind was a gentle breeze, great for sailing.

Paz and her clients thanked the islanders of Bird's Wing for their hospitality.

"You can stay longer if you wish. Some of us will go out fishing in just a few minutes. Each of our fishing boats can take two of you. We will be back by noon. We don't need to catch much, just enough for ourselves. Sometimes we catch a lot. Then we will sell them to the mainland. Or we smoke them."

Paz looked around the group. "We have no set itinerary. If you want to take up our kind hosts' offer, we can just spend another day here."

Wendy and Lonnie were the first to say yes with enthusiasm, and the others followed.

The tai chi group went fishing with the locals with nets. They came back around noon with great catches. They all chipped in to clean, filet, and prepared their lunch.

Pastor Fung checked the marine weather. He said to the group, "The weather will be good for the next forty-eight hours. We can sail to the Three Kings Islands. It will take about ten hours. We can spend the night there. There are thirteen uninhibited small islands. One of them has a very good protective cove, better than the one here. We can stay on the boat or camp out on the shore. The islands are all very beautiful with lush green growth, some with rocky cliffs and outcrops. All the beaches are carpeted with fine white sand with hardly a pebble."

"Pastor, can we take some of the fish with us?" Wendy asked.

"Yes. There is a gasoline generator which can power up the refrigerator on the boat. I have not shown you that yet. Also, Paz has provided us with fishing poles."

Ten hours later, they reached the Three Kings Islands on Pastor Fung's *Four Seas* sloop.

ONE YEAR LATER

A full board of the Phoenix Group was meeting in the penthouse of their building in Hong Kong.

Mr. Li wasted no time commencing the meeting. "Two years ago, we decided to accelerate this particular scientific project. We built two laboratories for the ten scientists, including Dr. Jeng of Stanford here today. We were fortunate that these esteemed scientists had a similar wish to ours, that is, to be able to control certain infectious viruses and design specific drugs for their treatment. Actually, our scientists came up with the idea. With Dr. Jeng's leadership they have accomplished much since they joined us. I will let Dr. Jeng have the floor."

"Thank you, Mr. Li." Dr. Jeng went to the sideboard and took a bottle of mineral water. "We, the board and our scientists, share the same idea about controlling an epidemic. It is a challenge, it's never been thought about in the field of medical science. We took the challenge. With your support we are proceeding well in tune with our agenda. We believe we will have the final products in another year, plus or minus."

All the board members clapped their hands with big smiles on their faces.

"Congratulations, Dr. Jeng and to your colleagues," Mr. Simpson said. "Does the scientific community miss their colleagues?"

"I don't believe so," Dr. Jeng answered. "There are many of us. Retirement, job transfers, etc. are a daily occurrence. Many are tired of research or burned out. It's nothing unusual. Their absence of publications or at conferences is not unusual. Besides, academicians are complacent individuals."

"Not like in business," Lloyd of Kuala Lumpur said.

"Correct, Mr. Lloyd," Jeng said. "Let me briefly summarize our progress."

"Please, take your time, Dr. Jeng," Mr. Li said. "We all are very excited. The outlook is good, better than good."

"I am uploading an outline to our monitors," Jeng continued after taking a sip. "You may remember, we decided to narrow our choice of infectious agents to either the Ebola or Zika virus. Neither of these is endangering us any longer in their present forms. There are effective vaccines and we know the vectors. Precisely, it was for this reason that we selected both as our bioweapon. They are both RNA viruses. But their methods of reproduction, replication in molecular biology terms, differ. In molecular biology terms, Zika is a positive sense while Ebola is negative. In layman's language, the reproduction of Zika takes one step and Ebola two.

"Let me explain. The Zika virus RNA, i.e. its genes, can make an exact copy of itself after it enters a cell using the biological machinery of our cells. Ebola has to make a complimentary copy, that is, a pair. Then this new partner makes a new strand which is exactly like the one entering the cell. It is like making the bronze statue in the center of our conference table. The artist makes a clay model, he then casts a mold. He then pours melted bronze into the mold."

"Dr. Jeng, a very good explanation to us laymen," Mr. Hector L. said. "Please continue."

"Our scientists were able to switch the mode of the reproduction of Ebola and Zika. We made the Ebola reproduction one step and Zika two. A switch. Because of this switch, their protein coats which wrap around the RNA will not be the same as the originals. We will make a chimeric virus too. If you were infected by our virus, the current vaccine would not be effective, and the immunotherapy would not work. The only vaccine that can work will be those produced by us, the pharms of Mr. Simpson and Mr. Nelson. We have already accomplished this stage."

"Dr. Jeng," Mr. Fu of Thailand said. "I am extremely pleased and impressed. I am sure we all are. One more year or two? Regardless, it is great."

"Thanks, Mr. Fu," Jeng continued. "Now, we need to work on two more steps. The first is the carrier system. The second is to incorporate radioactive elements into the virus as insurance. It means if the infection does not work, the radiation will take over. Or they do it together.

"The first step. The scientists could not do it in their own labs as with the switching of the viral RNA. So they retired to different locations. The lab in Melbourne will do the delivery system, the drones, micro-drones. Three or four of them will work there using digestible materials, proteins. The lab on Bird's Wing Island will do the radioactive isotope insertion because of its isolation from civilization. They will travel back and forth between the labs to coordinate the protocol. In about a year, I hope, we will have the finished product. My science colleagues and I will be done. The board will take over regarding how to make our bioweapon work for us."

"Dr. Jeng. Thank you. You have selected the right team, the right people to do the job," Mr. Li said. "If I may, I am going to nominate Dr. Jeng to be one of us. We have been talking about that for a while. Any comments?"

There were no comments, just affirmations and handshakes. Dr. Jeng became the newest board member of the biggest conglomerate in the world, the Phoenix Group.

"Thank you," Dr. Jeng said. "I will end my sabbatical leave and go back to Stanford. I will continue to coordinate with our scientists. It is better that way. That means I will do more travelling. By the way, do not forget the contribution of Dr. Carl. We had many conversations before he passed away."

"Dr. Jeng, you can always use my Cessna whenever you need," Mr. Simpson said. "We won't forget Dr. Carl either. His family will be well taken care of with the generosity of this board."

"There is another development. I'm not sure whether it is good or bad yet," Mr. Li said. "But I think it may not concern us."

Mr. Li continued, tapping a key on his computer. A new screen appeared.

"We were monitoring all new mergers as well as new travel agencies. One of us, I don't remember who, thought the government may use travel agencies to find our scientists. One of the new travel agencies, Paz Exotic Travel, is the only unusual one. We checked the agency. Paz was a VP for the defunct Global Foundation. She is using her old contacts as local guides. Her first trip was to Costa Rica. Nothing special is drawing our attention. Her second trip was sailing in the archipelago around New Zealand. This particular trip was requested by an exercise group of senior citizens, a tai chi group from California. She used a retired pastor, David Fung, and his sloop. Pastor Fung took the group sailing around New Zealand. One of the stops, not on the itinerary, was Bird's Wing Island. According to our tracking, they stopped at the island to shelter from a storm. Actually, none of their destinations were scheduled. Anyway, on Bird's Wing Island, Paz's clients were very courteous. They did not ask who lived in those buildings where our scientists are staying; one of the houses is our lab. They did not even wander over because, according to the islanders, they said they respected their privacy although our scientists were not there."

"Mr. Li, do you think we need not be concerned?" Mr. Simpson asked.

"I don't know. That is why I brought it up."

"Do you have any details about the group?" Mr. Fu of Thailand asked.

"As I said, members of the group were senior citizens. A lady name Wendy was the contact with Paz's travel agency. A man named Lonnie, an eighty-three-year-old tai chi master was their instructor. They just sailed with Pastor Fung and his grandson Liam as first mate. They did a lot of sailing and fishing. They had no scheduled stops. Sometimes they just stayed overnight on a small island."

"Nothing out of the ordinary then," Mr. Nelson said.

"Where is Paz's home base?" Mr. Lloyd said.

"She has a residence in New York City." Mr. Li said. "She appears to be operating alone. She could do it because she had a lot of contacts and experience while with Global Foundation. She has an associate on the tour, a lady named Bonnie. Our computer guys found that she is the widow of a biotech engineer with some tech firm which is no longer operating. She sold her house in upstate New

York and bought a small house in Costa Rica after her husband passed away. Nothing unusual there either. There are numerous people like her in Costa Rica."

"In that case, from our information, Paz Exotic Travel may be OK. Let us wait to see where she goes next," Mr. Fu said.

The Phoenix Group had a good meeting and a new board member, Dr. Jeng of Stanford.

TWO SURPRISES

Paz and Bonnie had a great tour sailing around the New Zealand archipelago. Most importantly, they discovered one of the houses on Bird's Wing Island was hot, i.e. radioactive or contained radioactive materials. If it were not for the storm and the prototype of a detector for low-level radiation from the Lawrence Livermore Laboratory, they might not have been able to make that discovery. The level of radiation was too low for an ordinary Geiger counter.

An encrypted email came to Harrison's computer.

Jeng has surfaced. Came back from his sabbatical leave in an unknown location. He was elected a board member of the Phoenix Group. Did we make a mistake? Checking.

"That is interesting," June said. "We thought Jeng may be the central figure, like John with us."

"He may still be a leader, an organizer, or the brain behind the project," Harold said. "Based on what we were told, he has made many trips to Kuala Lumpur. But what John said about his sabbatical leave to an 'unknown' location intrigued me."

"We are making progress. All credit to Paz and Bonnie," June said. "We now know three scientists are on Bird's Wing although we do not know who they are."

Harrison came over with another encrypted message from John. Another surprise.

Paz, would you take Bonnie to New York. Visit Shum's hotel and the old Global Foundation building in Manhattan.

After reading the email, it was shredded.

"Bonnie, let us go to Manhattan," Paz said.

They bought tickets to New York and left the next day.

"Bonnie, stay with me in my condo," Paz said. "I am keeping it for a while. It is uptown near 244ᵗʰ Street. It's a great location. We just walk out and have everything we need, great restaurants, groceries, and even a small art museum featuring street artists. This museum was funded by a retired Chinese restaurant owner who liked art. He has had that restaurant for some thirty years in this neighborhood. He actually financed some of the work. Nothing like the Guggenheim, of course."

"Sounds good. John and I used to visit Manhattan once in a while. It is a great city."

"I will show you where the Global Foundation was. We will go to Mr. Shum's hotel nearby to have coffee for old time's sake. Mr. Shum must be in his nineties now. He is still healthy. His sons are taking over his hospitality business."

"He must be an unusual man."

"He is. Very generous too."

The weather was good. The usual crowds of New Yorkers walked a little faster than those in Costa Rica. Paz and Bonnie walked at a leisurely pace.

"Here is the old Global Foundation. It is a law firm now." Paz pointed out the old Manhattan brownstone to Bonnie. Paz and Bonnie continued to walk and crossed Broadway. "Here it is, Mr. Shum's hotel," Paz said.

"Wow, such a massive waterfall. Chinese Feng Shui. Water is money." Bonnie was impressed.

"Let us have a light lunch in the coffee shop."

Half way through their lunch, Paz looked across to the lobby. "Bonnie, a surprise. There is Mr. Shum. I will go over to say hello."

Paz walked out of the coffee shop into the lobby with a giant waterfall.

"Mr. Shum." Paz stopped in front of Mr. Shum.

"What a surprise, Paz." Mr. Shum gave Paz a big hug. "What a pleasant surprise. I heard that you have formed a travel agency. What are you doing here?"

"I still have my condo in Manhattan. I wanted to show my associate, Bonnie, where I used to work and your hotel. She is in the coffee shop."

"Joe," Mr. Shum, who was using a walking cane, said to a middle-aged gentleman walking next to him "You remember Ms. Paz? I will be with her. I will call when I need you. Thanks. Let us go to meet your associate, Paz, walk on my left side."

Bonnie stood up as they approached the table.

"You must be Mr. Shum, Paz has told me a lot about you."

"Hopefully not too bad! Please sit down." Mr. Shum waved to a waiter. "These are my good friends. Everything is complimentary."

"Yes, Mr. Shum."

"Are you ladies staying here?"

"No, Mr. Shum. Bonnie is staying with me."

"Ms. Bonnie, where is your home?"

"I sold my house upstate after my husband passed away. I have bought a small granny house in San José, Costa Rica."

"Taking any tours lately, Ms. Paz?"

"Yes, only two. The first one in Costa Rica. Daisy the marine biologist helped me with the clients. I don't know if you met her or not. She helped us when a presumed-dead volcano erupted in Costa Rica. We went down there. She was our contact then."

"I don't think so," Mr. Shum said.

"The second trip was sailing around the New Zealand archipelago. Bonnie was helping me. Pastor Fung was our local guide. We sailed in his sloop. That was a great trip."

"Got a third one?"

"No, not yet. I don't want to just take anyone. I want to be sort of selective because we don't have a set itinerary. We want to go to places where few or no tourists have gone."

"Ms. Paz, you still look great and healthy too."

"Thanks. I have been lucky."

"By the way, what are you ladies' plans for this week?"

"We have none. We will just hang around Manhattan," Paz said.

"I have a proposal. My son is supposed to go with me to Melbourne the day after tomorrow to look at some sites for a hotel. Something came up in Boston. He has to be there. Remember the twin architects, E and E Design? They will go with me. Do you want a ride? There is plenty of room in our Gulfstream."

"I have never been in a private plane. Paz?" Bonnie turned to Paz with a question. "I was in New Zealand with you. I've never been to the mainland."

"Since you have no tour yet, come with us. Paz's friends are my friends. Bonnie, did Paz tell you we were both on the board of the Global Foundation?"

"Yes, Mr. Shum. Paz wanted to reminisce about old times. That is why we are here."

"Good. Paz, the day after tomorrow my chauffeur will pick you ladies up at 7.00 AM. That's not too early I hope. We will fly out from a small airport north of here. Pack for a few days." Mr. Shum stood up. "Paz, please walk me to the elevator. Joe will meet me there."

SECOND HUNTING TRIP

Mr. Shum and the twin sister architects were at the small airport on the outskirts of New Rochelle, north of New York City.

"Paz, have you met Elizabeth and Esther?"

"No, I don't believe so." Paz shook hands with the twins. "This is my friend and associate, Bonnie."

"Mr. Shum, ready when you are," Bran, the pilot, said.

"OK. Let us go."

While they were in the air, Mr. Shum gathered his guests around him.

"Thanks for coming along. My son could not join us. But I have you! I want to look at some properties around Melbourne. I heard that the old waterfront, the warehouse district, may have properties for sale. I want to see what they are like, maybe to build a hotel. That is why I have the twins with me. We will hire a helicopter to fly over it first. Then do a land assessment and one from the bay. It will probably take a couple of days. I have already made reservations at the Hilton for us."

"Ladies and gentlemen," Bran said. "The flight will be smooth for the next several hours. Mary has set up a simple buffet."

"Thank you, Mary," Mr. Shum said. "It is a long flight with one stop in Hawaii to refuel. And if you are tired, just adjust the seats and take a nap. I will after I have something to eat."

Mr. Shum's cell phone alerted him to an email.

Package waiting upon arrival. John.

A long flight on the Gulfstream was not the same as in a commercial plane. The passengers were not tired. A limo was waiting when the plane taxied into a private hangar in the general aviation area at Melbourne International Airport.

Mr. Shum picked up the package from the reception counter in the Hilton. There was a note attached: *Please give this to Ms. Bonnie.*

"Ladies, we will do a flyover tomorrow morning. Then we will take my son's yacht and cruise along the waterfront. If you twins think there is a possibility of building a resort hotel, I will start to negotiate with the owner or owners when you twins find out who they are. I understand this old warehouse district is only partially used. Most shipping has gone to the new container terminal. With the new container ships, the merchandise can go directly from the dock to the destinations. There is no need for storage of the goods to be sorted out later. Eight in the morning, OK?" Mr. Shum said. "Ms. Bonnie, this package is for you."

"Thanks. See you tomorrow morning."

Paz and Bonnie shared a suite while the twins had another.

"Ms. Bonnie, would you walk with me on my left side to my suite? I don't want to fall again."

"Of course, my pleasure," Bonnie answered. "Paz, would you take this package to our suite? Thanks."

While Mr. Shum and Bonnie were walking to the elevator, Mr. Shum said in a quiet voice. "Ms. Bonnie, John wants you to handle this instrument. I don't know what it is. Instructions are inside. You can keep it as long as you need."

"Of course."

When Bonnie entered her suite, Paz had already unpacked the box and laid out all the parts on the table in the living room of their suite.

"Bonnie, it looks like a spy scope."

Bonnie sat down and read the instructions.

"Paz, it is a spy scope. It has night vision lens that can see inside of a darkened building as long as there is a window or an opening. There's a camera with it too. Camouflage colors and pattern, military. We need to put the parts together."

After the ladies put the spy scope together, they both lifted the instrument to ascertain its weight.

"Not too heavy, a little bulky. We need to get a travel bag for it," Bonnie said.

"Let us go shopping after a shower," Paz said.

"Paz, I have never been on the mainland here. I am looking forward to it. Even as a spy!"

"The helicopter trip tomorrow should be a great scan of the city, a bird's eye view."

Melbourne is a city well sheltered from typhoons by Port Phillip Bay with a narrow inlet. Large modern container ships and oil tankers have not come into the port of Melbourne for a number of years because of the narrow entrance to the bay. It is difficult for the giant ships to turn around.

Mr. Shum hired a big commuter helicopter for his architects, Paz, Bonnie, and his own pilot, Bran. Bran was an Australian born in Melbourne. He knew the city and surrounding communities like the palm of his hand.

"Mr. Shum, the warehouse district over there, three o'clock. That used to be a busy port. Big container ships and oil tankers don't come in now. It is too crowded and they are difficult to maneuver. And the entrance to the bay, six o'clock, is narrow."

"A beautiful city, the bay too," Paz said.

"Now, the big ships dock in the new container port with pipes from the tanker to the storage tanks. We will fly right over it in a minute."

"Andy," Bran said to the helicopter pilot. "Would you follow the shoreline of the bay and hover over the old warehouse district. Afterward, fly over to Geelong's new port facility."

"OK, Bran."

"Beautiful bay, Mr. Shum," Esther said.

"Without the giant ships, this bay is great for sailing, small boats, and jet skis," said Elizabeth adding her comment to her sister's.

As they hovered over the old warehouse district, Esther made an observation to Mr. Shum. "Uncle Shum, the district is not very big.

I can see some dilapidated buildings. A few seem to still be used. There are two with landings from the bay, probably under a quarter mile apart on a curved shoreline. They cannot see each other."

Elizabeth added her comment. "Uncle Shum, some of the buildings can be torn down. We could make the area into a park with a big boulevard leading to our hotel. We can also have an entrance from the bay. That probably needs approval from the city. We need to check the city ordinance."

An hour later, they finished the helicopter tour of the bay and the warehouse district. They flew over the city before landing.

"Mr. Shum," Bran said. "You son's yacht is docked at the yacht club, about twenty minutes from the hotel, also about twenty minutes by taxi from the heliport."

"Good, we will have lunch in the yacht club. Afterward, we can take a cruise in the bay."

After lunch, the party boarded the yacht. This yacht had the skin of a Chinese junk with modern navigation gears. There were three other similar ones. They all belonged to Chinese multimillionaires.

"Ms. Bonnie and Ms. Paz, I hope you brought the camera," Mr. Shum said quietly while they were quite a distance behind the young people, the twins, Bran, and the captain of the yacht.

"We have it," Bonnie said, pointing to her newly purchased travel bag.

"Uncle Shum, we took many pictures. We will take some more from the yacht. Those will be good for us to design the landing entrance from the bay in the event you decide to build a hotel here," Elizabeth said.

Unlike western yachts, the Chinese junk/yacht has an elevated aft deck with small windows at the sides and back. The deck in front of this elevated structure was modified into the style of a western yacht. The dinghy was hung fore instead of aft. Mr. Shum's son kept the mast with an imitation of a Chinese square sail. The sail was rarely used.

"Mr. Shum, I will take pictures from the aft chamber. It is more stable with a tripod and from a dark interior," Bonnie said quietly.

"Bran, would you ask the captain if we can use the sail today? A slow boat!" Mr. Shum said.

A few minutes later, Bran came back. "Mr. Shum, the captain said there is a good breeze. He too likes to sail instead of using the motor. It's slow and a bit more rolling then using the motor."

"Bonnie, would that work?" Mr. Shum asked quietly.

"No problem, my camera is very sensitive," Bonnie answered almost in a whisper.

Bonnie went aft with her equipment, found a window, and set up her spy scope.

As they came near the warehouses, Bonnie began to scan the buildings, looking into windows and doors.

The boat was about one hundred feet from shore. When they reached the landing of the warehouse where the Phoenix Group built its laboratory, the double doors to the landing were open. So were the windows. Several workers waved to the people in the Chinese junk/yacht. Mr. Shum and others waved back.

"Amazing," Bonnie said to herself.

Bonnie had almost five minutes to look inside through the door and the windows of the warehouse with her spy scope.

The twins had a different perspective in their observation. They wanted to build a hotel while Bonnie wanted to know what was inside the warehouse.

After the air and sea tour of Port Phillip Bay, Mr. Shum and his party went back to the Hilton Hotel.

As soon as Paz and Bonnie went into their suite, Bonnie immediately wrote down her observations in her own shorthand. Paz then relayed them to Harrison in the encrypted format that Harrison had written for all the conspirators, the Volunteer friends, and Paz.

Observation from air – rooftops all the same. Observation from sea level – through the open door at one of the warehouses with a landing, image of several analytical ultracentrifuges, several nucleotide analyzers, tabletop centrifuges. Maybe a couple of safety hoods. Pictures of people inside not clear. Workers outside not scientists.

Harrison handed the sheet with the above information to Harold and June in the pavilion.

"I deleted the incoming message from Paz. Here is the copy."

"Thank you, Harrison," June said. "By the way, how are you getting along in this motel-home?"

"Great, June. It is actually bigger than my pad in New York. A lot more fresh air too."

"June, this is like a lab, like mine and yours."

"Better let John know."

"Harrison, would you email that to John? Thanks," June said.

SUSPICION BECOMES FACT

Air Force One landed at Beijing International Airport to the standard official welcoming party. The president of the People's Republic of China and his first lady were about ten yards from the foot of the mobile stairs. As the US president and his first lady stepped onto the ground, the band played the Stars and Stripes while the president of the People's Republic of China and his first lady walked toward the US couple.

"Welcome to China, Mr. and Mrs. President," the Chinese president extended his hands to both while introducing his wife, a lady with a great disposition. She was an actress of some repute before she married the president of China.

All four people walked along the red carpet to inspect the honor guard. A convoy of Red Star limousines was waiting at the far end of the tarmac away from the area for the commercial passenger terminal.

While the presidents and their first ladies were led to a big elongated Red Star limousine, the scientists were led to another Red Star at the end of the convoy.

"Drs. Alex, Calvin, Robert, and Somers, welcome again to Beijing." Dr. Wang stepped forward to the scientists. "Mr. Morrison did not come with you?"

"No, he has some politicking to do," Somers said. "He is indispensable to our science, maintenance of the funding, especially!"

"A good man to have," Dr. Wang said. "I hope you are not too tired. I would like to show you our newest molecular biology laboratory just outside the campus of Beijing University. Let us take that big limo at the end of this entourage."

A surprise. Dr. Lee was in the passenger seat while Mei Mei was the driver.

"Welcome, my American friends." Lee turned around to greet them. "We recruited Mei Mei to be our driver. It will take an hour if there's no congestion. I thought we would have a brief confidential meeting on the way."

"Great idea, Dr. Lee," Robert said. "You got my email. I will give you more details now."

Robert continued. "According to our source, one of the buildings on Bird's Wing Island in the New Zealand archipelago is radioactive or contains radioactive materials, low level. We don't know if they are from a solid or liquid source. Three couples from America are on that island. A large yacht has visited the island more often than the usual rich people's outings. Local islanders never asked about their business. They know them as retired good friends. The islanders never wander over to that side of the island. The wives of the Americans socialize with the islanders, but not the men. A warehouse by Port Phillip Bay in Melbourne houses a lab with analytical centrifuges, nucleotide analyzers, and other standard lab equipment. There are people working there but we have no clear pictures of their faces. Not yet anyway. The warehouse district is no longer a busy port. Only a few small general cargo ships use it. About half of the warehouses there are vacant. There is a new container port in a district called Geelong which giant tankers and container ships use.

"With this information, we know for sure these two labs must be related, that is, housing the missing scientists. And Jeng of Stanford has reappeared from a sabbatical leave. Jeng may be the chief coordinator of this suspicious project. The nine other missing scientists are also connected. Here is a hand-drawn figure." Robert handed out copies of what Jack drew for the Volunteer friends.

Robert continued. "We will put them in the shredding machine later. This is the clandestine part."

"Dr. Robert," Mei Mei asked. "How sure are we that these ten missing scientists are our persons of interest? There must be many molecular biologists retiring or changing jobs all the time."

"Yes, true, Ms. Mei Mei," Robert answered. "We checked them all. Only these ten stand out. Our source also postulated their goal. Here is a summary."

Robert handed a thin folder to each one in the limo. The information in these folders was the result of the literature search/detective work of the Vols.

"We will shred them too, later. Or maybe not. We need to find a solution to neutralize this possible agent or agents. An antidote? Whatever is needed," Robert continued his narrative.

Within a few minutes, all the SAGRC members finished the content in the folders.

"We need first to narrow down the agents, infectious agents, or poisons," Alex said. "Then we should proceed to sort out some specifics. I don't like this radioactive data. Why incorporate, I assume, radioisotopes into the agent, the bioweapon?"

"And it emits low-level radiation?" Wang added his comment with a question mark.

"Our source detected low-level radiation from the Bird's Wing Island lab. Does it mean isotopes were used to mutate, to break or to incorporate into some macromolecules?" Calvin put forth a question to the group.

"We don't know. It was low gamma. That is about all," Robert said. "Not beta because it could not go through bricks."

"Yes. Either C^{14} or tritium can be easily replaced in either protein or nucleic acids," Alex said. "If so, the macromolecules would be radioactive. That might exert a secondary effect."

"As insurance?" Lee of Beijing expressed her opinion.

"There is one thing for certain, pretty certain," Mei Mei said while keeping her eyes on the road and without turning toward her passengers. "It is not similar to the bioweapon that was given to us several years back."

"If that is the case," Wang said. "This new bioweapon, I assume that is what it is, will not be targeting individuals. If not individuals, populations?"

Calvin suddenly had a thought. "It is still based on the powerful CRISPR-Cas9 tech. If not targeting individuals, it has to be a population. In that case, I would use existing macromolecules, a virus. We have to think like them!"

"That is why there are a couple of immunotherapy experts in this group?" Somers added her opinion with a question mark.

"Maybe, just maybe, we should assume it is virus," Robert said. "That would involve vectors. Am I thinking right?"

"Are you thinking what I am thinking, Dr. Robert?" Alex looked over to Robert. "Instead of killing—euthanize is a better word—individuals, this bioweapon is targeting a population. That would create an epidemic. They want to control, or elicit, or create an epidemic?"

"Yes. Dr. Alex."

"If they can create an epidemic, viral in nature, that certainly will involve immunotherapy. Dr. Somers," Lee turned to look at Somers. "We will be dealing with the protein coats and the drones as vectors. The nitrogen in both can easily be substituted with radioactive N^{15}. More stable too."

"Yes, Dr. Lee. Is it a double-edged sword?"

There were a few moments of silence as the giant limo glided silently along the newly paved road. Two motorcycle security guards came close to each side of the limo, one of them signaling Mei Mei to roll down the window.

"Please follow me."

A few minutes later, Mei Mei's limo slowed, turning to leave the convoy with the presidents and their entourage.

"We are going to the Beijing Hotel, the others to the American embassy, then Zhongnanhai. They do their politics and we do our science," Wang said.

"After our meeting, we will take a commercial flight back, no more Air Force One," Calvin said.

"We shall be at the hotel in twenty minutes, barring any traffic on the cross-ring roads. So far we are OK," Mei Mei said. "I will return this big tank. There will be other cars for us if we need them. Or we can take a taxi. Dr. Wang, tomorrow at eight?"

"Yes, ladies and gentlemen," Wang said. "In the conference room in the hotel. There will be breakfast there too. We will learn from our American friends, a breakfast meeting! Later in the afternoon, we will have a press conference announcing our recent developments in pancreatic cancer."

Mei Mei stopped the big limo in front of the VIP entrance, left of the main entrance of the flag ship Beijing Hotel. This hotel had been remodeled inside. The outside was still the same classic Chinese façade.

Mei Mei handed the car key to an attendant. "We don't need this anymore. Please return it to the VIP carpool. Thank you."

"Yes, madam."

"All of us will be in this hotel for the next couple of days," Wang said. "It's more convenient. Our meetings will be on time. Traffic in Beijing is like Manhattan except our drivers don't like to follow the dotted lines on the roads. We have five ring roads now. Sometimes it will take almost an hour just to come from Ring 5 to Ring 1 here via the so-called express cross-ring connections."

"Dr. Wang, a sign of progress!" Alex made a small joke.

Alex and Mei Mei were the youngest members of SAGRC. Either before or after their meetings, they would go out shopping or do whatever young ladies did. They became good friends in a short time span.

Wang addressed everyone as they paused in the lobby waiting for their room keys. "We don't have a welcome dinner for our guests. Please go to the restaurant; sign your name and room number. There's no tipping. If you go outside, there are many good eating places. There also, no tipping."

CONNECTING THE FIRST FEW DOTS

"Elizabeth and Esther," Shum said to the twins. "What do you think about the location?"

"Definitely a good location, looking out over the bay," Elizabeth said. "Easy to design too. Flat ground. We may need to create some small rises. We can even use some of the existing roads. They'd need to be paved, of course. Whatever you like, Uncle Shum."

"There are a couple of smaller, non-paved roads. We may be able to dig out the soil and make them into a small creek connecting to the bay, an aquatic recreation venue. Loop around the hotel, maybe." Esther added her thought.

"We don't need all the acreage though," Shum said. "We need to talk to the city. Half of the warehouses are vacant. Maybe the city can do something. They may already have a plan. Will you ladies go to the city tomorrow? Find out who owns what and where and how much acreage?"

"We will be glad to, Uncle Shum," the twins answered in unison. "We will call for an appointment right now before they go home."

Elizabeth thumbed her cell phone. Within a few minutes, she had made a connection with the city.

"Thank you, sir. Nine in the morning."

They went back to the Hilton.

"Bran, we will not need the plane for maybe a couple of days. If you wish to see your folks, please do. I will call tomorrow. I need to know what the young ladies find out first. Bonnie and Paz, take a tour if you wish. But first, dinner tonight at seven. I have already made a reservation at the best Chinese restaurant in Melbourne, may even be in Asia. We will take a cab there. See you here in the lobby."

"Bonnie, let us get lost for the next two hours," Paz said.

"What do you mean?"

"There are bikes for rent from the hotel. We will bike over to the warehouse area. Bring your special camera."

"Right."

"Elizabeth and Esther, would you join us for a bike ride? We have two hours before dinner," Paz said to the twins.

"Thanks for asking. We need to do some prep before we go to City Hall tomorrow. Specifics, a possible plan to show the city with building-related matters. A sketch of what we saw from the helicopter and from the bay," Elizabeth said. "But we will have dinner with you and Uncle Shum. We'd never miss a great Chinese meal."

"Paz, look at these bikes, they even have a GPS on them."

"And a walkie-talkie too. The bellhop told me that the range is just a two-mile circumference with the hotel in the center. If we got lost, we can call. I think the warehouse district is not that far. Let's see from this GPS."

"No hills either."

"Ready?"

"Ready."

"And the bike lanes are well marked."

Within twenty minutes they arrived at the warehouse district. There were still shops and restaurants in the district. Bonnie put the radiation detector in the basket at the front of the bike. They biked near the walls but did not stop. Several warehouses appeared to be vacant. A small back door of the one which had a landing was open. That was the one with the centrifuges and nucleotide sequencers. They could not see in. There were no beeps from Bonnie's detector. They looped around the district one more time and back to the hotel.

Paz emailed John what they saw—no faces and no detection of radiation energy in the warehouse district.

John transferred that message to Surgeon General Pei.

After a great Chinese dinner, they all retired to their suites.

Elizabeth and Esther had to work.

"Uncle Shum, we will present a rough plan to the city tomorrow. We have not finished yet. Do you want to look at it before we go to City Hall?" Esther said to Shum.

"No need. Just tell them who wants to build. I believe they may know me although I have no hotels in Australia. My son owns a few condo units here. That is about my only connection here. You may tell them I own the Orchid Garden in Boston and the New Asia in New York. Tell them you are my architects."

"OK, Uncle Shum."

The next morning after breakfast, Paz said to Bonnie. "We still have not seen any faces here or on Bird's Wing Island. I noticed yesterday there are small sailboats for rent. It's not far. Maybe we should rent one and sail close to the warehouse of our interest. Take our chances with your spy scope. Do you know how to sail?"

"No, I usually sat around as counterweight when John did the sailing. I picked up some techniques here and there. Those sailboats for rent are usually simple to handle. Let us do that. If we run aground, we can call for help. The bay is pretty calm."

It took the ladies about forty-five minutes from the sailboat dock to the warehouse district. The wind was breezy but not strong, ideal for small sailboats. They sailed very close to the landing of the warehouse with biochemical instruments. The door was open. Bonnie laid low over the gunwale not wanting to raise attention just in case. There were people moving around inside. However, it was still too dark inside to make out faces.

As luck would have it, a man came out. Bonnie quickly snapped a series shots. The ladies waved to the man who returned their greetings.

One face. That was enough.

"I think this is Dr. Wing of Singapore," Paz said. "Just to be sure we can compare this shot with the pictures we got from John."

It was Dr. Wing of Singapore.

Paz emailed it to John.

Now they knew there were two labs, one here in Melbourne and the other on Bird's Wing Island.

But there was still no proof that these scientists were carrying out any rogue activities, or who was behind their activities.

However, they had connected the first few dots: Bird's Wing Island, Melbourne, a face and the possible nature of a bioweapon.

Where would the other dots be? Would they fall into what the line should be? Ending up at the Phoenix Group of Hong Kong? Or some other rogue organization?

While Paz and Bonnie were doing their snooping around in a sailboat, Elizabeth and Esther went to City Hall armed with their preliminary plan for a hotel.

"Thank you for giving us a chance to talk to you, Mr. Dumont, at such short notice." Elizabeth said. Elizabeth was usually the one who did most of the talking.

"You are welcome. Twins?"

"Yes. We are the architects for Mr. Shum who owns several hotels around the world except in Melbourne. He is interested in building one here."

"Mr. Shum? The philanthropist as well?"

"The same, Mr. Dumont," Elizabeth answered.

Elizabeth continued. "We took an aerial picture of the old warehouse district. Mr. Shum's son told Mr. Shum about it. We also took a boat ride to see how the place looks from the bay. We think there is a great possibility of building a resort/hotel where the warehouses are. What we would like to know is:

"One, does the city have any future plans regarding the use of the district?

"Two, if your city does have a plan, what might it be? Residential or commercial or both?

"Three, we have drawn a rough plan; if you have time to look over it today, we would appreciate it very much."

"Yes. This old warehouse district is half vacant now. All the container ships and tankers are over in the new port in the Geelong district. Give me a minute." Mr. Dumont picked up a phone. "Rose, would you bring me the preliminary plan for the old warehouse district?"

A few minutes later, a middle-aged lady came in with a folder.

"Thanks, Rose." Mr. Dumont then turned to the twins. "This is our preliminary plan for the district. It is too big for commercial use and too small for residential. The city thought it may use it as a park. That would be a big one. My idea was for all three." He paused, flipped open a folded page. "This is the dimension of the district. You can compare that to your aerial photo."

"Thanks."

Esther laid the computer-enlarged aerial photo and the city's drawing side by side.

"Mr. Dumont, we sort of outlined what we thought we might do with the district," said Esther using a small pointer to show Mr. Dumont.

"Here would be our hotel. This would be the boulevard leading to it, landscaped of course. Slightly curved. A footpath along the shore. A park adjacent to the hotel proper all the way to the shoreline. An entrance to the hotel from the bay in addition to the main entrance."

Esther continued to trace the photo with her pointer. "We noticed that there are three narrow, unpaved streets sort of winding around some buildings. We talked about digging them up to make a recreation aqueduct connecting to the bay. Such as for small paddleboats for kids, kayaks, etc. that are not safe in the bay. We will design a couple of rises, little hills. Mr. Dumont, what do you think?"

"Looks pretty good. You ladies just did that last night?"

"Yes, sir."

"I cannot give you the answer right now. You know all municipal work takes time. The council, city engineering, environmental departments, and others, like politics. You know."

"Yes. We do. We can present you with a plan in two weeks, not just a rough drawing. However, we do have to know certain facts. That is, which area belongs to the city, who owns which warehouses, the existing shops and restaurants, etc. We don't handle this. Mr. Shum's financial staff will ascertain the financial part."

"We can answer that. But it will take a little time. We can give you the owners and the addresses. In an hour, maybe—wait, I think we have a list." Mr. Dumont called Rose. "Rose, do we have a list of the owners of all the properties in the district?"

"Wait a minute, please, let me check the big folder."

A minute or so later, Rose called. "Yes, Mr. Dumont. Do you want me to make a copy?"

"Please. We will give it to these young ladies."

"Here it is. I think that is what you asked for." Mr. Dumont handed the list over to the twins.

"That is perfect, Mr. Dumont," Elizabeth said. "Here is our card. We are in New York. Can we present a formal proposal with an architectural plan to the City of Melbourne in two weeks' time to start the conversation?" Elizabeth said.

"That will be fine. As soon as I receive it, I will talk to my staff. Then we will present it to the City. Be patient. The government here doesn't work very fast. It may take weeks."

"I think we are even slower in New York," Esther said with a big smile.

They shook hands.

It was a very informative meeting.

"Good work," Mr. Shum said to the twins. "Would you make a copy for me? Paz, Bonnie, do you ladies want to spend a few more days in Australia? Elizabeth, Esther, and I have to go back tomorrow to start work."

"We will go back with you. Mr. Shum." Paz said. "I am thinking of taking a group to the Amazon."

"Ms. Paz, do you know if Professor Alvarado is still involved in the Amazon? If so, I bet she will help a lot. She knows the rain forest better than anyone in the world."

"I am not sure. But I think she is still active. She does not look like the retiring type, like you," Paz said.

"That is the trouble with us, no hobbies!" Mr. Shum said with a smile.

"You keep us working too, Uncle Shum," Esther said.

Before they left for the US, Paz emailed John.

The warehouse of interest belongs to Chan Brothers Engineering, Inc. Hong Kong, which may have done the modification into a lab.

SMOKE BUT NO FIRE

"Dr. Pei, your golf partner John for you," Anna, Dr. Pei's secretary, said over the intercom.

"Please put him through."

"Dr. Pei, I cannot make it for our regular game today. I have come down with the flu. How about Saturday, the day after tomorrow?"

"I think I am free. I know I will be free because my wife is going to her grandniece's graduation. See you, 7.00 AM as usual."

Dr. Pei then called his secretary. "Anna, would you check if I have any appointments on Saturday?"

"Dr. Pei, you have one. A talk to a group of interns from Emery University Medical School."

"Can you call Dr. Tilford to see if she can do it? Show them around, etc."

A few minutes later Anna called. "Dr. Tilford will be available."

"Thanks. You know where I will be if needed on Saturday."

Paz and Bonnie went back to Costa Rica after their fruitful amateur detective work in Melbourne.

"Harold, that spy scope really worked. The low-level radioactivity monitor too," Bonnie told June and Harold.

"We have to email the information to John," June said.

"I already did," Paz said.

Harrison came over. "Good to see you ladies back. I have information for you."

"What do you have, Harrison?" Paz asked and went over to give Harrison a hug. Paz had been like a mother to this genius geek.

"Someone in Hong Kong is monitoring your travel agency. I cannot find out who. It was like an old-fashioned phone answering service. It appears to serve more than one concern; it may not, or they just use it as a façade."

"To monitor the Paz spy-agency," Harold said with a great smile. "I think you should lead another tour to some place without any suspicious purpose or intention, Paz."

"How about Brazil, the Amazon? I've had that in mind for a while."

"Do you still keep in contact with Professor Alvarado?" June asked Paz.

"Not really. I did not ask her if she would be interested to be my local guide of our travel agency. Maybe I should ask her now. The Amazon will be a great destination. And she knows the Amazon and many poachers there. I told Mr. Shum that when we were in Australia."

"Professors? Poachers?" Bonnie raised an eyebrow.

"Sorry, Bonnie," Paz said. "Professor Alvarado was on the board of the Global Foundation. She was instrumental in identifying a small tribe in the Amazon as our first sacrificial lamb."

"Why poachers?"

"Professor Alvarado was, still is, I hope, in charge of the conservation of the Amazon, the Amazon Conservation Agency, a quasi-government organization. She makes use of the knowledge of the poachers who roam around the rain forest looking for animals. They encounter or see many small tribes that never have been exposed to the outside world. I think Professor Alvarado pays them for the information and gives that to the government if necessary. The Brazilian government knows the unlawful business of the poachers. However, the government also needs information on the Amazon. They need to protect the rain forests and at the same time make use of them. So the poachers serve a useful dual purpose."

"So, Paz, you and I would go into the Amazon with the help of Professor Alvarado and the poachers?" Bonnie asked with a somewhat excited expression.

"Whoever monitors Paz's agency must have a suspicion or taking a precautious measure. This outfit is also monitoring mergers, emergent businesses, and start-ups," Harrison said.

"Paz and Bonnie have organized a tour to New Zealand requested by a tai chi group in California. The tour included Bird's Wing Island. They then went to Melbourne. Melbourne was with Mr. Shum and they found out the owner of the warehouse. The latter was innocent enough. They, the terrorists, may not have knowledge about the Melbourne trip. This unknown 'phone service' may not be monitoring Mr. Shum." June was thinking out loud.

"So far, sailing around New Zealand may have raised the suspicion of the rogue people. However, I don't think anyone on that tour knew Paz and Bonnie were sneaking around the island at two in the morning. So, an innocent tour to the Amazon like the one here in Costa Rica would provide a good cover for Paz Exotic Travel, P.I.!" Harold said.

"We had luck, too. We had to shelter from the storm and stayed overnight on Bird's Wing. I bet these rogue people knew about our staying there. Not our plan. Our luck!"

"Harold, you all have learned to be spies!" Bonnie said. "I will get there in time!"

"I will send out an ad for it. First come first served on an Amazon tour."

"Paz, I am excited already. I have never been to South America," Bonnie said.

Dr. Pei and John were driving their golf cart to the second hole on their favorite course in Arlington.

"Dr. Pei, I have some very interesting information on the missing scientists. My contacts have uncovered the possible locations where they are doing their work. One site is on an island called Bird's Wing in the New Zealand archipelago. There is a building that emits low-level radiation. The native islanders told them that three retired American couples built this 'hot' building and their residences on the island. This island is not under the jurisdiction of New Zealand although New Zealand, as a courtesy, also monitors its environment like others under its jurisdiction. The islanders do not go over to that side of the island and don't ask questions.

"My friends did not see anyone there because these three couples were visiting folks in America when they sailed around the archipelago. Actually, it was pretty much accidental. They had to seek refuge from a storm when they were near Bird's Wing Island. If it were not for the storm, they would have had to find an excuse to visit that island. I told them about the yacht."

"John, that is indicative that our suspicion is true."

John continued. "In Melbourne one of the missing scientists, Dr. Wing of Singapore, was in that particular warehouse in the old warehouse district. My friends also saw ultracentrifuges and nucleotide analyzers in that warehouse, plus some standard laboratory wares. It is an active lab. This warehouse with the lab belongs to Chan Brothers, Inc. Hong Kong. The Phoenix Group is part owner of this engineering firm."

"That was great work by your friends, John." Dr. Pei was very pleased about the development. "But still we have no proof."

"That is true. We need more."

"We cannot just go into these suspicious laboratories to have a look."

"Right. Another development. One of the missing scientists was a Dr. Jeng of Stanford. He reappeared and became one of the board members of the Phoenix Group in Hong Kong."

"John, that is a very important indicative revelation. I remember that your friends were able to study the work of these missing scientists and came up with a hypothetical intention of the rogue group. Now, with Jeng on the Phoenix board, we should look into whether Phoenix has a connection with the scientists or the rogue group. Or perhaps the rogue organization is in fact the Phoenix?"

"That should not be hard to find out."

"How?"

"I will ask my friends if they noticed who supported the research. Research papers always cite the supporting agencies. I am sure they would have noticed and recorded it although they did not give us the information. That would be easy to find out if the Phoenix group is involved. Such as so and so institutions or organizations were sponsoring the research. If any of them is subsidiary of Phoenix, it should be a public record."

John sent Harold an encrypted email with his smart phone.

Have you any information on the support of their research?

Answer from Harold:

Singapore Biotech, Inc.; Hong Kong Biotech, Inc.; Immuno Inc.; Alpha Pharm; Cardiotech, Inc. (Kuala Lumpur); Singapore Medical Science, Inc. Some by the Cancer Foundation, NSF, National Institute of Health as well.

John showed Dr. Pei the list from Harold. Dr. Pei said, "I will email this to our intel people. It won't take them long to find out as to the relationship of all these biotech firms to Phoenix."

Eight holes later, as they sat in the club house having a light lunch, a message appeared on Dr. Pei's phone.

All concerns are connected to one Phoenix Group holding company, Hong Kong.

"John, we can connect all the dots and end up at Phoenix. That is a good indication as to who may be behind this bioweapon project."

"Yes, that is still no proof that Phoenix is doing anything illegal. Companies supporting scientific research is nothing new or illegal. In fact, scientific communities welcome the financial support. I am sure if we check into more detail, there may be more companies of interest other than those companies that my friends emailed to us."

"And that is nothing illegal either."

"We have smoke but no fire. We have thunder but no rain."

"Remember the bioweapon, John? Years ago when some unknown group used it to blackmail the governments to cease their war games? It worked. It was a noble act. But who could predict the repercussions we are having now? A repercussion from a noble intent. An echo of peace."

John kept silent for a moment.

"Dr. Pei, did SAGRC come up with a postulate for the bioweapon, if indeed it might be that?"

"Like your consultants' conclusion, they are on the same page. It would seem to involve immunotherapeutic technology. Most likely it will involve a virus to infect a large population."

"A population, a large population, an epidemic, man-made?"

"It is possible. Zika, Ebola, swine flu? Maybe even bringing back polio!"

Nothing was said for a few minutes. They looked at each other, shaking their heads.

THE AMAZON TOUR

Paz sent an ad to several major travel magazines as soon as she and Bonnie went back to Costa Rica.

There have been requests for us to lead a tour into the Amazon. If interested, please email us ASAP because we can take no more than ten people, adults, healthy, no exceptions. $4000 pp. 10-12 days.

Within a week, more than fifteen people responded. Paz selected ten. She emailed her guests.

Please arrange your own transportation roundtrip to Manaus. One week from today. Let us know the schedule. Look for Paz Travel sign. You will be met at the airport.

Paz addressed the group in the lobby of the Hilton Inn in Manaus. "Welcome to Brazil. Have any of you been here before?"

An elderly couple raised their hands. "We did a cruise from here to Miami several years back. That was it."

"Any others?"

"I was with the Peace Corps when I was a junior in college," a middle-aged man said.

"We have three tour guides," Paz said jokingly. "This is Bonnie, my associate. And here she is! The real one! Friends, I want to introduce to you our real guide. This is Professor Alvarado. She is the director of the Amazon Conservation Agency. She knows the rain forest better than anyone."

All the travelers clapped, looking very excited.

"Friends of Paz and Bonnie are friends of mine. Welcome to the Amazon. I will give a general talk this evening here at the hotel. An informal one. Tomorrow we will begin the tour of the Amazon. It will be daily almost ninety-five degrees Fahrenheit and ninety-nine percent humidity and no rain."

"We can feel it already," one of the travelers said.

"Let us meet in the conference room on the second floor, six o'clock. We will have a buffet dinner. Then during coffee and dessert, Professor Alvarado will talk to us. If you are not too tired after freshening up, take a walk. Get used to the weather. Or rather, get acclimated to the Amazon weather," Paz said to the group.

On top of the Phoenix Tower in Hong Kong in the conference room, Mr. Li and his two trusted staff members, Mr. Piazza and Mrs. Poon, were looking over some of the information from their computer center.

"Let us see what is new. Mrs. Poon," Mr. Li said looking over to Mrs. Poon, a middle-aged lady.

They all opened the same page on their monitors in front of them.

Mrs. Poon read from her monitor. "Mergers of two food giants in America. Startup of a delivery service here in Hong Kong, like Uber but with orders from clients for grocery stores and restaurant take-outs. Merger talk by two major banks in Europe. Travel agencies. Nothing new. Paz Exotic Travel is taking a group of ten to the Amazon."

"Mrs. Poon, would you get more detail on Paz Exotic Travel? Their clients." Mr. Li said.

Mrs. Poon hit a few keys. "Our computer guys have followed our instructions. They have checked into the background of all the participants."

Looking over the list of the participants, after a few minutes Mr. Li said to his associates. "They do not seem to have anyone unusual in the group, or anyone with an interest related to our activities."

"Anything new from SAGRC?"

Mrs. Poon hit a few keys.

The monitors showed the arrival of the US president with his entourage at Beijing International Airport. Standard welcome routines were shown.

"Mr. Li, note the last limo. Face identification has revealed that these four Americans getting into the limo are members of SAGRC hitching a ride on Air Force One. Our intel said they later separated from the president's motorcade and went to the Beijing Hotel. They will be meeting with their counterparts from China."

"We need to monitor every movement and word from them," Mr. Li said.

Mrs. Poon then showed SAGRC and the presidents of both China and the US the announcement about the early detection of pancreatic cancer.

Dr. Wang, the Chinese technocrat representing SAGRC, made the following announcement.

We are pleased to announce that the consortium, with the assistance of many scientists in China and the United States, has successfully developed an early diagnostic protocol of the deadly pancreatic cancer although a successful method of curing it has not yet been reached. Please go to our website to download the protocol.

The TV camera then scanned the audience and those on the stage. Waiters and waitresses were seen hovering around the ballroom with trays of hors d'oeuvres and drinks. It was a celebratory social event.

After a few minutes, the TV moved to another program.

The SAGRC scientists adjourned to a conference room in the hotel.

"Ladies and gentlemen," the director of the Chinese Academy of Sciences put his hands together with a beaming smile. "Another great success. Congratulations. I am glad to convey the same from our premier."

He went around shaking hands. "I will leave you alone for your discussions."

"We have much to discuss," Dr. Wang of China and the United Nations started the meeting. "We will take as much time as needed. Make yourselves comfortable. The monitors in front of you are all dedicated to our task. They are secure with no connection to World Wide Web or any other internets or satellites. After our discussions, they will be wiped clear, i.e. after we download our discussions onto the flash drives."

"Our 'consultants,'" Somers said, not knowing that the consultants were the Volunteer friends. "They have given us an excellent assessment of what this unknown rogue group's plan may be. It certainly would involve immunotherapy. If so, the agent or agents may be viral in origin. They are not bacteria because we have conquered a wide spectrum of bacterial agents, including the superbugs. I am inclined to think of Zika, Ebola, HIV or polio."

"Editing their genes?" Mei Mei asked.

"Change their phenotypes?" Alex added her question.

"The protein coats?" Lee of Beijing added hers.

"Bypass or non-reactive for current immunoglobulin against them?" Robert of Tennessee said.

"Or all of the above?" Calvin said.

"I am also inclined to think that they would use a virus as a tool, perhaps for an epidemic?" Somers said. "We have ample immunoglobulin for all of the above viruses in stock. I recall asking Dr. Pei, our surgeon general some time ago."

"Unless they were able to edit their genome," Alex said. "That could be the amino acid sequence of the protein coats."

"Then they will create an epidemic with whatever genetically modified virus they choose. Our immunoglobulin stock will not be effective," Somers followed the trend of thought.

"I agree with our consultants' postulate that it is of viral origin," Alex said. "But which virus? I don't think they can create or edit all four."

Alex knew their consultants, the Vol buddies. She knew how they thought because she was one of them albeit peripherally to the real lab work.

"Furthermore," Alex continued. "They can, and we can too, of course, switch the genes between the viruses. That is not difficult with CRISPR tech. They could create a brand-new virus."

"Yes, you are right, Dr. Alex," Calvin said. "Timeline?"

"Two years?" Wang suggested. "Those scientists could have started the work before they retired. There are two labs now, one in Melbourne and one on Bird's Wing Island. Not too far from each other."

"Just assume that is what they plan to do. But that will be difficult if not impossible to prove without having real samples," Mei Mei said.

"True, Ms. Mei Mei. We know the lab on Bird's Wing Island is hot. That will be our next question. Why radioactivity?" Wang asked.

"And don't forget the artificial intelligence angle," Calvin added.

"Let us assume they have created a new virus from any one of the four we have talked about. They still need a carrier system, a vector," Robert said.

"A working hypothesis, yes, Dr. Robert. A new species of virus, a synthetic biological product. Even a modification of the same species can be considered a new species. Artificial mutation?" Lee of Beijing agreed.

"A drone? A drone that can think? A robot, very small, a nanobot?" Alex was talking to herself. "Then there's no need to use pheromone specificity as the bioweapon, the one that got us here!"

"I think we are on the right track. It is late, let us meet again tomorrow. Eight thirty here, OK?" Wang said. He had taken over the chair of this meeting because Morrison could not be with them.

"We did not arrange for your meals. If you eat at the hotel, just sign your name. If outside, keep a receipt. No need to tip," Wang reminded them.

The two young ladies, Mei Mei and Alex, went out together.

"Alex, I know a great local place to eat in the Hutong. I know the owner. Her daughter and I went to high school together. Interested?"

"Of course. Let's go."

The young ladies went to the Hutong. Hutong was in the old Beijing city. The government had a plan to raze it; but a group of historians and artists petitioned to keep it. Hutong has become a tourist attraction in Beijing with narrow stone-paved alleys just wide enough for two tricycles to pass each other.

A CHIMERIC VIRUS

"I hope you all had a nice evening," Wang said to the members of the consortium after they took their seats.

"I certainly did," Robert said. "Dr. Somers and I got the best suggestions from the desk. We even attended a Beijing Opera."

"Mei Mei took me to the Hutong to visit her friend and we had home cooking," Alex told her fellow members in the consortium.

"Let me see if I can summarize what we discussed yesterday," Wang opened his notebook and at the same time turned on his computer.

The others did the same.

"We pretty much narrowed down the agent or agents to be viral in origin, Zika, Ebola, HIV or polio. They may have edited their genome, changed their infectious characters, their protein coats, or other properties. With the changes, our existing immunoglobulins and vaccines will not be effective. They can create an epidemic that will be out of control. This implies this rogue group is the one who can control the epidemic. With their own designed immunoglobulin or vaccine?"

Wang paused to wait for other comments or filling in the blanks.

"I think, on the virus part, that we discussed just what you said, Dr. Wang," Somers added her comments. "I think we also touched on the exchange of genome. CRISPR can easily accomplish that."

"That would mean all the stocks of vaccines and immunoglobulins for all four viruses will be useless?" Robert asked, addressing no one in particular.

Everyone was looking at his or her notebook and computer.

After a few moments, Wang began to address the group again. "We also discussed artificial intelligence and the possible vectors, drones in particular."

"And why radioisotopes of low energy?" Calvin added.

"Where would they insert the isotopes? Into the genome or the vector, the drone?" Somers raised a question.

"Maybe both," Robert suggested.

"Why both, Dr. Robert?" Alex asked.

"I was thinking. Can they make use of the radiation from the isotopes as an insurance policy?"

"Now that makes sense," Calvin exclaimed. "A WMD, a bio-WMD of immense scale! Numerous dirty bombs made with viruses!"

"Who would benefit from this bioweapon?" Alex asked.

"Pharmaceuticals, and power, power to control. Their new world order?" Wang said, shaking his head slightly.

"Where would artificial intelligence come in?" Mei Mei asked.

"Another insurance policy?" Robert said. "To make sure the bioweapon goes to the right targets. Or change direction? Change target? That is, when the bombs encounter resistance or a defense line. I am being optimistic that we will form a defense line!"

"Dr. Robert, that is optimistic without knowing what the weapon may be," Wang continued. "However, it is not farfetched. Dr. Robert, I remember meeting someone sometime back when I went to your Oak Ridge National Laboratory in Tennessee. While we were taking a break in the corridor, a pretty big fellow was telling us, I forget who he was, that ORNL has a preliminary tool, or protocol, to chelate out tritium and carbon-14 from DNA molecules and replaced them with normal elements."

After a few seconds Wang exclaimed, "How can I forget? That big fellow was an ex-center of the Volunteer basketball team. His name is Dr. Russel. Maybe sometime in the future we will need to have him here."

"That is maybe one of our breaks. We need a few more," Robert said.

Right in the middle of their discussions, there was a knock at the door. A young lady poked her head in.

"Ladies and gentlemen, sorry for the interruption. You have visitors."

With that said, the presidents of the United States and China came in. Nobody else, no aides.

All the members of SAGRC stood up.

"Please be seated," the president of the PRC said, with a slightly apologetic demeanor. "We did not want the press to know. We actually sneaked out, pretty much, from our social event upstairs."

"Mr. President, why don't you take the floor?" the Chinese president said to his US counterpart.

"Thank you, Mr. President." He then turned to the group. "Thank you for letting us in. We have some important information to share with you. Some intel. It is not pleasant. Using the information from your consultants, you know what I mean although neither of us know who they are. Our intel has distilled the following."

The US president took a bottle of water from the sideboard. He continued. "Our intel has revealed that the Phoenix Group, a very large holding company in Hong Kong, is behind and funding this project. And yet, we have no proof. We can only connect the dots. But we cannot extrapolate them to the end point. Mr. President." The US president turned toward the Chinese president.

"We have smoke but no fire! Here is our intel." He reached into the inner pocket of his coat. "Five pages. The knowledge must remain within these four walls and the ceiling, we are the only ones who have it. None of our aides or secretaries or cabinet members know about the existence of this document. After you read it, shred it. The best way to keep a secret is not to know it. As the cliché goes, you never saw it.

"We have identified the possible scientists, laboratories and the firms that may provide the chefs and the kitchen staff. That may help your discussions. Ladies and gentlemen, we were here to say hello and thanks. That is all."

The presidents shook hands with everyone. They were in the conference room no more than ten minutes.

"Now, thank you ladies and gentlemen, let us go to meet the press. Do our PR." The president of the United States waved goodbye to the group.

The SAGRC members followed the presidents of the two superpower nations out of the conference into the pressroom down the hall to face the press.

Without much introduction or preemptive speeches, the Chinese president took the floor. "Our joint effort to combat deadly diseases has borne fruit. Thanks to these scientists [he looked at the SAGRC members behind him] and their many associates. Mr. President [he turned toward the US president], I cannot deny, and you cannot either, that our joint force has brought the results of conquering certain deadly diseases. Our effort does not end here. For the health of the world, we will continue to work together."

A round of applause was heard.

Hands were up to ask questions. However, the presidents waved their goodwill gestures and exited through the back door.

One of the officials wearing the standard Mao jacket went to the mike. "Sorry, ladies and gentlemen, we are behind schedule. Please email us your questions and we will answer them. I promise."

Having said that, he too exited through the back door leaving many press people disappointed.

The members of SAGRC also left the pressroom, going back to the conference room.

Wang took the papers that were given to them by the president of the PRC and went to the copying machine to make copies.

Wang handed the copies to the members of SAGRC, then sat down and read as everyone else was doing.

After about fifteen minutes, the members of SAGRC had read the information given to them.

"Well, we are actually in the ballpark," Alex said with a pleasant smile.

"There is a lot here. We need more. And we are supposed to just make the announcement, PR mainly. Then go home. I think we had better do that. We don't want the perpetrators to have any suspicion that we are onto them." Calvin exercised his expertise in security matters. Dr. Calvin had been in the FBI. After retirement at fifty-five, the mandatory age for FBI field agents, he became a marine biologist with a joint appointment at the University of Hawaii and the Pentagon as a biowarfare consultant.

"You are right, Dr. Calvin," Wang said. "Let us study them for another thirty minutes. Then shred them. We will go out, face the press to make our next announcement, our agenda."

Wang continued. "Our PR team will take us to the newly found tomb outside Beijing on a tour. Then you will fly home on commercial airlines. I have the tickets. Next week, Mr. Morrison will contact you for our next meeting."

A BIOWEAPON OF MASS DESTRUCTION

Paz went to her condo in New York City and Bonnie went back to her granny house in Costa Rica after their very fruitful sailing adventure in New Zealand, a successful trip to Melbourne, and a pleasant tour into the Amazon.

Two days later, all the Volunteer friends and Paz received an encrypted email from John.

Need to meet without me. New data. New Asia Hotel, New York. Buy tickets to US Open Tennis tournament. Meet third day into the tournament.

"June, tennis time," Harold said after they read the email from John.

"Bonnie," said June as she picked up her cell phone, "your email from John is with us here. Harrison said you need to upgrade your computer in order to maintain security for all of us. He will do it in a day or two."

"I'll come up. Thanks, June."

Other than the World Fair, the US Open drew the largest crowd to the Big Apple. Many visitors were actually not tennis players or played tennis. They came because the City took advantage of the time at the end of the summer and before the hurricane season descended upon the East Coast. New Yorkers knew how to throw a party! Numerous tourists were in and out of the three major airports, and a trillion cars drove through the tunnels and over the bridges to

Manhattan toward Forest Hill. Locals might complain, but they liked the way tourists spent their money generously!

The whole city was geared toward the annual event of US Open tennis tournament. This year the Big Apple was in an extraordinary mode because half of all the ranked players, men and women, were Americans. The chances of bringing back the trophy to America were high. Betting in Las Vegas was swamped; all the odds were on American players. Even those who did not play tennis got involved. Baseball caps and T-shirts with the US Open logo were seen all over town.

Paz bought tickets to the US Open for her clients.

"Mr. Li," one of the computer people monitoring 'persons of interest' for the Phoenix Group said. "Paz Exotic Travel bought tickets to the US Open for her clients."

"Thanks. Don't bother tracking who her clients may be. It's impossible anyway and not important for us."

"OK, Mr. Li."

Mr. Shum was in the penthouse of the New Asia Hotel to welcome all the Vols.

When all the friends were there, Mr. Shum addressed the group. "Welcome again to my hotel. I think Ms. Bonnie was not here the last time."

"No, Mr. Shum. They just recruited me recently," Bonnie went over to give Mr. Shum a handshake and a hug.

"Wow, Ms. Bonnie. Every single strand of your hair is red!"

"Thanks, you ought to see my mother's."

"You can use the penthouse as long as you need. I also have reserved several rooms for you. You can stay as long as you need. All on the house. When you go to the coffee shop or the restaurant, just show the maître d' your card. He will take care of everything. You may tip the waiters if you want.

"If you need anything, call this number," Shum told the Vols. He then used his cell phone. "Joe, I will be down in twenty minutes or so. Have my car ready to go to the airport," Mr. Shum said.

"Yes, Mr. Shum," Joe answered on the other end of the line.

"I have something from John," Mr. Shum opened his briefcase and pulled out a brown envelope. "John gave this to me a few days ago. I did not open it. The best way to keep secret is by not knowing."

Shum handed the envelope to Harold who was the nearest person to him.

Shum looked at everyone. "John only told me that you may have to do a lot more legwork. He mentioned that the New York Public Library, Columbia, Hunter College, and NYU would probably have most if not all of what you would need. I hope you finish in time for the finals."

With that said, Mr. Shum left the group.

Harold tore open the envelope containing five sheets. He went over to the copying machine and made several copies.

"Let us take a look and decide how we go about getting more information."

About fifteen minutes later Jerry said, "That is a lot of information. I wonder how they obtained it."

"You did not hear this from me." Jack said. "There is a very secretive small department within the Pentagon that can go around finding things. I bet this is from that department. Only a few top people know who the members are. Most of them are anonymous. But there is a limit to what they can do. That is where we came in."

"This summation of the work of the missing scientists and others goes back some five years or more," Harold said. "We need to do what we did before, a division of labor again. The Big Apple is full of people like us. We will not draw attention from anyone."

"Let us go to work. Just like before, no online searching," June reminded everyone. "And John has attached courtesy library cards for us."

"How did he do it?" Bonnie asked.

"John is still in the thick of things," Jack said. "But he is staying away. Once in a while, you may read about his golf outings with his friend, Surgeon General Pei. They have unusual hobbies other than golf."

"I read about that too," June said. "John is interested in rare medicinal plants in the Amazon while Dr. Pei is interested in ancient Chinese medicine."

"John is, like we say, hiding in the open. I bet that is how he gets and delivers information," Harold said.

"Dr. Pei is the conduit," Jerry said.

"How clever," Bonnie said.

The Vols began reading the hard copies in the stacks of the libraries in the Big Apple. After two days of legwork, the Vols had compiled a detailed list of research for the scientists on their list in addition to what they had searched earlier.

Harold made a suggestion. "Why don't we each give a summary; no need to have the names, just the works. Then we can compare notes. Bonnie?"

"Here is what I have. The RNA of the Ebola virus was sequenced. They identified the nucleotide for the coat and the sequence for replication. In addition, the control and regulating introns and exons."

June followed Bonnie. "These scientists were pretty ingenious. Using CRISPR-Cas9, they switched the replicons of Ebola with Zika. That is, from a positive sense to a negative sense. So far, they have not been able to make them reproductive. They're probably working on it now."

Ruth told her colleagues from her notes: "The paper by Nasatir, Toledo, who five years ago coauthored several papers with Bishop, Harvard, theorized that they could build in artificial intelligence into the DNA molecule. Actually, we have read that already. What they said was that having specific protein receptors in the viral coat, that protein could sense changes of the microenvironment, I assume that would be intracellular, the replicon to replicate or just remain dormant until the proper condition presents itself, whatever that may be."

"Jack, what have you got?" Harold looked over to where Jack was sitting.

"I also read a paper by Nasatir. He coauthored with Trent, the ecologist. They theorized then that AI could be built into an oligonucleotide-glycoprotein complex in the viral coat or cell membrane. I told myself, that is about ten years ahead of the work at that time. Now, it is ten years later. I am afraid to even guess what their progress may be, assuming there has been progress since." Jack's narration was not without pessimism.

"Jerry?" Harold asked.

"Guys, their research, I hate to admit it, was like ours. Not to glorify ourselves but I saw our reflection in the mirror," Jerry said. "Dr. Wing of Singapore and Xavier of Rockefeller coauthored two papers, I think it was six or seven years back, on radiation resistance of certain biomolecules. They gave a number which I could not find more information about. It was RRN-1. I guess it might mean radiation resistant nucleotide."

Harold casted his eyes upward, talking to himself. "That is very interesting. I was reading a little-known journal last year. I ran into the isolation of a bacterium from a larva bed that was still red hot. I thought that was probably pseudo-science, or some science reporters pulling our legs."

"No, Harold. It is now known that there are two species of bacterium that are heat-resistant," June said.

"So," Jack added, "finding or creating a radiation-resistant nucleotide or protein would not be unusual."

"Well, the peptide in Mad Cow disease is heat-stable," Ruth said.

"Hey, remember *Deinococcus radiodurans?*" Bonnie suddenly got up from her chair. "How could I forget that!"

"All it takes is to move that radiation-resistant sequence or sequences from *D. radiodurans* to the viral genome or maybe even mammalian cells." June said. "Is that possible, Bonnie?"

"Then," Harold added. "Incorporate radioisotopes into the bases or the sugar phosphate backbone!"

"*Voilà,* you have your chimera virus, Ebola/Zika, with radioactive nucleotides or proteins. A dirty viral bomb!" Jack exclaimed.

"And an infectious one with a brain!" Bonnie emphasized the point made by Jack.

"I almost forgot a couple of papers by Stiff, one by Cliff, and another one jointly authored by them," Harold said. "They were able to create a glycoprotein with the peptide from the Mad Cow disease with an affinity to the glial cells in the brain!"

"We had better give John this information ASAP," Jack said.

"Jack, why don't you summarize our findings to John," June said.

"OK," Jack said. "You know what, we checked their current work, remember? And what we found? Not much of a hint of what they were doing before that. It is a well, very well researched task. I bet they started as soon as we gave the world our protocol."

Their legwork paid off, but not without creating extreme pessimism. This bioweapon of mass destruction was deadlier than the Vol buddies anticipated. Not only that, they all felt guilty because they themselves laid the groundwork for these bioterrorists, whoever they may be.

Their noble task had become the tip of the devil's spear!

A Dirty Viral Bomb

"Dr. Pei, we need immediate action," John handed Dr. Pei an envelope as they were finishing up their golf game.

Dr. Pei took a quick read.

"Indeed. I will get the ball rolling. I will contact Caleb at the NAS."

Caleb Morrison, president of the US National Academy of Sciences picked up the phone. "Would you arrange a meeting of SAGRC, ASAP."

"Yes, sir," Caleb answered.

In the conference room at the US National Academy of Sciences.

"Ladies and gentlemen, sorry for the short notice, especially our Chinese friends who had to drop their scheduled work and fly over. I did not want to send emails even though they are encrypted. We need to start working on a neutralizing agent or special antibodies to counter whatever they, the bioterrorists, have in mind." Caleb handed each member the same information that John received from his Volunteer friends.

It did not take long to read the report from their consultants, the Vol friends, who were unknown to the group except for Alex.

"An infectious, dirty bomb with artificial intelligence! Bigger and deadlier than the one we talked about," Robert said.

"Our consultants did a thorough job," Alex said. "This rogue group has planned this for some time, probably since soon after the world was given the bioweapon protocol by the unknown group of scientists. Remember?"

"We need to immediately set up teams to formulate counter measures." Caleb stood up and went to the front of the conference room unveiling a big monitor on the wall. "This is our blackboard."

Caleb continued, hitting a key on his laptop. "Here are the scientists who may be doing the work. I think they will be willing to sacrifice their time to help us. I made the list as soon as I got what we have here. Please make suggestions, shuffle things around, etc. I will contact them ASAP after our discussion."

The SAGRC members studied the list. They keyed in suggestions into their monitors which were linked to the monitor at the front of the conference room.

"I believe we need to have one individual here as a team leader after we select the appropriate scientists for the tasks ahead," Caleb said.

Calvin stood up and addressed the group. "I will arrange for security for everyone. Not me personally, I will contact my old friends and colleagues in the FBI. By the way, they are all retired agents. That is just a precaution. Using existing agents from the FBI or other agencies will be too obvious. This group must have bottomless resources. Maybe even informers in our governments. They started their prep earlier, much earlier than we thought. Those scientists, the missing ones, have actually interacted and collaborated on the dirty, infectious bomb for at least five to seven years, maybe longer. We know the force behind this bomb may be a giant holding company called the Phoenix Group based in Hong Kong."

Caleb said to the group. "We will just work on the science part. Let Beijing and the White House take care of the Phoenix Group. Actually, there is still no proof that the Phoenix Group is the culprit. Just because their subsidiaries funded much of the work does not give us hard evidence that will hold up in court."

"Dr. Somers, would you head up the immunotherapy team?" Caleb asked. Caleb knew in great detail the expertise of each of the scientists in SAGRC and many others in many institutions.

"Yes. Glad to. I will contact my colleagues ASAP after this meeting."

"Dr. Alex, artificial intelligence?"

"Yes, Caleb."

"Dr. Lee, gene editing and splicing of Ebola and Zika?"

"Yes, Caleb. I think it will be better if I work with Mei Mei."

"Of course. I think Dr. Robert should be the one on radioisotopes."

"Yes, Caleb. We, that is, including the Oak Ridge National Laboratory, have the best tools for that."

"Dr. Wang and I will coordinate between D.C. and Beijing."

"Yes, Caleb. Perfect arrangement," Dr. Wang said.

"Shall we meet again soon? We need to because these scientists are ahead of us. However, we have more resources in both science/technology and personnel." Dr. Wang posed his question to all.

"By all means," Caleb said. "Next week, same day, same time, here. There will be a general meeting of the heads of various disciplines here. That will be a good cover. Will that fit your schedules, Dr. Lee, Ms. Mei Mei, and Dr. Wang? You need to come all the way from Beijing. Again!"

"That is OK. We need to do what we need to do," Lee said. "Besides, we need to start working in the lab. Double time, as you Americans say."

"Me too," Mei Mei said.

"I will be here at the UN. No problem for me," Dr. Wang said.

"I assume Dr. Alex, Dr. Calvin, Dr. Robert, and Dr. Somers will be OK as well?" Caleb looked over to where they sat.

"Ok with me," Alex said.

"Me too," Dr. Robert said.

"Of course, me too. I have a condo here five blocks away," Dr. Somers added.

One week later, the SAGRC members mingled with hundreds of scientists in the US National Academy of Sciences building. When the general meeting began, the members of SAGRC went to the conference room on the second floor.

Somers was the first to take the floor. "We have plenty of antibodies for the Ebola and Zika viruses in stock. But we do not know if this serum will neutralize the chimera or whatever has been synthesized by these terrorists. Our group decided to produce different combinations of chimera. It was not difficult because we have all the tools, including CRISPR. We even reverse-transcribed their RNA into DNA. We are not yet able to infect cells in vitro. We want to see if the chimera virus makes the same protein coat or a different coat from the original virus."

Dr. Alex was second. "My team was able to transcribe the *Deinococcus radiodurans* DNA into RNA. Then we cut the RNA into several short segments. With the modified recombinant DNA tech for RNA and CRISPR tech, we were able to create a number of modified Ebola and Zika genomes with segments of the genome of the radiation-resistant bacterium, a chimera of three origins. We will be testing their infectious potential as well as their radiation-resistant potential."

Dr. Robert was the third to take the floor. "We did similar experiments as Dr. Alex except we cut the radiation-resistant bacterial DNA into segments first; we then inserted the reversed transcriptase products into the virus genome. We actually have a molecular hybrid, a segment of DNA, in the chimeric virus. In addition, we incubated some in radioactive tritium, carbon-14, P-32 and N-15. We shall be cloning them to ascertain their radioactive level as well as infectious potential. Dr. Alex and I have exchanged our data."

"Ms. Mei Mei had a family problem. I will speak for us," Lee took the floor. "We reverse transcribed the viral RNA into DNA, some with the whole genome and some with different nucleotide length. Then we transcribed them back into RNA segments. We made chimeras to see if any of them will be infectious. We will microinject the chimeras into HeLa cells to ascertain their infectious potential. Some of them are being done now by my associates in Beijing."

"Dr. Lee," Somers said. "I will give you our samples to microinject into HeLa cells. We are not so proficient in microinjection techniques."

"I will give you ours too, Dr. Somers," Lee said. "I have a suggestion, we will test to see if all the chimeras have the same degree of antigenicity. Will our animal model produce the same immunoglobulin as what we have in stock? That is a lot of tests."

Somers went to the sideboard to fetch a bottle of water. She said. "It will be a lot of work. But I think we can do it. First, we can study the protein coats, their amino acid content and sequences. We can now do hundreds of samples in a week. More if we have more amino acid analyzers and peptide sequencers. Since my lab has been doing that routinely, why don't I take all the samples. In addition, we will find private labs to help. We won't give them information, just the samples."

"Dr. Somers, that is wonderful," Robert said. "I think I can even get some labs in Tennessee to help too. There are a number of these gadgets at ORNL."

"I think we can do it in probably no more than a couple of weeks," Lee said. "We needed it yesterday, as Americans like to say. They are far ahead of us. We need this."

"How do we really know if that is their goal? Their product?" Alex asked.

"We don't know. But I think we are in the ballpark," Caleb said. "I will ask appropriate agencies to collect more data, including financial data. I am sure we can get a good picture. We need to gamble a little."

With that said, SAGRC would be busy, very busy. The most difficult part was to keep it all secret.

"For security's sake and to keep them from knowing, we should not label anything even close to Zika or Ebola or have any characters associated with these viruses. No Zs or Es. Just numbers, codes," Calvin suggested.

"Or, tell our associates that we are trying to predict what may change in the next twelve months. If they ask." Caleb said. "In fact, I was thinking on the way here. CDC will issue a directive to those who are interested in immunotherapy for different kinds of cancer cells. A shotgun approach. Since SAGRC has actually accomplished a great deal, SAGRC will take the lead. We can even contract the work out to private labs. It is the strategy of hiding in the open. No mention of viruses. We will just call them specific antigens, etc."

"Great idea," Robert said. "I can do the infectious potential in my institute. Each graduate student will take a number of samples. All our labs are safety level 4."

Never in the history of science has a gambit been used to flush out the rats in science!

SCIENCE AND PEACE

With the secure line, the red phone on the desk, the president of United States called Beijing.

"Premier Li, good morning. How is the traffic?"

"Traffic" was a private code between these two world leaders. The public did not know that.

"Congested as usual. But there is always a gap."

That too was a private code.

"We know it is the Phoenix Group, the largest holding company in the world, behind the work. But we have no proof. Smoke but no fire, as your president said."

"Yes. We still have one aspect we have not investigated thoroughly. That is their financials, their subsidiaries, etc."

"But that will not prove their ambition because we still don't know what their scientists are making. Or, in fact, whether they are supported by the Phoenix Group directly or indirectly."

"True. But we do know what instrument they are using. From that we may deduce the product. Didn't the SAGRC group come up with a hypothesis?"

"Yes, they did. Not only they did, they are proceeding to do what they think the terrorists might have been doing. They are trying to think like them."

"Never in our lives has peace been precipitated by the work of a group, still unknown to us, of ingenious scientists using modern biotech with the ancient precept of human sacrifice. It was certainly a noble act, at least in their minds. We never figured we would face such an immense repercussion."

"I agree with you, Mr. Premier."

"Let us both proceed to thoroughly analyze their financial realm. Much of it will be in the public record. Then we will let the scientists examine the nature of their research that is supported by the Phoenix Group and or its subsidiaries. We should get a pretty good picture."

Carla, personal secretary to the US president, called the National Academy of Sciences. "Mr. Morrison, please, this is the White House."

"One moment, please."

"Caleb here. Carla?"

"Yes, good morning. According to our calendar, you will be reporting to the Senate Health Committee in two days. Can you come with Dr. Calvin? No announcement, please. Come in the west entrance. 7.00 AM. OK with you?"

"No problem, Carla. We will be there."

Next day, Caleb of the NAS and Calvin, ex-FBI, arrived through the west entrance of the White House.

"Thanks for coming in such a short notice," the president said, shaking hands with his guests.

"I will be brief. Here is some information on the financials of the Phoenix Group. I would like your SAGRC group to peruse them and correlate them to the scientific activities of the missing scientists. I understand this rogue group has a lead for more than seven or more years. That is, they may be able to threaten the world peace in a year or less."

"Yes, sir," Calvin said. "We are trying to think like they do. Not one hundred percent, Mr. President. We think they have been developing chimera viruses, radioactive ones from Ebola and Zika. In addition, they have incorporated artificial intelligence into the bioweapon. We also assume that our existing vaccines and antibodies may not be effective. We are also developing chimeras with genes from *Deinococcus radiodurans*, the radiation-resistant bacteria. In two to three weeks we should be able, we hope, to find vaccines or antibodies to counter or neutralize the postulated rogue chimera virus."

"Good work. Compare and ascertain the science, including the laboratories with this financial information. I hope there will be a close correlation. Unfortunately, it will be very difficult to prove if the Phoenix Group is behind the work."

"We will do our best, Mr. President," Calvin said.

"By the way, only Premier Li and I had this discussion. You know what I mean."

With that, they shook hands.

Their brief meeting was not on the agenda of the Oval Office.

"Dr. Calvin, please take a look at it," Caleb said. "There must be no inquiries from SAGRC. I will have our consultants do the legwork. Then we, SAGRC, will discuss the report from our consultants; we will then give it to our bosses."

At the last hole in their game, Dr. Pei handed John a thin folder. "Here is the financial aspect of Phoenix. See if your friends can come up with some kind of correlation with their postulated product or products."

Paz was in New York City in the process of selling her condo and moving to Costa Rica. John sent Paz an encrypted email.

Meet me at Guggenheim at 4PM today. OK if no answer.

At 4.00 PM, John handed Paz a thin envelope, the same as the one Dr. Pei gave him.

"Harold, I've got something from John." Paz handed the folder to Harold as soon as she stepped out of the taxi from the airport in San José, Costa Rica.

"Thanks. You are leaving tomorrow, right?"

"Paz, good to see you." June came over and gave Paz a hug.

"You guys have work to do. Harold got the folder from John."

"Well, we'd better get busy," June said." Harold, have the meeting here or in one of Mr. Shum's hotels?"

"More convenient here. For Jack, it's a long way."

"It's a long way for Jack anywhere."

"Let us read this file first. If they can do it wherever they are, that is the best."

Harold and June went to their living room. There were only two guests. They had taken a local tour and would not be back until dark.

It did not take long to read the briefing material.

"June, it is essentially what we have done except John needs to know where the grants or support came from and the nature of the firms or institutions supporting the research. Just more detailed information."

"Yes. We have the source of support of some. We should have done it in more detail than we did."

"I don't think we need to come together on this. We can just divide the labor as we did. We still have that list. Since we are not in New York, and neither are the others, we may not be able to collate the answers."

"I don't think we need to obtain one hundred percent of the information. Seventy percent or so should give us a good idea."

"Right. Let us draft a short message to them. We and Bonnie shall try down here to get as much as we can. Harrison may be able to go online without being traced to us here. That is, if we need it."

June went to Harrison's bungalow. "Harrison, we have work for you. Would you send this message to Jack, Ruth, and Jerry in our encrypted format?"

"Of course."

We need more info. Need to find out more detail—who is supporting the research and the nature of the supporting organizations—of those you did in New York last time we met in the New Asia Hotel. Also, see if you can find out where they get their supplies from in the Method and Material section. Just email John directly. John will do the rest. John will ascertain if there are relationships between their work, the supporting organizations, and the source of materials, directly or indirectly.

Within minutes, the Vol friends received it.

Within forty-eight hours, John received the answers, approximately seventy percent. That was all SAGRC needed.

Dr. Pei hand delivered a copy of the email from John to Caleb in the National Academy of Sciences building.

"Thank you, Dr. Pei," Caleb said.

At the entrance Caleb said to Dr. Pei, "Dr. Pei, everything is ready for the Academy of Medicine meeting next week. You may be interested to know that I had an interesting visitor yesterday. She was one of the physicians to the Chinese astronauts. Dr. Kung from Beijing. She just stopped by to see the academy as a tourist. I happened to be in the lobby. We chatted. I told her about your meeting next week. She wanted to know if she could be an observer since she will be in town. She is retired but still active with the retired astronauts and their families."

"Absolutely. I would love to meet her. In fact, I may be able to fit her into one of our informal 'tea-time' programs. That will be a great surprise for us. I am sure some of the space-medicine and NASA med people would like to talk to her."

"Here, she gave me her cell phone and email."

A middle-aged man with non-descript features was nearby listening to the conversation. No one paid attention to him. He recorded every word said.

A week later, the regular quarterly meeting of the SAGRC was held in San Francisco at the University of California School of Medicine.

"Again, thank you to our friends and colleagues from China," Caleb opened the meeting.

"Thanks, Mr. Morrison. It is just a short flight from Beijing. Besides, it gives us time to work on our projects," Mei Mei said.

"Dr. Calvin has read what I have for you, for us. I will let him chair this one. I will be an observer and take notes," Caleb told the group and handed a thin folder to each SAGRC member.

Twenty minutes or so later, Alex said, "Our consultants did a marvelous and detailed analysis. All the research, the money, and the sources of experimental materials, the institutions etc. are all intertwined. For example, one of the pharms supported the research of Nasatir on artificial intelligence; it also sponsored the research of White on material science. They are in close proximity to each other in Ohio. But that does not really matter. The matter is their research was unrelated, on the surface."

"That is the impression I also have," echoed Robert.

"On this particular one, this pharm makes generic drugs for diabetics?" Somers questioned.

"The only connection is that this pharm is a subsidiary of the Phoenix Group," Lee said.

"Stiff was a research fellow at a research institute in Europe. That institute was involved in aging research. Please note, this aging research center was supported by a shipping company. Why?" Robert said. "And this firm's president is the husband of Mrs. Biotti, a board member of the Phoenix Group. Shipping, ship builder, and aging research?"

"This Italian firm is partly owned by the company of which Mr. Nelson is the president, and he's a board member of the Phoenix Group. In addition, Mr. Nelson sits on the board of Vouit Pharma in Europe." Wang of the UN added his comment.

"Mrs. Biotti has been in D.C. socializing with many of our high officials."

"Our consultants also revealed that most of the chemicals and biomaterials for their research were from three companies:

Omega Chemical, Alaska Bio-Supply, and Malaysia Medical Supply, Inc. Alaska Bio-Supply is not in Alaska, it is in Hong Kong," Alex said. "Our consultants really did a thorough job! Mr. Morrison, do you have any idea how they did this?"

"First, I don't know who they are. It was a lot of legwork with no online searches, most likely," Caleb answered.

"That is the reason we were told not to do their job. I am sure they, the perpetrators, monitor each one of us closely. If we did, the Phoenix Group may find out and close up shop immediately," Calvin explained.

"Even with all this information, we still have no definitive proof that the Phoenix Group is behind the work. Supporting scientific research is not illegal. Neither are all the business transactions and interactions among the firms," Caleb said.

"How big is this Phoenix Group?" Somers asked.

"I don't know exactly," Caleb answered. "It is the biggest conglomerate in the world with fingers in every business venture. Probably governments too."

"Many of their business are public records. I think the US and China can gain more information than what we get just from the public records," Lee said.

"Scary!" Alex exclaimed.

"We will give our bosses what we have. We have given them our scientific postulate on what the product or products may be, and their possible medical effects plus the possible timeline. They will do what they need to do." Caleb concluded their discussions.

SUPERPOWER CONSPIRACY

"Good morning, Carla." The president walked into the Oval Office after his breakfast following his routine morning exercise at 5:30 AM.

"Morning, sir. You have a busy day."

"That is new?" the president proceeded to his desk and turned on the monitor.

"Sir, there will be a trade group from China in the morning. After your staff meeting at eight, Madam Ambassador of China will bring the trade group over. The group includes Dr. Wang, the technocrat and a member of the SAGRC."

"Carla, can you check if Caleb Morrison is available?"

"Yes, sir, I will. I think Mr. Morrison is scheduled for a congressional oversight meeting or something."

"See if you can set up a meeting with Caleb, Wang, just me and Madam Ambassador after the trade meeting. Fifteen to thirty minutes. Be discreet please."

"Understood, sir."

At nine o'clock sharp, Madam Ambassador arrived at the White House with her entourage of the trade group from China.

"Please follow me, Madam Ambassador," a crisply dressed Marine stood attention while the chief of staff of the White House escorted the group to the Oval Office.

"Welcome, ladies and gentlemen. What can we get you, coffee, tea, lemonade?"

"We are fine, we just finished breakfast. Tea will be fine," Madam Ambassador from China said politely.

"Please, have a seat," the president said. "I understand your trade group will meet with our people in the Department of Commerce later."

"Yes, Mr. President. They will leave for their meeting shortly. Dr. Wang and I would like to have fifteen minutes or so with you. I hope you have the time."

"I certainly do. In fact, I was going to ask you the same."

After fifteen minutes of courtesy discussion of bilateral trade in technology, the trade group left.

"Carla, are Caleb and Calvin here?"

"Yes. They are. I will get them."

"Madam Ambassador, I think you have met Mr. Morrison."

"Yes, my pleasure."

"Caleb, please."

"Yes Mr. President, Madam Ambassador. We have a definitive indication, but no definitive proof, that the Phoenix Group in Hong Kong is our target. Our scientists have uncovered from where the work has been funded."

Caleb continued. "Mr. President and Madam Ambassador, our scientific investigators, including SAGRC and others, have postulated that the missing scientists have been supported by the Phoenix Group indirectly through its subsidiaries. Most importantly, they started their work a few years, maybe more than a few, before we knew about them, perhaps as early as when we were given the protocol of the bioweapon by the still-unknown scientists. We think they have synthesized radioactive chimeric viruses with the genomes from Ebola and Zika with the insertion of genes from a species of radiation-resistant bacteria. In addition they may have been coded with artificial intelligence. These radioactive chimera viruses may be just as infectious as their parents. The real danger is that our existing vaccines and antibodies will have no effect on them. With that hypothesis, we have also synthesized chimeras of different types. We have made vaccines and antibodies against our own synthetic products. We have accomplished all this thanks to the very hard work of many scientists here and in China. They dropped their own research and helped us. The chimeras of the perpetrators are very deadly, a dirty viral bomb with artificial intelligence. They may even have coded AI into the vectors as well."

"Our people on both side of the Pacific will be thankful," Madam Ambassador said with a grateful expression.

"We know the locations of the laboratories; one is on Bird's Wing Island in the New Zealand archipelago and one in Melbourne." Mr. Wang cleared his throat. "Bird's Wing Island is not under the jurisdiction of New Zealand. In fact, it does not belong to any of the island nations in the Pacific. Strange it may be, but that is true. I took the liberty of asking Secretary Tongo of the UN if the UN can take it under its wing, so to speak. Mr. Tongo said it is the UN's duty. We understand that this giant Phoenix Group may have control of no less than twenty to thirty percent of global enterprises in various sectors, finance as well as technology.

"Madam Ambassador, Mr. President, if we shut down its business, that would probably mean thousands if not millions of workers will be unemployed."

"We can shut down their laboratories, confiscate the chimera virus and all the equipment," Madam Ambassador said.

"And yet, we still don't have definite evidence that the Phoenix Group is behind the deadly task," the president of the US said.

"Mr. President, I talked to Premier Li on this. He has suggested we let the Phoenix Group continue to exist, for the millions of people they employ worldwide. Since the headquarters of this conglomerate is physically located in Hong Kong, we will be responsible for the Phoenix Group. Is it agreeable?" Madam Ambassador politely asked.

"Yes, Madam. I talked to our vice president also. We will let Australia take care the Melbourne lab. Dr. Wang?"

"Yes, Mr. President. Mr. Tongo will use the United Nations peacekeeping force for Bird's Wing Island."

High-level discussions needed no details. The details would be worked out by their staff.

No News is Bad News

A week before the general board meeting of the Phoenix Group, Mr. Li received a call from the governor of Hong Kong.

"Mr. Li, how are you? I hope you have a minute."

"Of course, Mr. Soong. Always a pleasure to talk to you."

"The reason I am calling is I have a directive from Beijing. We have discovered a fairly large natural energy source near the Inner Mongolia border. You know, a very desolate region of desert and rocks, an unusual geoformation. Beijing is asking for advice from many industries as how the best way to retrieve the minerals, transport them, etc."

"Right offhand, I can say that we would like to help. As you know, we have multiple business endeavors, including petroleum and mineral explorations."

"I understand you will have a general board meeting in one week. I wonder if I can come to spend no more than thirty minutes with a few of my staff to present to you my directive from Beijing. I want you to understand that you are not the only company Beijing will have conversation with on the same topic. Discretion is therefore necessary, at least for the time being."

"Of course, I fully understand. I know that region. It is a challenge, not an easy task. I am sure our board will be glad to hear what you have to say."

"Thank you very much, Mr. Li. Until next week."

"Oh, yes. Mr. Li. We are only messengers."

At the top of the Phoenix Building, all the board members, including Mrs. Biotti and the non-voting member Hector L., were assembled in the conference room. After the servers left, they stood around making small talk before their meeting. The mood was good, actually very good indeed.

Mr. Li as usual took the floor. "Welcome again. I believe this will be our best meeting. You know what I mean. Before Mr. Soong comes with his staff, I think Dr. Jeng has some good news. We all know it already, but not in detail. Dr. Jeng, please, you have the floor."

"Thank you, Mr. Li. I am sure we all remember the unique bioweapon developed by some still unknown scientists. Based on their protocol, our ambition has paid off. With our current control of some twenty to thirty percent of all global enterprise, we can achieve more, not only in business but in politics as well."

All the board members smiled broadly and clapped their hands lightly.

"I believe our pharm colleagues have already an ample supply of vaccines for our chimera viruses. Right, Mr. Simpson and Mr. Nelson?" Jeng asked.

"Yes. More than enough. And we have also vaccines for the original ones as well." Mr. Simpson answered.

"It won't take long for the world to know that we are the only ones who have the right vaccine for our chimera viruses. We should be in control," Mr. Nelson said with confidence.

"In one month, no more than two, we will be able to unleash our own bioweapon. First in Africa, then North America. We will go to the forthcoming United Nations General Assembly to propose a new world order—ours." Jeng spoke cheerfully.

Not much needed to be said.

There was a knock at the door. The secretary poked her head in.

"Mr. Li, Mr. Soong and his associates are here."

"Please show them in."

Mr. Soong came in with four other people, one lady and three men, each carrying a briefcase.

"Thank you, Mr. Li. Let me introduce my associates here." Mr. Soong said. "This is Mr. Ling, our consultant on pharmaceuticals, Mr. Yeh on technology, Mrs. Lee of economics, and Mr. Hsieh, our communication consultant. Mr. Hsieh, please."

"Thank you. I will connect what we have to your monitor on the wall here. I hope, Mr. Li, there is no linkage to any other monitor. Am I correct?"

"That is right. The one on the wall is just a blackboard. The monitors in front of us are however connected to our mainframe, that is, if we want it."

Mr. Soong stood up and said. "I talked to Mr. Li. Your group will not be the only one Beijing will seek advice from. Therefore, this is confidential. Maybe it would be good to turn off your monitors and computers."

"We understand," all the members agreed.

"Mr. Soong, this room is also soundproof," Mr. Li said.

"Lady and gentlemen, we know that your Phoenix Group has been extremely successful in whatever your business endeavors are, pharmaceutical, transport, oil, financial, and more. You know better than I do."

There were smiles on all the faces of the Phoenix board members.

Mr. Soong continued. "You practically control at least twenty percent of the global enterprise. You employ millions of people. If the Phoenix Group was to sink, close up shop, so to speak, there would be chaos on Wall Street, in the London stock market, and of course here in Hong Kong. In other words, we don't want your Phoenix Group to go under. As the Americans say, you are too big to fail! We are here to deliver a message. We are, I repeat, messengers."

While Mr. Soong was talking, Mr. Hsieh was connecting a satellite receiver to the big monitor on the wall.

"Ladies and gentlemen, this is a live feed," Mr. Hsieh said.

On the monitor was a split screen. There was no sound.

"I believe you will recognize Bird's Wing Island on the left and a warehouse in Melbourne on the right. At this moment, activities are synchronized to happen simultaneously, maybe a few minutes apart. No more." Mr. Soong said.

"Wait," Mr. Li. "What is this all about?"

"Mr. Li, these are raids simultaneously in two locations. We believe that in these two locations unethical operations, possibly illegal, are or have been carrying on, which will harm the welfare of the world. We are here on the orders of China and the United Nations. As messengers, I repeat."

No words came from any of the board members. They were stunned, waiting for the bad news to come.

"The building you are looking at on Bird's Wing Island contains radioactive materials. It does not belong to New Zealand, although New Zealand extends the courtesy of protecting its environment; it however has no jurisdiction. There is really no documentation as to which country this tiny island belongs. Therefore, the United Nations has agreed to send its peacekeeping forces to vacate the building and take procession of the equipment inside. New Zealand is providing the transportation and necessary assistance. Three scientists, their wives, and two associates will be allowed to remain in their residences on the island for the time being."

Mr. Soong continued in the dead silence of the conference room. "On the right you can see a warehouse in the old warehouse district of which only half is still in operation. The one you are looking at, according to the city record, belongs to Chan Brothers Engineering, Inc. Hong Kong, of which your organization is a part owner. It is listed in City Hall as a warehouse. However, it is being used as a laboratory instead of a storage or distribution center. Therefore, it is illegal. The City has identified six scientists working in the laboratory, possibly working on microorganisms, viruses, maybe Ebola and Zika. The definitive identification will be known within twenty-four hours. These scientists have been detained at a hotel for the time being. Any questions?"

No questions. Deadly silence. Expressionless faces on the Phoenix board members.

"Allow me, please," Mr. Ling stood up to take the floor. "Both Ebola and Zika are deadly viruses as we all know. To produce a chimera with a gene from the radiation-resistant bacteria, *D. radiodurans,* plus radioactive isotopes in the chimera organism is a highly imaginative scientific work. This is our hypothesis based on the limited data we have. We may be wrong. We have vaccines and antibodies to neutralize the effects of Ebola and Zika. For the chimeras, we don't. We can, of course, manufacture them with the chimeras on hand. Mrs. Lee, please."

"Thank you, Mr. Ling. Beijing and the United Nations believe we should not allow any deadly infectious organism, or organisms, to be used for whatever purpose they have been designed. Our governments admit that just knowing that your group is part owner of the warehouse in Melbourne cannot definitively prove your Phoenix Group is behind the work there or that on Bird's Wing Island. But we do have the right to confiscate all materials and equipment in these properties. The scientists who have been engaging in making this bioweapon of mass destruction, we presume, may be prosecuted. Of course, it is still hypothetical. On the science aspect, Mr. Ling is more qualified to tell us the facts. Mr. Ling."

"Thank you, Mrs. Lee. My colleagues and I have read a number of scientific papers by these ten retired scientists." Mr. Ling handed a list of their names with their aliases and a brief summation of their research to all members of the Phoenix board. "You will notice their names have changed since their retirements. In addition, we also realize that some of their research programs have been supported directly or indirectly through your subsidiaries; that includes Dr. Jeng's research in the audience here. Some research programs were also supported by private and government organizations, for example, the American Cancer Foundation, the US National Science Foundation, and others. In fact, governments are grateful that much worthy research is supported by private industries. Any questions?"

Still dead silence in the conference room.

Mr. Soong again addressed his audience. "Ladies and gentlemen, China and the United Nations, and the United States I may add, realize, I repeat, that the holdings and business ventures of your Phoenix Group contribute greatly to global economy by employing many thousands if not millions of people. It should remain as it is. We believe, but again we have no proof, that the retired scientists are under the auspices of the Phoenix Group," Mr. Soong said. "Mr. Yeh, please."

"Thank you, Mr. Soong," Mr. Yeh stood up to address the board. "I am in charge of sanitizing both laboratories. As you may notice on the right, the workers are putting many vials into an oven-like box. These hundreds of vials are kept in deep freezers at minus one hundred and twenty Centigrade. This oven-like box is an annealing oven that glassblowers use. These vials and the material within will be destroyed by heat on site. We don't want to take any chances of broken vials or contamination in transit. Of course, we shall transport to the US CDC and keep a small number for analysis and for future reference. It is routine. I am sure Dr. Jeng is familiar with the work at the CDC in Atlanta in America. The lab on Bird's Wing Island, you are looking at it, is being cleansed and sanitized just as a precaution. We know the scientists working there are highly qualified to carry out protocols with radioactive materials. We will let the United Nations and New Zealand to decide their future uses on the island. As to the lab in Melbourne, I believe the city has a plan to raze the buildings and make the area into a hotel and park complex."

Mr. Soong stood up while Mr. Hsieh was disconnecting the receiver from the monitor on the wall. "Concerning the scientists and their associates, all of them will be detained at this moment. Their laboratory notes, computers, and communication equipment like cell phones, etc. will be confiscated. We think all the information and discussions here today should remain in this room for the benefit of your vast business ventures and those millions of people working for you. And of course, for the welfare of the world. Are there any questions?"

There was only silence in the room. Dead silence.

"All the materials, I repeat, including all computers, personal as well as those for the experiments, will be confiscated. Everything from Bird's Wing Island, including the scientists, will be turned over to the World Court in The Hague for consideration and/or investigation. Those in Melbourne will be turned over to the City of Melbourne. As far as we are concerned, we have finished our work ordered by both China and the United Nations. We will give our recorded conversation here to the World Court and Melbourne. If you wish, we will give you a copy as well. As I said earlier, we are merely messengers. All of us here have signed confidentiality and secrecy documents. There will be no public announcement from any one of us—the United Nations, Australia, New Zealand, China, or the United States—as I understand it. Thank you for your time. We know the way out unless you have questions."

There were no questions.

All the board members of the Phoenix Group remained seated, stunned, looking at each other as Mr. Soong's entourage left the room.

Within this ultra-luxurious conference room at the top of the tallest building in Hong Kong, there was only dead silence. With some imagination, one could hear and feel the collision of atoms in the air!

How did they find out?
No news is bad news!

Epilog

For the first time in history, the use of a science gambit, a gamble, has prevented the release of a bioweapon of mass destruction. Peace and humanity are again given a chance.

For the time being.

Is the synthetic chimeric virus a product of evolution mediated by *Homo sapiens*, one of the species in the Animal Kingdom?

Will synthetic biology, including the synthesis of partial human characters and artificial intelligence, dominate our lives in the future? In what perspective?

May it be a forthcoming evolution?

Will artificial intelligence accelerate natural evolution?

Or is it part of evolution?

Will there be a revolution because of the synthetic evolution?

What would Darwin say if he was around?

QED 2018

ABOUT THE AUTHOR

Harold H. Lee was a professor of biology at the University of Toledo, Ohio, USA. In addition to his teaching duties, his laboratory research led to his earning of several US and Canadian patents in biotechnology, including cell cultivation technology and bioremediation with natural biodegradable materials. After his retirement, he began to contribute articles on the practice of Tai Chi Chuen, a moderate callisthenic, to health in various health magazines. His first novel *Casualties of Peace* was published in April 2017. *Echo of Peace* is the sequel of his first book. *Hong Kong Boy* is his second novel. He resides in Mission Viejo, CA, USA.

HONG KONG BOY

By Harold H. Lee

Using the background of the seafaring spirit started in the fifteenth century by the famous General Zheng He, the Columbus of China, the author presents his family history spanning three generations in a story format. He describes his grandfather's work and life in North America and in China, his father's education in America and work in China before, during, and after WWII. He considers his grandfather and parents as migrants while himself a transplant.

Together with the author's unusual path into science, his scientific endeavors and his life story, *Hong Kong Boy* illustrates the changing society in America.

COMING SOON...

TIBET EXPRESS

By Harold H. Lee

Three ex-diplomats with cybersecurity experience and international connections start a business of cybersecurity for medium-sized institutions like hospitals. Having gained access to the institutions' computer systems, they begin to blackmail them with ransomware.

Four young people hack into the Tibet Express, a magnetic levitation or *MagLev* train, causing a sudden deceleration.

When the four young hackers cross paths with the three cyber thieves, a dangerous cyber gambit begins set against a backdrop of Hong Kong and Macao.

Made in the USA
San Bernardino, CA
26 July 2018